THE IMMORTAL CHRONICLES

VOLUMES 1-5

GENE DOUCETTE

The Immortal Chronicles
Volumes 1 - 5
By Gene Doucette

GeneDoucette.me

Copyright © 2014-15 Gene Doucette
All rights reserved

Cover by Kim Killion, Hot Damn Designs

This book may not be reproduced by any means including but not limited to photocopy, digital, auditory, and/or in print.

The Immortal Chronicles is an ongoing series of novellas written by Adam, the immortal narrator of Immortal, Hellenic Immortal and Immortal at the Edge of the World.

More information on all books by Gene Doucette can be found at the end of this volume.

CONTENTS

IMMORTAL AT SEA	1
HARD-BOILED IMMORTAL	41
IMMORTAL AND THE MADMAN	89
YULETIDE IMMORTAL	161
REGENCY IMMORTAL	229
About the Author	295
Also by Gene Doucette	297

IMMORTAL AT SEA

I don't like boats all that much.

I used to be okay with them. Working as a fisherman was one of the first things I did that could qualify as a profession, back before there was anything like money. This was for trade, because the idea of doing something *for profit* also didn't really arrive until there was money. The basic idea was, I would catch more fish than I could eat personally so that those fish could be used to get things from people who had a surplus of something else.

It was an interesting progression. We began as hunter/gatherers, but that was a really unpleasant way to live, especially when the head count started to go up and bigger and bigger game was needed just to keep everyone from getting lethargic. From hunters we became settled farmers with land we considered ours, and that worked much better because then it was easier to divide up the responsibilities. Some of us farmed, some of us protected the farms, and some of us left the farms and went out and hunted. If we were near water, the hunting we were doing was usually fishing.

We did not, at first, need a boat to fish. We just had to wade into the nearest river with a sharp stick and wait for something to swim by that looked edible, hopefully before something came along that felt the same way about us. It worked well, but was time consuming. There weren't a *lot* of fish close to the shore, and nets worked better than spears, especially in deeper water.

That's when boats came along. The water got deeper, the nets became more efficient, and somebody figured out wood floats, and then it wasn't all that long—all right that's a lie, it was an achingly long time—before we were navigating them across the Mediterranean, and fishing with them on the Sea of Galilee and so on. (I was a fisherman in Galilee for a little while. Yes, it was the right time period, and no I never met him.)

I was okay on boats back then, for the most part, because I could almost always see land from where I was. I'm not a great swimmer, but if I can see the shore, I'm usually a good enough of one to reach it. I needed that reassurance—seeing the shore—because ultimately, I didn't trust any boat to remain afloat.

Here's the thing: if you've been around for long enough, you're bound to experience a few unpleasant things: fires, earthquakes, avalanches, volcanoes, sometimes all on the same afternoon. Boats, I can tell you from first-hand experience, sink. A *lot*. Sometimes it's because whoever made the boat for you made a crappy boat. Maybe *you* made a crappy boat. There is also the occasional psychotically malevolent storm that doesn't care how well designed your boat is. When you encounter something like that, and the thing you were relying upon to keep you alive ends up sinking, you really want to know you're not too far from the safety of solid ground.

Oh, and here's another thing to worry about when you're in a boat: sea serpents.

I've had arguments about this before. *Whales*, I've heard. Whales, and giant squid, and seals and all of that, and I'm willing to put my bet down on at least one or two of the things I've seen on the water being attributable to something mundane. But I have also seen sea serpents with my own eyes.

The first time was when I was a Carthaginian merchant. I had a small fleet of ships that operated across the Mediterranean, moving goods from the African coast to Greece and the safer ports of the Roman Empire. It was probably my first really successful business enterprise, and it only ended because it's always been hard for me to settle down too long before people start to worry about the fact that I haven't aged.

I only very rarely rode my own boats. The whole point of being a merchant is that you get to hire other people to do unpleasant things like combat nature in an environment humans aren't really supposed to occupy, which is how I feel about the surface of large bodies of water. (Also, the tops of mountains, and the moon.) I was on this trip because it was destined for the Greek coast and I had business in Athens involving a religious cult that liked to worship me from time to time. (Long story.)

The boats moved across the sea through a combination of wind and rowing. The sails were square-rigged and relied much more on favorable wind currents than the modern fore-and-aft rigs everybody uses now. We planned the market schedule around favorable winds because rowing was an enormous pain in the ass.

The captain, whose name I can't recall, was a Hebrew whose personality was the kind of mixture of scrupulous honesty and degenerate violence that makes for a good sea captain. He was the one who put a name to the thing in the water.

We were roughly halfway across the sea when we lost the wind. In Atlantic crossings (later, when people started crossing the Atlantic in ships) these are called doldrums, but on the

Mediterranean we called it whatever curse word we had in whichever native tongue we preferred, and then we pulled out the oars.

Well, *I* didn't. I watched. Because I owned the thing. And since there was no below-deck to speak of other than the hold where the supplies were, I had nothing much else to do except stand next to the captain and look out over the still waters of the sea, occasionally check in on the two boats behind us—which I also owned—and listen to the drum. One of the sailors manned the drum from the prow, pounding a rhythm the oarsmen were trained to follow. It was animal hide pulled over the mouth of a barrel, and it made for a deep bass that reminded me of at least one or two animal sacrifices from more savage days.

Some time passed in which we did little more than listen to the grunt of the oarsmen and the drumming, when a cry went out from one of the sister ships.

"What is it?" I asked the captain.

He squinted at the trailing vessel. "Is that the Assyrian? Pah." He spat, as one did. "He is an idiot. Who cares?"

My vessel captains were unreasonably competitive with one another, something that was not obvious unless at sea with them. Ashore, they acted quite comradely.

The captain cupped his hands around his mouth to shout. *"Did you drop something? Go back and get it! We will wait!"*

A second later, a torch was lit on the other ship. The Assyrian captain performed an up-and-down sweeping motion with the flame, then turned to the third ship, trailing behind both of us, and did the same. Then he doused the torch.

"What does that mean?" I asked.

The captain turned pale.

"Drop oar!" he commanded. "Stop the drum! Run still!"

The first mate silenced his drum and repeated the order. All the sailors, as one, pulled their oars in, stowed them on the deck, and then fell to their knees and covered their heads. Entertainingly, it looked as if they were bowing to us.

"What—"

"*Shh!*" the captain silenced me. He was listening to the sea, as much as it was possible to do such a thing when not in the water.

I looked at the other ships and saw they were doing the same thing: oars in, hiding on the deck.

Then I heard something. At first I thought one of the other ships had failed to silence their drummer, but the faint thrumming wasn't coming from above the water, it was from beneath the surface, as if the sea had developed a heartbeat.

The captain stepped to the railing of the foredeck and peered over into the water, looking for whatever it was that made the noise. He gestured me over, and pointed.

A terrible beast was moving below the surface. It was serpentine in nature, if not in size. It was easily the largest animal I'd ever seen. (I had seen larger trees, but for the most part they didn't move.) It slid through the water the same way a snake might across land: back-and-forth sideways motions. It crested twice, a spiny back that rolled over the surface.

I saw the head only once, briefly, on the second circuit. It was a little like a horse's head, if the horse had a head the size of an elephant. The heartbeat—if that was what it was—got louder on each close approach, but never changed tempo.

And then it was gone.

For close to an hour we remained silent and motionless on the water, just drifting and hoping it didn't come back. Then the captain gave the all clear, the drumming resumed, and the sailors got to rowing again.

I asked the question that had been on my lips the entire time. "What was that thing?"

"It is tanakh," the captain said. "And when you next speak to us about our commission you remember the risks we face out here."

Tanakh, my captain said, was in the habit of destroying entire fleets, and it was only through the superior seafaring knowledge of he and his fellows that my riches had not ended up at the bottom of the Mediterranean long ago.

Had I not seen the serpent myself I'd have taken it for the usual exaggeration of a man trying to justify a higher bid. I still thought he was going a little over-the-top since I'd not seen the creature even acknowledge the boats he was swimming with, but that's a little like saying *prove to me that bomb can explode*. At some point you have to take an expert's word for it.

For a while I became obsessed with this Tanakh. I am unreasonably well versed in many of the myths and legends of many of the early cultures of man, partly because I'm *in* a lot of them, partly because I was there when the thing that spawned the myth happened. But there were fewer legends about sea monsters than I expected, and a lot of them sounded like a different creature.

The pursuit of one of these legends later brought me as far as China, where I ended up in a small village and confronted what turned out to be a water dragon. They are (or rather were, since dragons are extinct) only a little similar to the tanakh, but much smaller and more akin to alligators. They also go away when you hit them on the nose.

I didn't expect that to work with a real sea serpent, and I also hoped I would never have a chance to find out.

It was the early fifteen hundreds before I had another opportunity to contemplate the wisdom of being on a ship on a large body of water. This is not to say I didn't spend a lot of time using boats in the interim, only that the voyages were mostly uneventful.

Sea travel was impossible to avoid completely. I did spend a long time moving overland in Eurasia, along the Silk Road and so on, in a conscious effort to stay away from boats, but some places couldn't be walked to. England, for instance. Also, the land route from India to Europe was time consuming and dangerous, especially in winter, so the wiser course was often to charter a merchant ship to North Africa.

In 1530, or thereabouts, I was making a living as a traveling scholar/poet. Back then, "poet" meant something slightly more general than it does now. This was especially true in my case, where I interpreted *epic poem* to mean *writing fictive prose however I want*. I hardly ever completed any actual writing, and when I did it was actually non-fiction stories about my own life that nobody took seriously as non-fiction.

Being a poet was mostly just a good way to get women into bed with me, but being a scholar was what paid the bills. By this time in Europe there was a decent amount of gold bouncing around in the hands of a lot of uneducated people. These people placed value in an educated man who didn't answer to the church. (Meaning, not a priest or a cardinal. *Everybody* answered to the church.) I was hired to teach reading, to consult important texts, to adjudicate legal issues, and so on. I had patrons in houses in Italy, Portugal, Spain, and parts of France, and none of the houses knew about my freelancing. It was a good gig, and easy enough since all I had to do most of the time was figure out what my employer wanted to hear and then find a way to tell them that. It was a lot like my time as an astrologer, in that sense.

It all fell apart because of a greedy Spaniard—Juan Pedro de Hoyos, of the house Hoyos, an old line that may have since died off. Juan Pedro was a self-defined entrepreneur who had it in his head that he could challenge the Portuguese grip on the Indian spice trade. He was hardly the first or the last to dream up such a notion, but he was the only one that I know of to screw it up before he even got to India.

My involvement was partly my own fault. I told Juan Pedro once that I had been involved in the spice trade "long ago", by which I meant five hundred years. He took this to mean I had active connections I didn't have any more, because everyone (as it later turned out only *nearly* everyone) I associated with in those days was long dead, but I couldn't tell him this. I wasn't telling *anybody* my age if I could help it. I wasn't concerned about not being believed, but there was a valid fear that if I was believed, the person I told might feel that it was best for all concerned if I were burned at the stake. Just to be safe.

I became one of the secret weapons he hoped to leverage in building his spice empire. The second secret weapon was Juan Pedro himself.

If you haven't met a royal person—or a very wealthy person, which is fundamentally the same thing—in your lifetime, this might be difficult to grasp, but a lot of them think they are deeply, profoundly amazing individuals. The evidence for their amazingness is their vast personal wealth.

This mindset goes way back, as far as Babylonia at least, in the lines of kings who thought themselves granted kinghood by whatever deity they worshipped. It was never, *I am king because my father before me was king*, it was always, *The gods want me to be king because I am better than everyone else on Earth*. That's how it was for a rich man like Juan Pedro de Hoyos, who didn't have to feel bad about being rich for one second of his life on the planet, because his riches were proof that he was just a better person than the rest.

His plan, then, was to go to India personally and meet with whichever spice merchant he could find—or maybe he was hoping I knew a guy—and when they saw his awesomeness they would be compelled to trade with him instead of anybody Portugal was sending over.

The third thing he was bringing was money, and on that he was at least thinking straight, because once everyone finished laughing he was going to need money to secure any trade arrangement, and probably to buy up the nearest brothel for a few days when he discovered no Indian merchant was going to screw over the Portuguese for him.

I would have skipped the voyage if I could have. He'd been talking about it for months and I honestly didn't take him seriously because he had also been talking about sacking Rome with an army and declaring himself pope, and building a palace of gold in the Americas. I had no reason to think this plan of the three was the one he was actually going through with. That was why, on the day of the supposed departure, I was still in the city rather than in some safe place where he couldn't find me.

"Are you ready for our adventure, Giovanni?" he greeted me when I arrived at his estate that morning. (Giovanni was the name I used in Spain and Italy. I used another name in Portugal, a third in France, and a five or six others depending on where I was. I mostly use Adam now.) Since he was my patron, in theory I should have been living on the premises, but I insisted on a villa off the property. I wanted the freedom to disappear if I had to, and arguably my advice was worth the extra expense. This did me no good when I failed to disappear on the day of the voyage, but it was a good idea in principle.

"You're going through with this?" I asked him, as a carriage pulled up to take us to the dock.

"Of course! But you have packed no clothes! Not to worry, I'll send men to the villa for your things so we can leave straight away."

I spent the ride to the ship trying to think up a way to excuse myself, but couldn't come up with one. In reality, I worked for several people and performed a variety of jobs, but as far as Juan Pedro was concerned he was my only source of employment, so naturally where he went, I went as well. He thought it was charitable, since if he left without me I would be out of work.

When I saw what was waiting for us at the dock I discovered myself equally short of ideas for what to say.

He had gilded his ship. This is another foolish thing very rich people do sometimes: they put gold on *everything*. Conspicuous wealth as a display of importance is something the western world picked up from the Romans. It was later perfected in both Constantinople and the Vatican, and is still really popular now. It's also been stupid for nearly that long.

"Impressive is it not? Imagine how impressed the Hindus will be when they see this at port!"

"Very impressed, milord," I said. "I only hope the merchants are willing to give you a fair price when seeing how much gold you have to spare."

Juan Pedro laughed and clapped me on the shoulder. As always, the point I was trying to make had rushed past him unnoticed. "Indeed!"

We were soon aboard, and to his credit Juan Pedro had built for us an impressively comfortable cabin and had packed a formidable quantity of Spanish wine, which I began drinking immediately. This helped, but only in the sense that it made it harder for me to contemplate going anywhere, and as we sailed from the docks I gave up any thoughts of tossing myself overboard and swimming back to shore. India wasn't really that bad, I decided, so why *not* take a trip there?

This wasn't one of my better decisions.

~

It was two or three days before I made it out of the cabin for any reason other than to relieve myself or change out a chamber pot. I'd have gone out sooner but Juan Pedro had been wildly sick almost from the moment we took to sea, having made the unwelcome discovery that boats rock about a lot and seasickness is a real thing. I had the glorious job of making sure he didn't choke on his own vomit, and also that when he did vomit it went into a receptacle and not onto one of the plush pillows lining the room.

When we weren't discussing how miserable he was we talked about Greek philosophy. Juan Pedro wanted to be a great thinker, but he couldn't get out of his own way.

"It seems to me if Plato didn't know what a chair was, he should have asked around. I would have told him."

"This is what you've concluded?" I had left him with questions to self-interrogate on the nature of forms and objects.

"I have. I thought of it just recently, between bits of sickness. I believe nausea to be a great clarifier."

"The point isn't whether or not Plato knew what a chair was, it was how *we* know what a chair is. You recall he made the same point regarding animals, and so on."

"I would have explained it to him. It's amazing to me that people have been talking about Plato all this time and the man didn't know how to tell a dog from a cat from a chair. It seems to me the point of philosophy is to take something obvious and make it sound complicated."

This was actually a decent insight. Plato was nearly as insufferable as Juan Pedro—for wildly different reasons—but he would have loved arguing this point. (Although Plato loved arguing *any* point.) And in a way I was just as surprised as my patron was that people were still talking about him.

Still, he was missing the central thesis of Plato's higher forms, which was not a vast surprise.

"Plato is arraigning the notion that there is a deeper truth to basic reality," I said. "It may be easier to imagine this as a conversation with the Aristotelian perspective—"

"Yes, yes. Aristotle. I remember him."

"Yes." He didn't remember Aristotle, because we hadn't actually talked about him yet. "Maybe it's best if you just consider, for now, the possibility that there is more beneath the surface. Think of reality as this ocean. Below the waves are things we can't see which affect the things we can."

This wasn't close to being a correct analogy, but I was working with what I had.

"All right. I will think on this. Thank you, Giovanni. And I may need a clean bucket."

∼

I was on the portside railing later, having replaced Juan Pedro's bucket with a clean receptacle and left him to sleep and think about how stupid Plato must have been. I was drinking wine from a tin cup and staring at the land in the distance, trying to figure out what land I was staring at. The captain stepped up beside me.

"How goes the prince?" he greeted. The captain was an aged Italian named Grillo who confessed in the first conversation we had that he'd not been to sea for fifteen years. Juan Pedro insisted Grillo was the best captain alive, based on whatever sources he used when putting this adventure together. The same sources told him to buy the ship we were sailing, which was supposed to be the fastest Spain had to offer. I had doubts on the second point because surely the fastest ship in Spain wouldn't be quite so easy to buy.

"The worst appears to be over," I said. "And if not, I'll have to continue to drink his wine for him."

Captain Grillo laughed and clapped me on the shoulder. "You relax and drink, we will reach India in no time."

Incidentally, in this era, *no time* meant *several months*.

Nodding at the land before me, I asked, "When do we head for deeper seas?"

"Oh we won't go much deeper than this. I like to keep the shoreline in view. We're on a dead run for the Cape of Good

Hope. I've charted it out; we should hit the winds right on schedule."

"Well that's good. And if you should *need* to go deeper?"

"For a storm, we'd be better off seeking shelter close to shore rather than further at sea. That or battening down and riding it. Not to worry, I know how to navigate."

"Good, then," I said, forcing a smile. I was wondering if I was actually too far away to swim for the land I could barely see, then remembered all the giant things in the water beneath us and decided I didn't like that option any more than I liked the idea of staying on board.

What Captain Grillo was doing made absolutely perfect sense. In the days before proper timepieces it was extraordinarily difficult to navigate East-West travel, which involved correctly calculating one's longitude. This was important because while a map could tell you where a land mass—or a reef—was, it didn't tell you when you were going to arrive at it. To do that you needed the sun or the stars, and you needed to know what time it was at a fixed location. (The standard now is Greenwich Mean Time.)

The easier solution was to just keep land in view the whole time. This was reasonable when traveling North-South from Europe to the horn of Africa, and in a perfect world it's what I would have done too. It certainly satisfied my concerns about deep oceans and the things that live within them.

But other things lurked near the shore of the African coast.

"Fastest ship in Spain, you say?" I asked Grillo.

"Indeed!"

"I do hope you're right."

It was a few weeks of mostly peaceful, storm-free sailing before we saw the other vessel. It turned up behind us having, I assume, rounded North Africa from Algiers or thereabouts.

"It's the Portuguese!" declared Juan Pedro with a laugh, the first time he saw them. "We're already leagues ahead, by India this gap will surely be a month or more."

"I'm afraid that's not likely," I said. The captain was shaking his head at me, just subtly enough to escape Juan Pedro's attention. "I've been looking at the ship for days now, and it seems to me it has either kept pace or gotten larger each day."

"Captain, is this true?"

"It appears to be so, yes," he said mildly.

"Then go faster, why don't you?"

"Yes, lord, of course. I'll give the order straight away."

Once Juan Pedro had disappeared back into his cabin, the captain turned on me. "Why did you do that? We could have easily kept him in his cups below deck until they passed."

I laughed. "Passed? Captain, who do you think is behind us?"

"I don't know. The have a shallow draft and a wide hull, and they are clearly carrying a lighter load, but I don't recognize their colors. Perhaps it *is* the Portuguese. What does it matter?"

"It matters because that ship will not be passing us. Why do you suppose the Portuguese route turns wide from shore before here? Or why if they travel this route it's only with escort vessels?"

"Pirates?" he gasped.

I had considered giving warning many times, but I couldn't decide what was the greater risk: pirates, or Grillo's navigational skills. My trepidation regarding open ocean travel was clearly a factor in my decision to keep quiet, but it's also not always wise to challenge a captain on his own ship. And after a while I convinced myself that he was right, and a straight run for the horn was the most logical choice.

"If you sail the Barbary Coast you risk Barbary pirates," I said.

"But I ran this route for years without issue."

"Maybe you did. Maybe you did it in a faster ship, or in worse weather, and maybe nobody was foolish enough to nail gold plates to any of the boats you captained."

"We have to go faster."

"I would say so, yes."

~

The ship couldn't actually go any faster without dumping provisions overboard, and that was an option nobody was prepared to consider. Juan Pedro did his best to encourage us to sail more rapidly by banging the drum, which only proved he knew nothing about how boats worked. He had bought a ship that once had oarlocks, but they were sealed up and there were no oars on the vessel. The drum remained, but it served no purpose aside from calling everyone's attention in the event of a speech. So his banging of the drum in a somewhat rhythmic fashion to get the sailors to address the wind more effectively—or whatever he was thinking—did no good other than to annoy everyone.

We decided—*we* being the captain, myself, his first mate, and definitely not Juan Pedro—to head for deeper seas. As the captain first noted, the pirate ship had a higher draft, which was partly the way their ship was built but also due to a difference in provisions. We were heavy-laden with enough goods to get us around the Cape of Good Hope and to the east coast of Africa before needing to resupply, but the pirates couldn't go that long. It was thought that if we sailed away from the African coast—a coast where they could expect to stop for resupply—we might reach a point where the pirates would be forced to either turn around or face starvation.

This idea had a drawback to it, which was that if they reached that point and did *not* turn around, we would be the only source of food in their vicinity, and they would literally have no option but to run us down or starve. We might well outrace them to that point-of-no-return, but we couldn't compel them to actually turn around.

If it worked, we could turn north and then back east and return to Spain with our ship and our lives and no spices.

Unsurprisingly, when I informed Juan Pedro he expressed active hatred for this plan. "I say we let them catch up to us!" he said. "Surely they will see that we pursue greater riches. They may even join!"

"Juan Pedro, do you trust my advice?" I asked him.

"Of course, Giovanni."

"Trust your captain to make the best decision for his ship, and for you."

"But I hired the captain!"

"You did, as you also hired me. And I am advising you not to try and counter his command. It will fail, and since we are looking to throw things overboard to lighten our load, the louder you protest the more you look like unnecessary ballast."

We did throw a few things overboard, but thankfully not the wine. Any beverage that wasn't salt water was welcome aboard a long sea voyage, and our survival of this long aquatic siege might hinge upon potable drink. I did, however, curtail my impulse to start drinking all of it.

It wasn't actually all that long, as sieges go. It felt much longer, because we could see the pirates constantly, and if one stared at their ship for long enough it was easy to become fooled into thinking they had slowed, or stopped, or were turning. But we didn't get close to that point where they would have been forced to turn around. They reached hailing distance on the third day after our decision to turn east. It happened when the ships were both slowed due to a failing wind, but unlike our vessel, the pirates had open oarlocks, and oars, and people to use them. So for the final few hours we got to hear their drum pounding louder and louder, until it was silenced.

"Hello, gold vessel," shouted a man—in Spanish—from halfway up the rigging of the pirate ship. "You can stop running now."

The man was squat and portly, brown-skinned, tattooed and scarred. When he spoke Spanish it was with a Moroccan accent.

"Let me talk to him," Juan Pedro asked.

"Be quiet," I said.

Captain Grillo faced the pirate ship and spoke to no one in particular. "This ship is the sovereign property of Spain! Keep your distance!"

The man on the rigging laughed heartily at this. None of the other men on his ship did, which either meant they were in a much more foul mood than their spokesperson's demeanor suggested, or none of them spoke Spanish.

"Captain Grillo," I said. "Do you speak Arabic?"

"No."

"Then may I?"

He looked surprised, but acquiesced. I stepped up next to him.

"*Allahu Akbar*," I greeted.

"*Allahu Akbar!*" the man answered. He continued in Arabic. "*You are Muslim?*"

"*I am when it suits me.*"

This elicited more laughter. "*I thank you for your honesty, sir,*" he said.

"*Are you captain?*"

"*I am. Whose ship is this?*"

"*No man of great import.*"

"What is he saying?" Grillo asked.

"He wants to know whose ship it is."

Juan Pedro jumped up. "He wishes to speak to the lord of this vessel? I will talk with him!"

"Let me speak for you my lord," I said. "This is why I'm here."

"*Is that he?*" The pirate captain asked.

"*It is. I fear he is an idiot.*"

"We would have run you down sooner, sir, but for the sheer insanity of a gilded vessel on a pirated sea. My first still expects the navy to appear, as surely this must be a trap."

"It is no trap," I said. "Alas, I am beholden to a patron who thinks it wise to cover his ship in precious metals and hire the one captain in Spain who doesn't anticipate pirates. My patron would make for an excellent ransom, and serves no other purpose in this world. The rest of the crew is likely worth nothing except as slaves."

"What is he *saying?*" Juan Pedro asked.

"I'm negotiating your surrender."

"*My* surrender? I will fight these dogs to the death!"

"I will let him know your feelings on this," I told him. To the pirate captain I said, *"forgive me, he appears to have already forgotten you speak Spanish."*

"He sounds stupid enough to be worth a great ransom indeed. A man such as yourself no doubt fetches a good coin as well."

"This is unfortunately not the case, captain. I have no family with holdings, only what I myself possess. I have no real desire to be sold into slavery either, as I have been a slave in the past and do not relish the experience."

He looked confused. *"This is an odd negotiation, sir. Name your terms."*

"Terms? We have nothing to negotiate with. Drown them all if you like. If you drown him..." I pointed to Juan Pedro, who probably thought I was saying something flattering. *"...you might even have a pleasant voyage back to Algiers, as he is completely insufferable. No, I speak to you now because I would rather be a pirate, thank you."*

About half of the pirate crew laughed aloud at this. Notably, the captain didn't.

"Why would I trust such a man as you on my crew when you spare so little loyalty for your own?" he asked.

"Apologies, captain, but trustworthiness does not strike me as a highly valued attribute for a pirate. But very well. There is treasure hid

aboard this ship that is worth as much as the ship itself. I know where to find it without first tearing it apart stem-to-stern."

"Again, you have given me no reason to trust you."

"You have naught to lose. Let me cross peaceably and I'll tell you where it is, and then we can discuss whether to value me as more than a head to sell to a slaver."

"Have your crew lash the boats, and you will be the first across. Then we will see."

I turned to Captain Grillo. "The boat is going to be taken, but I am still negotiating. I may be able to spare you all, but you will have to do what I say. Assist them in lashing the boats together."

"We can fight them off once they come close," Grillo said. He looked much more eager to die in a battle than as a slave, and I didn't much blame him.

"If it comes to that, yes." In truth, I had no plan and nothing with which to negotiate for his or the crew's lives. If they chose to perish fighting for their golden ship I was in no position to stop them. But my own position was marginally better.

"Juan Pedro, I need you to do something for me right now," I said.

"What is it, Giovanni?"

"The wood bunk on which I sleep has a loose board. I need for you to pry open that board and place your purse beneath it. When you are done, repair the board as well and as fast as you can. Do you understand?"

"I'm afraid I do not."

"They need to be sure that there's more value in your ransom than in your death. If they find themselves sufficiently enriched by your purse and the gilding, you will not survive the afternoon, I promise." It was a pretty good lie.

"Yes of course," he said. "You feel I am to be ransomed?"

"It's an honorable outcome for you, my lord. If you die today who will tell the world of your bravery? In ransom, you can tell them yourself."

He clapped me on the shoulder. "You are a good advisor, Giovanni."

"I thank you. Oh, and one more thing. I will need your sword."

Even lashed together there was still a gap between the ships wide enough for a man to fall through, so a plank was laid for me. Happily nobody from either side took the opportunity afforded them by proximity to begin fighting with one another. I was counting on the pirates preferring diplomacy to bloodshed, with the risk of violence coming from the Spanish side. If this seems illogical, keep in mind the pirates make money off each man they sell into slavery, while many men would rather die than end up a slave. If I felt like negotiating a peaceful arrangement, the people in need of convincing were on the boat I was leaving, not the pirate ship.

I wasn't bluffing about becoming a pirate, by the way. I had never really thought about becoming one prior to this, but it didn't strike me as the most terrible profession imaginable, and I'd done plenty of things in my life that were worse than what I might find myself doing on a pirate ship. It was well within my skillset.

I didn't end up becoming one, but I might have had things broken differently.

This was not the first time I'd been aboard a vessel taken by pirates, but the last time had been on a Greek ship in the Mediterranean, and the total number of pirates had been less than ten, none of which proved to be very good swimmers. This was a larger ship, with a lot more pirates. About half the crew I saw moved freely—there were many men chained to oars, which was the likely fate of most of the Spanish sailors—and the number of those free men approached thirty. It was unlikely I could out-fight every one of them. Maybe half that number, if I was very lucky.

I'm really not bragging. You have to understand that in order to have lived for as long as this without any special invincibility or anything—I can't get sick, but that's about all—I had to learn how to fight, and I had to be very good at it. Basically, in hand-to-hand combat or anything involving a blade I'm in pretty good shape.

I also had a pretty good blade. The sword I borrowed from Juan Pedro was the finest piece of steel I'd ever seen. He didn't even understand how rare it was, and had never—so far as I knew—used it in actual combat. I wasn't sure yet whether I'd brought the sword with me to buy my way onto the pirate crew or to fight my way through it. Possibly I was just looking for an excuse to hold it for a while before I died.

From the starboard side I was led—by what had to be the two largest men aboard— to a table on the foredeck, where the captain sat waiting for me.

"Please," he said, in Spanish. "Have a seat, my learned friend. We speak your tongue now. None of these men know it."

"*I have many tongues,*" I said, in Italian, as I sat. "But Spanish is fine."

He raised an eyebrow at me. "You are quite a mystery: a scholar who wishes to be a pirate. Do you know how to use that sword?"

"I do."

"That's good. When I fight you for it I want to feel as if I've earned the right to wield such a fine blade. How did you acquire it?"

"I told the fool on the other boat I had need of it, and he believed me. You're Moroccan?"

"Yes. I am Yassine. You are Giovanni, I have heard them say. You are Italian? And yet claim to be an occasional Muslim. And fluent in many tongues. And by your claim, you are good with a sword. I admit you would be a fine asset to the pirate trade. It's a shame, I really have no option but to kill you."

"I agree, that is a great shame. Even if I tell you where there's gold hidden aboard the other ship?"

"Even then, yes. We'll take the ship, sail it to port, and tear it apart. We *would* take the men and the goods and just sink it but for the conspicuous riches nailed to the hull. We have little use for it otherwise."

"You could resell it."

"Would you buy a ship knowing it wasn't fast enough to outrun the pirate selling it to you? No, sailors are too superstitious. The problem, Giovanni, is if I let you aboard as a fellow, there will be a mutiny, especially after the entire crew heard you ask. The only reason we're speaking peacefully right now is to keep those Spaniards from developing a sense of purpose. So long as you live and they think you're negotiating for them in good faith, they'll stay their hand."

"Then we seem to have an impasse."

"Not really. I can kill everyone on your ship or you can contrive of a way to keep them alive for long enough to be subdued. You I will have to kill in either case, but I can give you a brave death for your troubles."

"That's very charitable."

"I'm as reasonable as events allow."

"If your only reason for speaking to me is to get me to help you take the Spanish peacefully, I'm afraid I have to disappoint you, Yassine."

The two men who had escorted me were standing at a distance from the table. If I stood at that moment and drew Juan Pedro's Damascus steel, the only person I would confront would be the captain, and my sense was this was intentional on his part, because he felt confident he could take me.

If we began to fight, however, I expected this would be a signal to the rest of the pirate crew that it was time to take the Spanish boat by force, and while this would leave me with fewer men to fight, it would complicate the entire affair significantly.

Basically, I didn't see any way I was going to be surviving the next hour, not in the middle of the ocean. Anywhere else I could expect to fight my way to a hasty escape on foot, but I couldn't swim to safety from where we were; it was too far.

"That's a pity," he said. "I had hoped you felt more charitable toward your crew."

I stood, and put my hand on the hilt of the sword. "I've lived too long for charity."

Yassine stood as well, and put a hand on the side of the table, the intent being to lift it aside so that we might have room to fight one another.

From my vantage I could see the Spanish ship, and I knew they could see me. As soon as I drew, they would do the same, and then it would be chaos.

Before any of that could happen, though, a sailor from the pirate's mast gave a shout. It was either an incoherent cry, or it was in a language I'd never heard, the latter being extremely unlikely.

"What was that?" I asked.

Yassine squinted skyward. *"What do you see?"* he shouted.

The lookout made the same weird cry, and then pointed at the water.

"A whale?" I asked.

"I don't know. He's been addled by the sun for years. We put him up there to stay out of trouble."

The starboard side of the pirate ship was lashed to the port side of the Spanish vessel, and most of the crew of both boats had amassed on those sides, so it was a moment or two before anyone on the pirate ship bothered to look into the water on the pirates' port side.

"Captain!" the man shouted. He tried to explain what was out there but he had no word for what he had seen. *"Come quickly!"*

The captain joined his crewman at the port rail, and I joined them. This seemed like a good time to start fighting pirates, but I was a little curious what was going on in the water myself.

"Allah be praised, what is that?" Yassine asked.

What we saw was only a tail snaking past us in the water, but it was a huge tail.

Then I heard the sound.

"I have encountered this thing before," I said. "Listen."

A steady low thumping could be heard from the water, as it had been so many years before on the Mediterranean.

"What am I hearing?" Yassine asked.

"The heartbeat of the ocean."

"Poetry doesn't help explain what it is."

"The word for the beast is tanakh in Hebrew. You have maybe heard it as tiamat, or rehab. Or leviathan."

"You have seen a thing such as this before? Or do you speak now as from books?"

"I've seen one such beast before, yes. We are in grave danger."

"*Your* danger has been nothing but grave for most of the day. You will forgive me if I take this as exaggeration."

"You can take it however you like. We can drown together after that sea demon tears apart the ship, and in the next world you can tell me I was right. Or you can listen to me now and skip the drowning part."

He shook his head. "I've seen many a great beast in these waters. I learned long ago not to fear the whale for its size, as it doesn't care for us. You've chosen the wrong man to frighten with your stories."

"All right. But the whale doesn't circle back for a second look."

The tanakh was doing exactly that, which was not lost on Yassine. It was also not lost on the other pirates, some of whom had begun praying to Allah.

"Fine. Tell me what we should expect from the heartbeat of the ocean?"

I didn't actually have a solid answer for this. The last time I was aboard a ship near one of these the only solution was to be as quiet as possible. I had since devoted years to learning more and had come up empty, and those years of study had partly been specifically for this moment.

"We will need to be silent," I suggested. "And we should untether the Spanish ship."

Yassine laughed. It was a loud, roar-at-the-sky laugh that was so exaggerated all the seamen around us felt compelled to laugh along with him, despite having no idea why.

"Oh, you are a shrewd man, Giovanni. If I didn't know better I'd accuse you of conjuring that water snake for your benefit."

"Listen and think, captain. You can catch the Spanish ship again at any time, but right now with the two hulls lashed together neither can move and both present a much larger target."

"Target? To an indifferent sea creature?"

"This beast destroys navies, captain. I swear to Allah and on the steel of this fine blade that I am giving you the best advice I know. Untie the ships, and if we survive the afternoon you can recapture them as easily as a hawk to a sparrow."

Swearing to Allah after admitting I'm only a Muslim when it's convenient wasn't going to get me far, but swearing on the blade had an impact. It was a very good blade.

"Come then," he said, after studying me for a little longer than was comfortable. "We'll untie your ship. But you will stay here. I believe you pose a greater danger on their ship than by my side."

Together we joined the men on the starboard side of the pirate ship, where I ordered the Spanish sailors to untie their boat while Yassine ordered his men to let them.

"Are we freed?" Captain Grillo asked me from across the narrow distance.

"No," I said. "There's a thing you must do. We're going to drift, and you are going to need to be as quiet as possible until I signal otherwise. There's something in the water."

"I don't understand."

"Giovanni!" Juan Pedro shouted. "Come, leap across! We will catch you and make our escape!"

"For God's sake, don't shout!" I said, unfortunately shouting as I did so. "Listen, both of you: check the depths, a creature is encircling us."

"We have seen no such creature," Grillo said.

"Look harder. I've seen it twice. You can hear it as well if you are careful and run still. Keep quiet, and keep your men quiet, and when the thing has passed we can continue with this negotiation."

"Be wary of what's beneath the surface, Giovanni, yes I understand!" Juan Pedro said. Then he winked at me and ran to help the crew untie the ropes.

It wasn't until after we'd drifted apart that I realized my patron had managed to apply my philosophy lesson incorrectly, and at exactly the wrong place and time.

"Very well," Yassine said, as we stared at the Spanish vessel being carried slowly away from us. "We are untied. What shall we do next? Set fire to our boat?"

A low thrumming traveled through the deck of the ship, the bass note of the tanakh. We looked down and saw it passing beneath us. I checked the other ship, only a boat-length away, and saw Grillo's face as he realized there was indeed a great beast swimming around.

"Now we stay as still as possible. Tell everyone to stay where they are, try not to speak, and wait for it to go away. And we can hope that the people over there do the exact same thing."

"Did you tell them to?"

"I did. But Juan Pedro de Hoyos heeds only his own counsel sometimes. Tell me, how are the winds?"

The pirate captain looked up at the flag atop the main mast. "They have improved, but not significantly."

"Could we make decent speed to the coast?"

"Check for yourself, scholar. Tell *me* what the winds say."

I looked at the flag, and the sails, and back at Yassine. "My direct experience with sailing doesn't include an extensive understanding of stem-to-stern rigging. I know square rigs, and I understand rowing. That these ships can travel by sail in a direction that is not the exact same direction as the wind is still a matter of witchcraft to me."

He squinted at me, wondering if I was joking. "How old do you think you are, Giovanni?"

"Older than I look. What is your answer?"

"We would make better speed with the oars than with sail under these conditions, regardless of our destination. But now I'd like to know if I have placed my trust in a madman."

I ignored the question. "Moments ago I told you to hold everyone still and quiet, but if the Spaniards try and run, you need to be ready."

"To chase them down?"

"No, no. To get as far away from them as quickly as we can."

He shook his head. "You *are* mad."

The Spanish ship had drifted far enough from us for Juan Pedro to decide it was time to act, and all of a sudden their deck was a flurry of activity. And someone was banging that drum.

Yassine looked at me. "Why does he—?"

"He thinks it makes the ship go faster. They have no oars."

I'd mostly been ignoring the pirates that were frankly surrounding me for much of my time on the deck. I'd worried about convincing Yassine, in Spanish, not to act rashly. It was only after Juan Pedro and his golden boat started to race away from us that I really felt the presence of the others. Watching treasure sail away was not exactly in their nature.

"Why do we not follow?" the first mate asked the captain, in Arabic. There was a rumble of agreement from all around us.

"Don't worry," Yassine answered, looking at me rather than his first. *"We will follow soon. The scholar believes in vengeful sea demons, and he has bet me his life."*

This caused some loud discontent that might have escalated to my being tossed overboard, but then came a loud... hoot.

Hearing it now I'd probably mistake it for a foghorn, but back then I didn't know what I was hearing or what to compare it to. It didn't sound like any kind of animal noise I'd heard before outside of maybe a whale song.

All the pirates looked at each other, then at their captain, then at me, but nobody knew exactly what to do about the strange sound so we all just stood there and checked the water.

"There," one of the men declared, pointing to a spot in the otherwise calm waters between the vessels. It was the spine of the beast, breaking the surface.

It was heading straight for the other boat.

"Now would be the time to turn about, captain," I said.

"Why? It isn't interested in us. If, as you say, the key is to remain still, then why don't we continue to remain still?"

"And if, being made aware of one boat, the creature decides to look for a second one, you will have lost the only opportunity you had to put some distance between us."

The tanakh disappeared again beneath the surface. It was difficult to tell if it had driven deeper underwater or we'd simply lost sight of it because of the angle. The water still seemed to carry the slow beat of the creature, but with Juan Pedro pounding on the drum it was hard to tell the difference.

And then... nothing happened.

"I wonder if you have us concerned over no particular thing, scholar," Yassine said. He turned to the first mate, and said, *"Ready the sail. We can be on them again before nightfall."*

The pirates swung into action... for about three seconds. Then those of us who hadn't taken our eyes off the other boat yet saw something we'll take to our graves. The creature had swum under the Spaniards in order to surface vertically, nose-first, into the bottom of the ship. The impact raised them fully out of the water and several feet into the air before the serpent twitched and let them drop.

Ships full of men and supplies aren't supposed to be dropped into water from a great height. It can happen in a heavy storm if the waves are unpleasant enough, and generally speaking most ships are built to withstand that kind of impact. But in a storm the men are generally better prepared for unexpected gravitational shifts. Sails aren't up, hatches are battened down, sailors are lashed to the deck or below deck if there is one. Simply picking up a boat and dropping it made for a lot of broken sailors is what I'm saying. That, and a lot of broken pieces of ship.

We didn't hear Juan Pedro banging his drum any more after that. Just a lot of Spanish curses and general cries of pain.

Yassine no longer had any questions about the appropriate course of action.

"Quickly, you dogs! Set the sails, open the locks, we make for the coast!"

The pirate sailors were an orchestra of efficiency, as the oarsmen chained to the deck were prepped to row and men climbed the rigging to unfurl the sails, so as to use the wind to bring the ship around. Generally speaking using both oars and sails at the same time was only occasionally effective. If the sails were up when there was no real wind they might deter any forward progress made by rowing, so a coordinated effort between wind and man-power was usually needed. A good crew —and this was clearly a good crew—would find the right balance.

I had no particular function, so I maneuvered my way around the busy pirates until I reached the ship's open wheelhouse, where the captain stood.

"My first mate now believes the gilded ship was a trap all along and you are a wizard," Yassine said as he held the wheel.

"I would like to be a wizard," I admitted. "But if I could conjure a beast like that I like to think I would figure out a way to do it without endangering what I'm standing on."

In the distance, the Spanish were scrambling to get their boat in order again, but it seemed half their men were either wounded or in the water. Still, if the serpent was done with them they looked undamaged enough to make it back to Spain, barring any pirate intervention.

It wasn't finished, though, as became breathtakingly apparent a moment later when the head and about one third of the beast's body breached the surface near the ship, soared over the deck, and then came crashing down on top of it. The impact was explosive and thoroughly devastating, as the wood ship shattered like a toy balsa wood raft. Sailors that weren't crushed instantly were thrown a hundred feet from the wreck, only to sink as soon as they hit the water.

When the serpent went back down it took all evidence of a gilded Spanish ship with it.

We stood, all of us, dumbstruck in silence and paralyzed by what we had just seen. For a long while the only sound in the air was the screaming for help from one or two of the former occupants of the former boat.

"I really think we should be going," I said. Yassine felt the same.

"OARS!" he roared. He looked up. *"Trim sail!"* Then he shouted a bunch of other nautically pertinent commands. In all honesty, I couldn't tell you what they were, because as I told Yassine, I stopped understanding sailing long before this.

The first mate started pounding the drum, double-time, and that I understood. It got the men rowing much more quickly. Soon we were moving as fast as we could in what was still a mild wind.

A loud *HOOOOOT* sounded from the creature somewhere in the water behind us, a noise we hoped was a declaration of victory and not the announcement of another attack.

"Do you think it will give chase?" Yassine asked, shouting over the drumbeat.

"I told you I've heard tales of a tanakh destroying fleets."

"So you have. If we survive this day, and assuming I do not decide to kill you, we are going to talk about where you heard these tales. I've been at sea my whole life and I know less of this creature than you. I find this unacceptable."

"You may find the explanation equally unacceptable."

The man near the top of the middle mast—the same one who'd first spotted the serpent—began shouting and pointing at the water. *"It comes!"* he said.

"Hold on to something!" I shouted to everyone in earshot. I had nothing to hold onto—a rope attached to something heavy would have been nice—so I took off my belt and wrapped it around the nearest railing, then tied my wrist to it.

Yassine saw what I was doing and began lashing himself to the wheel. "First it will soften us."

The attack came a moment later. It's impossible to describe exactly what happened from the center of things, but I know that we were lifted, and then dropped again. Lifted from where, and dropped at what angle I don't know. I saw the body of the addled sailor from the rigging slam onto the deck and bounce into the ocean, a tangle of blood and unnatural angles, and I heard shouts and cries of pain from all around me in four different languages. I felt wood beneath me bend.

When it was over we were still afloat, and Yassine still had the wheel. The first mate had survived the assault as well, but I didn't know this from seeing him. I heard the drum.

"Are you all right, scholar?" the captain shouted.

"I'm not broken." In truth my shoulder felt dislocated, but it seemed like a bad time to bring it up.

"We are still sound. That eyeless bastard hasn't beaten us yet."

I got to my feet. "What did you call him?"

"A bastard?"

"Eyeless."

"Your books didn't tell you this? I saw his face! His head was near as close to mine as you are. He's an eyeless worm. I tell you, I'll not be sunk today by a worm!"

If he couldn't see, how did he find us? I wondered. And then I understood not only how that was possible, but why the Spanish ship had been targeted first.

"Stop the drum!" I said. Then I repeated it for the first mate, and in Arabic. *"Stop the drum!"*

He couldn't hear me, though, over that very drum, so I untied myself from the rail and raced to the prow.

The deck was a slick mess of blood and vomit, and with the rocking of the upset sea I nearly ended up in the lap of one of the oarsmen, and almost tripped over an injured second oarsman. Still, over my shouts and obvious distress the first mate wasn't listening to me. He had at least noted that I was there.

When I reached him, rather than try and convince him that the drum was a bad idea, I put my hand on the drum skin.

"What are you doing?" he asked. The first mate, not incidentally, was two heads taller than me, twice as wide, and from some sort of country where piercings were more common than hair. I didn't relish the prospect of confronting him physically.

I put my finger to my lips and pointed.

Over the mate's shoulder I could see the tanakh running straight for us. With the drum stopped the oars had stopped, and if I was right, both of those facts would make it more difficult for the creature to find us on the water.

I held my breath, and waited, as did the first mate and everyone else aboard, it seemed.

It didn't attack. The tanakh passed beneath us.

"It's the drum," I said. *"It's blind; it responds to the vibration of the drum."*

On the Mediterranean, we had reached a calm, which forced us to use the oars and to keep time on the oars with drums. My Hebrew captain knew to run silent to keep from being attacked, but he might not have known why it worked. Likewise, the creature attacked only after hearing Juan Pedro on *his* drum, and came after us when we did the same.

I turned to face Yassine on the bridge. Shouting, I said, "The drum calls it. Without it we should be…"

And then the world was turned upside-down. The deck lifted up and at an angle, and down I went, straight for the water. The first mate, standing next to me a half-second earlier, flew past and straight for the water. I didn't see him emerge again, but I was busy trying to keep myself from following him. I nearly did, but my hand found a loose chain on the deck. (It wasn't truly loose, it was attached to a shackle around one of the oarsmen's legs.) I dangled in the air for two or three seconds by the same arm with the dislocated shoulder—this was super painful, but it fixed the shoulder, which was nice—before the boat righted itself, and sent me sliding across the deck in the other direction.

I managed to get to my feet again. The boat was rocking madly and I could see cracks in the wood of the hull, but it had steadied enough for me to keep upright and to try and make my way around. The oarsmen were the only crew I could see at first, and they all looked like they'd been slapped hard onto the deck, as perhaps they had been. Nobody looked particularly prepared or capable of rowing. The sails and the mast were still intact, so there was hope yet that the vessel, although wounded, could remain afloat for long enough to reach a shoreline somewhere.

But there was no way we could survive a third blow.

I couldn't see any crewmen. The first mate was gone, although his drum was still there and the drumstick was attached to it by a cord. There were no men in the riggings.

"Scholar!" the captain yelled, pulling himself to his feet against the wheel. "I hope you have another idea!"

"Where is it?" I asked. "Can you see it?"

"He swings wide to starboard. I think he means to break us in two like the Spaniards."

I looked around the devastated ship for something that could help. With the strength of a thousand men I could maybe fashion the mainmast into a lance, I thought. Or if I had wings I could fly away, or with fins I could swim to shore.

None of those were reasonable options, but they highlighted an important point: I should try harder to stay off of boats.

The insistent pulse of the creature's heart—or whatever part of its anatomy caused the water to thrum—was banging in time with the blood in my ears. The tanakh was close.

That gave me an idea. It was a tiny idea, but as the only thing I hadn't tried yet I thought it was worth a shot. I ran to the drum, picked up the stick, and listened again for the heart of the sea.

It was two or three beats before I got the rhythm down, and thankfully the serpent was more than three of its heartbeats away from us still. I started hitting the drum to the same tempo.

"What are you doing?" Yassine shouted. "The drum only makes it more angry!"

"Clap to the beat, or stomp, or do something! We have to match his rhythm."

Yassine looked at the beast still fast approaching, shrugged, and started clapping in time with my drum solo. *"Stomp your feet, you dogs!"* he ordered, for the benefit of whatever crew still had their feet under them. I couldn't see anyone, but I heard the ship tune itself to the drumbeat, so there were still people conscious and able, somewhere.

"How are we?" I asked the captain.

"I am ready to sing, Giovanni, but the beast still approaches. May we go down with music in our hearts!"

I couldn't hear the beast any longer, because the beat of the drum was matching it. My hope was that it would have the same problem hearing us.

"Brace yourselves!" Yassine shouted.

The third impact never came, though. I heard the rush of ocean water as the creature emerged in parallel with us on the starboard side, and the boat rose with the sea, but it didn't attack. It ran beside.

"Hey, scholar? You are very clever, and this might work, but now that it sees my ship as another serpent, what do we do when it decides to mate with us?"

∽

The tanakh didn't decide to mate with us, but it did swim alongside for the remainder of the day and most of the night. We manned the drum in shifts, with every able-bodied soul aboard taking a turn. The drumming continued for hours after the last sighting, until we felt confident it had slipped away to wherever it called home.

It was another two days before the coast of Africa came into view. I happened to be holding the wheel at the time, which was symbolic if nothing else. The attack on the pirate ship had decimated the crew. Nearly everyone that wasn't dead or missing-and-presumed-dead had an injury of some sort, so Yassine had to cobble together a full complement of hands from what he had. That meant unshackling the oarsmen and trusting me.

"I have decided I'm not going to kill you, Giovanni," Yassine said, upon relieving me. He took the wheel in both hands, and I stepped back and limped to the rail to watch the shoreline grow larger.

"That's a great relief," I said. "As I steered your boat and wondered if we were about to be crushed by a giant serpent my foremost thoughts were that surely any second you were going to appear and run me through."

He shot me a look over his shoulder. "Don't get sarcastic, I can still change my mind."

"We're both too tired to fight to the death, Yassine."

"You have a bad shoulder. I can take you."

"And you're nearly blind in your left eye, your right knee

aches when it's cold, and I believe you have no feeling in at least two of the fingers on your left hand."

The captain laughed. "You are too observant by half. Do you still wish to be a pirate? Or was that only the best possible outcome given your circumstances? Because unless my first mate swam to shore ahead of us, I am need of one, and most of the crew will change over once we reach a friendly port. If I say you are the first mate nobody will question it."

"In honesty, after this voyage I'm not certain I ever wish to step aboard another boat."

"No, no, you're thinking about this all wrong. You've discovered a valuable thing, Giovanni. We both have."

"I have discovered that land is more valuable under my feet than seen from a distance."

"You've learned more, my friend. Listen to me: it's not so bad a thing, being a pirate. There are cruelties, for certain. And if there is a heaven, I don't expect to be welcome there. But it is lucrative. Now imagine being a pirate who knows how to tame a sea serpent? Come with me. If we can figure out how to *summon* it, we can own the sea."

"If I didn't know better, I'd think you were trying to talk me into something, Yassine."

"I'm serious."

"I know. But putting my feet back onto a ship and returning to those depths and then attempting to deliberately call that beast? That's insanity. You survived an attack from a force of nature and would try and make it your pet."

"I would try, yes. And with your help I feel as if I would succeed. With your patron dead, tell me, what else do you have for yourself?"

"I have my life. That's sufficient for now."

Yassine didn't manage to convince me to stay on as a first mate. We took to port in a friendly harbor—don't ask me the name of it, I don't know—and repaired his ship adequately to make the trip north to Algiers, where as promised he switched out his entire crew and refitted his vessel. The venture cost him dearly, financially, without even taking into account the gold he lost by not capturing the Spanish ship.

I hitched a ride with him to the Iberian Peninsula, intent on making my way on foot back to my own holdings in Spain and beyond. When we shook hands as friends and parted ways, and I expected it was the last I would see of the Barbary pirate captain.

I was wrong. But that's a story for another time.

THE IMMORTAL CHRONICLES

hard-boiled IMMORTAL

Gene Doucette

HARD-BOILED IMMORTAL

I knew she was bad news the minute she walked into the bar.

She was a redhead. I always had a thing for redheads. One in particular, actually. She was dead, but that didn't mean I wasn't holding my breath for a second or two every time I saw another girl with red hair.

This one was very much alive, and once she walked in she was also the life of the room. Men I'd been serving drinks to for years, who smiled so little if you told me they had no teeth I would've believed it, lit up like a kid meeting the world's cutest bunny.

The girl's name was Lucy and she was there to see a buddy of mine, who we'll call Al. That wasn't his name, but Al turned out to be kind of important, and this story is kind of embarrassing for him, so even though he's not around any more let's stick with Al.

The redhead was either going to get him killed, or she was going to get me killed. I could tell right away. Call it gut instinct if you want, but I'm alive today because I know what bad news looks like as soon as I see it.

Also, she was a succubus.

The year was 1942, and there was a war going on.

I don't like wars. I try to stay out of them whenever I can, and I give that same advice to other people as often as possible. I've even introduced myself that way a couple of times: hi, I'm whatever-my-name-is-in-this-era, nice to meet you and stay out of wars.

The people who most need to hear this advice almost never do.

Sometimes it's impossible to stay out of a war, though, and there are a couple of reasons for that. For one thing, there have been so many it's almost impossible to move around without stumbling across one from time to time. It's hard to appreciate—from a modern perspective—how very often war broke out, especially if you were trying to make a living anywhere in Europe or Asia. I'm pretty sure whoever said war was politics by other means had it exactly backwards.

Another reason it's sometimes impossible to stay out of war is every now and then the war is too big to stay out of. Like when they started calling them "world wars." This is not to say there were places in the world unaffected by the first or second Big One, just that it was hard to get to those places, and it was difficult to know where those places might be in advance of the actual wars.

Chicago wasn't such a place. I'd been in the Windy City on and off for twenty years, mostly because it was a decent place to drink. That was especially true during Prohibition, when you needed a city that was big enough and mean enough to support a decent collection of speakeasies if you wanted to get drunk in America and you weren't a Kennedy or a Capone. You're welcome to ponder the merits of trying to get drunk in the States when the States clearly preferred it if everyone got drunk elsewhere, and to be honest I don't know why I stayed either. Maybe I just didn't have the energy to move somewhere else.

Or it might have been that I stayed in Chicago because I had lost something there. The last time I saw the aforementioned redhead—the apparently dead one—she'd been on the far end of a dance floor in an illegal establishment that burned to the ground about ten minutes later. That was how I had arrived at the conclusion that she was no longer alive. It was a shame, because I'd only been looking for her for about ten thousand years, and you hate to see that sort of perseverance go to waste.

So I may have stuck around in Chicago as long as I did to see if I was wrong. Sure, I was pretty positive she didn't make it out of that fire, but I never saw a body. Plus, it was a great excuse to spend all my spare time checking out redheads and hanging out in clubs.

But by '42 I'd had enough of the wild life and had settled down into a monogamous relationship with a bar called Jimmy's. Jimmy was an old prick of a guy, connected, but in a kind of polite way. He mostly used his family name when he wanted to make someone nervous about their bar tab, but that was about it. So he was a prick, but a pretty honest one.

Jimmy needed a night guy for his bar, someone who could close up whenever the last drunk weaved out the door, no matter what time that was. I could bartend well enough to pour booze, and as long as he didn't mind if I drank on the job, everything was good. There was even a little space in the back where I slept after closing on nights when I didn't get an invitation to sleep elsewhere. No shower, but there was a sink in the back and a Y up the street.

It was a sweet little arrangement for a guy who'd just as soon sleep in a bar anyway and didn't harbor any particular ambitions beyond that, which described my entire existence for pretty much the last three quarters of the twentieth century.

It was at Jimmy's that I made friends with Al, a mostly forgettable guy except that the stuff in his head was the kind of stuff you never end up forgetting even if you want to.

Al worked at the University of Chicago, but it wasn't really clear if he worked *for* the university, based on some of the things he talked about after he'd had a few. Like "unlimited free energy", which is what he used to shout after about five or six beers, sometimes toasting the ceiling. For the longest time nobody understood what he meant, because he never filled in the details, so we figured maybe he was talking about a new brand of coffee.

It bugged me enough to ask him what he meant by it, but most nights he'd just shake his head and say he couldn't possibly explain.

My concern—because I'd heard this kind of talk before—was someone had sold him on a perpetual motion machine. I'd invested money in enough of those to know to stay away. Not that Al was someone I'd peg as a sucker for that sort of scheme. He was a chubby little prematurely balding guy that wore the kind of thick round glasses that made you think he was intelligent. And he was. Sure, I'd never seen him wear a suit that fit properly, he had a weird barking laugh and bad breath, and overall came across as a real goof. But when you talked to him and saw his eyes light up, you realized he looked that way and dressed that way because he was too busy thinking about things nobody had ever thought of before to worry about anything else.

One night he made his usual toast to unlimited energy, and I asked him as I always did what he was going on about, and for whatever reason—maybe he'd had just the right number of beers, or maybe he just couldn't keep it to himself any longer—he answered the question.

"Atomic power, Rocky," he said. "That's what I'm talking about."

Rocky was the name I was using. It made more sense in the Twenties, I'll be honest.

"Atomic," I repeated back. "Like with the atom?"

"I know a fella named Adam," said the slightly less drunk guy sitting next to Al. His name was Federico, and he wasn't talking about me, he was talking about another Adam. I hadn't started using the name yet.

"Not Adam, Freddie," Al said.

"I get you," I said. "Atom. The building block of matter."

Al laughed. "Yes, yes, if you are Democritus that would be correct."

I actually knew Democritus, but I wasn't going to come out and say that. I first heard the word—and the idea—of the atom from Democritus's own lips. I might have even been standing next to him when he invented the concept, I couldn't remember. There was lots of wine involved.

"So, atoms *aren't* the building block of matter, you're saying."

"Blocks, you mean like bricks?" Federico offered. "Hey everyone, Al figured out how to get energy out of bricks!"

"What, is he eating 'em?" Someone shouted from the other end of the room. Everyone laughed.

Let me back up and set the scene, because they don't make many places like Jimmy's any more. This was a poorly lit dive bar that was just about exactly as seedy as possible in a time before enforced health inspections and fire codes. The permanent cloud of smoke that hung over the room was so thick the bare bulb light fixtures had almost no chance. There was sawdust on the floor that was mostly there so nobody slipped on spilled drinks, the walls were too thin to keep the cold from the winters out, and there were nights when the rats outnumbered the people. Most importantly—and this was sort of nice—pretty much everybody there knew everybody else there at least well enough to borrow money from and call an asshole when such a thing was necessary.

The general feeling about Al, among the patrons, was that he was a decent guy. Maybe a little weird, and not the person you want next to you in a fight, but decent. And clearly he was the smartest guy there. This commanded a kind of respect that kept him out of most of the fisticuffs that might be considered ordinary in this sort of setting. And if it didn't—if someone decided to give him some trouble—*I'd* get involved, and by this time everyone there had a decent sense that it was a bad idea to get me involved. I commanded respect too, but a different kind.

"I am *not* eating bricks, thank you!" Al said, in response to what was some good-natured ribbing. "All right, all right, I will explain."

"Everybody shut up," Freddie said, "he's gonna explain."

"But all of you have to keep this under your hats because it's important but it is also secret."

There was a collective *ooooooh* from the room. Nobody there could think of any reason a guy who worked at the university would need to keep secrets, important or otherwise, but because this was the most interesting thing going on that night—nobody was loudly mad at their wife or had a beef with a local boxer, a horse, or a sports team—we tried to humor him. Sure, the war could pop up again as a topic of conversation at any time, but it was the topic everywhere, so nobody really wanted to bring it up if they didn't have to. Sometimes they *did* have to. Sometimes someone's kid was in a bad place and we had to talk about it.

But this night was for atoms and how to break them.

It's pretty much impossible to explain even a simple thing to a barroom of drunk laborers, so Al didn't have an easy time of it. The average education level in the place—once you took Al out—was somewhere short of high school, and I'm not even counting me. I never went to school of any kind, but I got extra credit for being around when everything they taught in schools was invented.

This isn't to say I understood all that he told us either, but I came a little closer than most.

"So the C here, that's what again? The speed of light?" A guy named Vinnie, who I was pretty sure broke other people's fingers for a living, was the one asking. He was holding up a napkin with Einstein's equation written on it, and shouting from the other side of the bar. For most of the evening Al had been jotting things down on napkins and passing them around because we were short on blackboards.

"That's right, Vin," Al confirmed. His mini-lecture had already gone past Einstein, but I might have been the only one clear on that.

"Light has a speed? How come?"

"It just does. And it's a big number."

"Like what, in miles per hour?"

"Yes, like in miles per hour."

"Hey, that's a good question," a Polish longshoreman named Henryk said.

"I'm nearly positive it isn't," Al said.

"No, no, hear me out." He grabbed the napkin from Vinnie. "So I get this. Mass is the size of a thing, right? And the speed of light is a really large number, so what you're saying is you add the mass and the speed of light together, plus the two, and that's an even bigger number, and that's how much energy there is in this lump of mass."

Al had been all the way up to chain reactions, but at this question he was about ready to cry.

"You almost have it, Henny," I said. "Except when you put the numbers together like that you're multiplying them and not adding them. And the two means it's square. Right, Al?"

"Yes, Rocky, thank you."

"What is a square?"

"A thing with four corners, Hen!" someone shouted from in back.

"C squared means it's C times C, so the whole thing on the

right is Mass times the speed of light times the speed of light. So it's a *really* big number."

Al jumped in. "The point being, to break the bond of an atomic nucleus is to convert a portion of the mass contained therein to energy, and the energy being released is tremendous. Does this make sense?"

Henryk and Vinnie were both nodding like it really did make sense. "So here is the good question," Hennie said. "Does it release even more energy in Europe?"

"No," Al said. "Why would it?"

"Because they use kilometers there! A kilometer is smaller than a mile, so the speed of light in kilometers per hour would be an even *bigger* number."

After that, Al pretty much gave up trying to explain the idea of free energy to the guys at the bar, other than me. I was always eager to hear more, and I understood most of the ideas he was bouncing around pretty well when he kept the math out of it, which he tried to do.

We developed this conversational approach where he'd explain something in a way I could understand, and then he'd have to stop and try to prove what he said was a real thing. I didn't need the proof, but he seemed to think it was important, which meant writing stuff down on more napkins. When he was done he'd hand me the napkin, I'd nod a few times, and either throw it away or hand it off to anyone else who looked curious. There was no way we were going to grasp the point he was making on those napkins, but it made him feel better to draw it out. Plus I think three or four of the times he was explaining something to me he ended up figuring out a thing he hadn't understood before, so I like to think I was helping.

I'm usually a huge fan of science. There have been some times when I've been dubious, like when someone doing something scientific decides to lock me up, and then I'm not so pleased. But that doesn't happen often, and since basically every last creature comfort modern people now take for granted came from someone performing an act of science, overall I'm pretty happy with what's come out of the discipline. I'm not even talking about the big inventions like cars and television and radio. Sure, those are great, but after the wheel I think the modern world was founded on indoor plumbing and flush toilets, and someone had to invent those too.

I was pretty positive the things Al had been talking about were even more important than toilets. I knew next to nothing about electricity, but I knew there were power plants in the world that produced that electricity. What he was describing sounded a lot like an improvement on anything already going on, which is what you'd think too if someone said they could power a city just by stacking a certain kind of metal in the right order. So I kept on digging for more details, and he kept giving them to me, up until the day he told me he couldn't any more.

But before he got to that, he had to tell me about the girl he'd just met. That these two things came together did not escape my attention.

"You have to meet her, Rocky. She's something else," Al said. "I mean it, she's a straight knockout."

"Is she now."

"I know you're thinking a guy who looks like me doesn't land a knockout, but my Lu-Lu, she loves me for my brains."

"That's something you've got plenty of. Lu-Lu?" I was pretty sure my buddy's standards were low when it came to attractiveness in women, only because he wasn't what I'd call handsome, so he was right about my skepticism. I also wondered if, with a name like that, the girl was Asian.

"It's Lucy. She likes it when I call her Lu-Lu. She's gonna come round, so you can meet her."

"Here? You should think about bringing her someplace nice. Someplace clean, maybe. Even the rats think twice about this bar." Bringing a girl he thought was pretty into a barroom full of guys who didn't know what tact was, was a bad idea, but I didn't say that.

"I'm telling you, it's love. I want you to meet her. I told her about you."

"Now why would you do something like that?"

He laughed. "She wants to meet *you*, Rock, because you're my good friend, isn't that how these things work?"

I didn't think it actually *was* how these things usually worked, and to support my side of a dispute on that point I could turn to any other guy there and ask them if they ever thought about bringing their wives or girlfriends around. The answer would have been no, because this was the kind of place men came to behave like men, which was to say they behaved here in ways that made you wonder how the species ever managed to reproduce.

"Sure, sure," I said, "of course, bring her by. I'd be happy to meet her."

"Good, cuz it's already set. She's gonna be here Saturday. It'll be a blast. Don't worry, Rock, I know what you're thinking, but she can handle herself. Oh, and before I forget: all that stuff about... you know?" He leaned over the bar to whisper: "The atomic stuff."

"Yeah, I was about to ask you about that. How's things?"

"You had best not ask me any more."

"So it's not going well?"

He got a little red in the face, which was a peculiar reaction. "No, it's going... We can't *talk* about it, you and me. Not any more. Look, Rock, I know I can trust you, okay? But some guys got in a little trouble for saying too much to the wrong people about... all of that. And now, I mean *right now*, it's becoming kind of a big deal. A couple of fellas came by the other day, made me sign a bunch of papers."

"Are you in some kind of trouble?"

"Me? No, no, no trouble." The way he said it made me think the exact opposite was true. "I just have to... I mean, now that we... Aw hell." He grabbed my hands and squeezed them tightly, like we were about to get engaged or something. "I can't talk about it Rocky, but things have changed, you get me? You can't tell anybody about this stuff."

I nodded. "I'll keep a lid on it, Al, don't worry."

"I know you will," he said, releasing my hands and clapping me on the shoulder. "You're a straight-up guy."

"I try to be. So who were the guys?"

"The guys?"

"The ones with the papers you had to sign."

"Oh them. Don't worry about it. They won't bother you. Don't even know about you."

I did worry. Worry seemed like an extremely healthy reaction.

Maybe it was more than worry. That's the kind of word you hear when a concern is unfounded, and this felt like the kind of concern based on reliable historical precedent. Specifically, when I felt like this I was usually right, and that thing—call it an instinct, I guess—has kept me alive for a really long time.

I knew something was wrong, is my point. I wanted to know what those papers were for and who made Al sign them and what would have happened to him if he *hadn't* signed them. Then I wondered when men with papers were going to show up for me, and exactly how much trouble that was going to be for me when it happened, and if I should leave town before it came to that. But Al wasn't talking about anything other than his Lu-Lu after that, so I couldn't press him. Instead, I drank a lot of alcohol, which was another thing that's kept me alive this long.

Then came Saturday.

Al showed up at the bar at his usual time, took his usual seat and had his usual beer, and acted like nothing special, so I was thinking the whole thing was off. I was a little relieved about that, but I couldn't have told you why.

It wasn't until he was in his third beer, sometime past eleven o'clock, that Lucy breezed in and instantly confounded my expectations regarding what a woman who would date Al would look like.

She was a knockout all right.

Lucy had long, straight red hair under a sporty fedora, a sharp skirt suit with a hemline that didn't make it past her knee and a slit that, if you were looking for it, you'd be alarmed to discover went more than halfway up the thigh. She had on three-inch heels that managed to look practical and a little whorish at the same time. Her round face seemed to have been constructed specifically to draw attention to a cat-like pair of emerald green eyes and an adorable button nose.

It was like seeing a unicorn in a dog kennel, because this was more than just a pretty girl. People who had no business doing so would write poetry for this kind of woman. Men would leave their wives for her, and if she asked nicely, wives might leave their men for her too. She could start wars and wreck ships and end careers just by smiling at the right people. She was trouble. I knew right away what kind of trouble.

～

Succubi get a bad rap.

We live in a world where people who don't know better call things "demon". It's annoying because there really are demons, but they don't look like succubi or incubi or vampires or anything else. They look like demons, which is to say they're big and ugly and violent, and also not actually associated with any hypothetical hell you might ascribe to.

These are all just different species, and it's really simple, and if mankind would just get past the idea of magic (and maybe of heaven and hell but to each his own) they would get along better with the other things they happen to share the world with.

So here's the truth. Your average succubus *loves* sex, but not as much as they love being adored. In that sense they're like any of us, except that succubi are really good at both—the sex and the being adored—to a degree that might *seem* supernatural.

If you spend enough time with a succubus who finds you interesting, you're going to be ready to give up everything else you've got going on in order to spend as much time as you possibly can with her, and that might seem like a spell or something, but there's nothing demonic or magical about it. It's an obsession, and it can get unhealthy, but that's all.

I should know. I've probably spent more time with this species than any man who ever lived, and while I have certainly been tempted to give up everything for one or two of them, I never did, and I was always ready to walk away if I had to.

Sure, it helps to be immortal; I can outlive a succubus if one turns out to be too tough to walk away from. Succubi have a longer lifespan than humans, and they tend to look about twenty-five for somewhere in the neighborhood of seventy-five years, so outliving them does involve a commitment, but it can be done.

～

"Evening, boys!" Lucy announced from the threshold. "How 'bout letting a girl through?"

Being a Saturday night, the place was pretty packed. Not jammed by the standards of any of the big bars and clubs downtown, but well occupied for the dive it was. I counted three other women in the place when she walked in—one of them was a hefty dame who worked the docks, had a girlfriend of her own, and nobody actually thought of as a woman—but when Lucy showed up it felt we were looking at a girl for the first time in our lives.

"Hey sweetheart, you sure you're in the right place?" asked the guy nearest the door. I didn't know him by name, but he looked like the kind of customer you didn't want to meet in a dark place.

"Ain't you sweet for askin'?" she said with a glorious smile, touching his cheek. "I'm lookin' for a little guy, kinda bookish, glasses, goes by Al. You seen 'im?"

"Over here, Lu-Lu," Al said. He leaned up on the edge of the bar and waved her over, while the patrons between him and the door tried to come to grips with the unlikeliness of this couple.

"Yeah, there he is," the man at the door said, pointing. "Hey! Make way for the lady!"

"Thanks, sweetie," she said. I'm pretty sure he blushed, but it was tough to tell with the lighting.

Al grabbed my arm. "Hey, Rock, didn't I say? She's something, huh?"

"That's how I'd put it, buddy. Something else, all right."

A space was made for her at the bar next to Al once Vinnie stepped aside, with something approaching reverence in his eyes. Lucy waltzed down the middle of the parted room looking like royalty walking through the courtyard in Versailles, and somehow everyone in this crappy little hole felt like they were in that French court with her. You'd think a girl who looked like that would feel threatened in a place like this, but nobody dared touch nobility without asking.

When she reached Al she kissed him on the check, and held her hand out to me.

"You must be Rocky," she said. I shook her hand.

"That's what they call me."

"Pleasure. Heard a lot."

"Me too. Looks like Al might've done you a disservice."

Al said, "Hey!"

"You need a bigger vocabulary to go with that big brain," I

said. "*Lots* of girls are beautiful. You're gonna have to find a better word than that."

"Awww, you're a charmer. You didn't tell me he was a charmer, Al."

"I didn't know he was!"

"I'd kill for a beer, Rocky baby," she said. "And hey, can anybody offer the lady a smoke?"

∼

Lucy picked up three marriage proposals—one from someone I was pretty sure was already married—and started two fights I had to break up personally, since I was the only guy there who was technically an on-duty employee. (There were other bartenders. Most nights the only way to tell which of us was working was to see who was standing behind the bar.) She also never went more than two seconds without a beer in front of her, a cigarette, or a light for that cigarette. When she had to excuse herself to freshen up in the ladies room I think a couple of fellas ran in ahead of her and cleaned the place.

The attention his girl was getting didn't bother Al in the least. He seemed flattered by the idea that of all the mooks there, this hot little number was on his arm. He also didn't mind that for all the attention she was getting and giving out, the thing she was most interested in doing was talking to me.

"So no last name?" she asked at one point. "Just Rocky."

"Never had much care for last names," I said, although the truth was I never gave "Rocky" one. It took a while before I got around to picking full names for myself.

"Everyone's got one," she insisted.

"Yeah? What's yours?"

"Mine's Smith. Lucy Smith."

"Smith. Popular name."

"Oh yeah. I come from a long line of Smiths."

"I'm sure you do." I didn't think she came from a long line of anything with a family connection.

"Big burly craftsmen, like these fellas here. Liked to get their hands dirty. Do you like to get your hands dirty, Rocky?"

"Depends on the work," I said. "And who I'm doing it for."

She winked at me, as if we'd shared a secret. We hadn't, so far as I knew, but maybe she was coming to an understanding about me that wasn't entirely warranted, all by herself. People make assumptions about me all the time that are only wrong because they don't have *been alive forever* as one of their options.

Or maybe we *had* shared something and I missed it. I'd been sipping the cheap vodka straight from the bottle all night, which nobody much minded since nobody else was going to touch the vodka anyway. (We mostly used it to stretch the bourbon.) This made it a little hard to keep my head around Lucy, since every wink and smile and gentle touch of her hand on my wrist made me want to giggle stupidly. Knowing what she was helped me keep my head a little, but only a little, because as long as I knew that I also knew she was only as monogamous as the situation warranted.

When she wasn't talking to me she was chatting up all the other regulars, which was a distraction all its own since when she and I weren't talking I felt something like jealousy. I tried to get close enough to figure out what she was saying to the other guys, but it was too tough because after all I was working. I only picked up a word or two. She seemed really interested in what everyone did for a living and what their full names were, two details that only seemed weird to ask for after the fact.

Closing down the bar that night was tough. I wasn't allowed to keep the place open all night, but if I had been we probably could have gone on until sunrise so long as Lucy and Al stuck around for it. They might have been up for that too, as they were the last ones to leave.

"Gotta take my sweetie home, Rock," Al said as I walked them to the door.

"It was a pleasure, Rocky," Lucy said, extending her hand. That my first instinct was to bow and kiss her wrist was something I kept to myself. "I hope we meet again soon."

"Bring her back, Al," I said. "I'm sure the gang would love it."

Al laughed. "Oh, I'm sure. But I think maybe you were right. She belongs in a higher class place, huh? I've got to treat her right."

He led her out. As she walked past me I could have sworn I caught another wink.

~

Cleaning the bar was a couple of hours' worth of work, and I spent all of it thinking about Lucy, and those men that turned up with papers for Al to sign.

It seemed to me if he was in some kind of trouble for saying too much to someone, the first person I'd check on would be the much-too-attractive girlfriend who could convince men to walk into traffic for her. That should have been good news for the bartender he'd sworn to secrecy, because I'm not nearly as persuasive.

Somehow, thinking about it like that didn't make me feel any better. If anything, meeting Lucy had me even more worried. I just couldn't figure out why.

Cleaning the bar mainly involved rinsing the glassware and getting the trash out to the dumpster in back. I could have swept and wiped down all the tables but nobody much cared if I bothered. The place was covered in a thick layer of nicotine from the constant cloud of cigarette smoke lingering in the air just below the ceiling, and had reached some sort of irreversible unsanitary threshold long before I'd started working there. Nothing I did was going to change that. So when I was finished with the basic picking-up and scrubbing, and after coming to no firm conclusions regarding my friend's girl, I put out the lights and headed in back to clean myself up and call it a night.

A couple of minutes later, just as I was about ready to retire to the cot in the corner of the storage room, I got the sense I was not entirely alone.

I popped my head out into the bar again, and looked around. It was darker than during business hours, but one light near the door was always left on.

"Hello?" I asked. "Anybody there?"

"Hiya, Rocky."

Lucy had taken up the darkest corner of the barroom, but I didn't need to see her to know who I was talking to. I'd say it was the perfume, or the tenor of her voice, and that could've been true, but I think I was sort of expecting her.

"Evening, Lucy. Little late for you, isn't it?" I walked out and stepped behind the bar. A match lit up her corner of the place, shining a little light on a beautiful pair of legs and a taller set of heels than she'd been wearing earlier. She sucked her cigarette to life.

"By now I'd say it's a little early."

"True enough. How'd you get in, if you don't mind my asking? Seeing as how you're trespassing right now."

"Would you believe the door was unlocked?"

"I'm the fella that locked it, so no."

"Then you did a lousy job. Buy a girl a drink?"

I pulled out a bottle I'd been hiding under the counter. It was a top shelf whiskey that was so top shelf the shelf it belonged on was in a different bar. I put out two shot glasses.

Lucy unraveled her legs and walked over, from no lighting to poor lighting.

The heels were four inches. The legs were without stockings. She had on a trench coat that stopped somewhere north of mid-calf, belted at the waist. And it was really tough to tell for sure because the light only touched her in quick flashes, but I was pretty positive she didn't have on anything under the coat.

She was all kinds of dangerous. I should have turned around and run out the back door. Instead, I poured two shots.

"You don't seem surprised to see me," she said.

"I'm good at spotting trouble, sweetheart," I said with all the bravado I could muster. By the way, we really did talk like this back then.

She held the shot glass up in the light to examine the amber contents. "Is that what I am, Rocky?"

I took the second glass, and together we downed our shots.

"All sorts of trouble," I said, as the whiskey burned its way down my throat.

She put down her glass. "Ooh, tickles. You saved me the good stuff. Hope I didn't keep you waiting too long."

"I've been waiting for someone like you for years," I said. It was a good line, I thought. I refilled the glasses. "Now you're here and I'm not sure if I should be sticking around or running away as fast as I can."

She pouted. "Please don't run, it is so hard to keep up in these shoes."

I stepped around the bar, which wasn't much work since we were at the corner of it anyway. Standing next to her, we were almost eye-to-eye, thanks to those heels she had on. Her green eyes sucked me right in.

"What do you want, Lucy?" I asked.

She smiled, took her second shot, and slapped the glass on the table. "It's not obvious?"

She stepped closer, her hip touching mine, the smell of the top shelf whiskey mixing with cigarette smoke on her breath.

There was nowhere to look that didn't involve a piece of her. I could fall apart when looking into her eyes, but when I looked down it was straight into a bosom that shouldn't have been that perfect without something propping it up. My left hand was on her thigh and working up and under the coat, and it didn't appear I had any control over that.

The touch of my hand made her tremble, and somehow find a way to get even closer. We were practically in each other's clothes. I reached for the belt of her coat, and hesitated there.

"Go on."

I was about to. It would have been the easiest thing, and there was a large—and growing larger—part of me that was ready to lose everything for this girl. But I knew something wasn't right. "No," I said, sounding a lot less sure of myself than I wanted to. "How about first you tell me what you *really* want?"

My hand came off the belt and found the shot glass, alcohol being just about the only thing on Earth than can trump a beautiful woman for me. I removed my other hand from her thigh, stepped back and downed my shot.

Lucy spun away from me, and it *did* feel like a spell being broken. Like I said, I could understand the idea of magic when it came to a succubus.

She took a drag of her cigarette.

"You ain't like most guys, are you Rocky?"

She grabbed the whiskey bottle by the neck and took a pull, which was maybe the sexiest thing she'd done all night. When she lifted her arm to drink the coat rose up nearly enough to show me everything she wasn't wearing under there.

"I'm not like most guys, no. You sure aren't like most girls."

"Well thank you."

She slid onto one of the stools, her legs parting on the way up into the seat, and I caught a glimpse of everything, because I was looking. She didn't bother to cross those legs, because she knew I was looking.

"You're with my buddy Al," I said. "What makes you think I'd go behind him like this? That'd be rotten."

She had the bottle on the bar next to her. To get a swig of my own I had to step in front of her first—all right I didn't have to, I could have gone behind the bar instead—and when I stood there her legs opened.

"Al's a sweetie, but I need more," she said.

"Do you."

"A lot more."

"How do you think he'd feel if he knew you were here?"

She put her hand on my cheek. "Aww, he's a big boy. Besides, who's gonna tell him? I know how to keep secrets, don't you?"

I leaned in to kiss her, and stopped just shy of completing the act.

"You know how to *get* secrets," I said. "I don't think you know much about keeping them."

Then I did kiss her. It was a deep kiss, the kind where you grab the back of the girl's head to make sure you don't push yourself all the way through.

Lucy's lips parted for me, and her tongue slid around mine like a cobra. Then her thighs were spread open and her knees had found their way up around my hips. In a second she'd be undoing my belt.

I don't really know how I managed to pull away right then. It could be sixty thousand years had taught me sex is not a good trade for death, even if it's really good sex and you haven't had it in a while, and even if it was with a redhead that reminded you of another redhead, just a little. It could also be my curiosity was actually stronger than my ardor.

I couldn't tell you for sure, but I did it. I pulled away, took a couple of steps back and left her hanging.

"What secrets did you get from Al already?" I asked. "'Cuz I don't have any he didn't give you."

She hissed a frustrated exhale through clenched teeth, closed her legs and pulled the coat down to hide her indecency.

"Why don't you have a last name, Rocky?" she asked.

Again with the last name. "Who says I don't?"

She extinguished her cigarette on the edge of the bar, which would have been a bigger deal if not for everybody doing it all the time. It was better than throwing it in the sawdust on the floor. "You said so yourself."

"Maybe I don't want you to have it. You want to tell me Smith is your real last name? Long line of smiths, right?"

I grabbed the bottle and started to walk away. When my head was turned she shouted, "*Hey, catch!*" I spun around just in time to intercept the shot glass before it hit my head. It wasn't until I put it down on the bar that I realized her shout hadn't been in English.

And then there was a gun in her hand.

"Do I want to know where you pulled that pistol from?" I asked.

"My sleeve, wise-guy. How's my German?"

"Is that what that was?"

"Don't play dumb. You may be a lotta things, Rocky, but you ain't dumb."

"*Your German's not bad,*" I said, in German. "But mine's a little rusty. You want to shoot me because I know another language?"

"I don't wanna shoot you at all, but since you're not responding to the usual persuasions, I've gotta consider other options."

"Hmm." I took a swig of the whiskey. "How about I tell you everything I know and you tell me everything you know, and then I take off that coat of yours and we have some fun?"

"Might be you lost your chance at that already. I don't sleep with spies."

"Me neither," I said, although strictly speaking I was pretty positive we were both lying. "So let's make sure neither one of us is first."

"Right. Pour me a drink."

"Is that an order?"

"I still have the gun, don't I? And stay on this side. I know you ain't got a piece on you, unless that was one I felt in your pants a minute ago, but maybe you got one behind the bar."

There wasn't one behind the bar, and I was glad for it. Back then I didn't much trust guns, which is what happens sometimes when you see a technology from birth. Guns used to be tremendously inaccurate noisemakers that were just as likely to blow up in your hand as anything, and that made me want to steer clear. It took me a long time to accept them as a better option than, say, a sword. I had the same basic problem with cars and domesticated cats.

I poured a shot into the glass she'd chucked at my head and stepped close enough to her to both grab the gun and put the drink down next to her. I only did the latter.

"So I'm gonna tell you some things I think you might already know," she said, as soon as I was far enough away to pose no threat as either an attacker or lover. "You stop me when I'm wrong."

"How about if I say I don't know anything and we forget about it?"

"You already know German, and that's a thing, Rock. There's a war on and all."

"A lot of people know German. It's a whole country, and it's been around for a while. You speak it, and so do probably ten other guys in the bar tonight. And before you throw anything else at my head, I also speak Italian. My Japanese isn't so hot."

"Right, fine. You also know my Al is kinda important."

"I wouldn't say that. He works on some things that are more complicated than I'll ever understand, and those things sound like they're important."

It wasn't that I couldn't see where she was going, but I was going to do all I could to derail her before she got there, short of getting the gun out of her hands. Romantically, that's not usually a big turn-on. (Okay, maybe it is sometimes.) That I was still thinking in terms of salvaging the possibility of sexual intercourse after she'd pulled a gun on me should give you an idea of exactly how compelling she was.

"That's funny, Al says you're the only one who *does* understand. Tells me all the time about how sharp you are and how great it is talking to you. How you ask the right questions."

"Lots of guys come in here and talk about things, Lucy. Most of them don't have much more to say other than how heavy the last thing they had to lift was, why their wives are disappointed, or what the cost of bread is. A couple of times of month someone with a kid overseas has to tell us all about him so we can feel bad when he doesn't come home. Al's the only guy I know with something to say that I haven't ever heard before, and that doesn't make me depressed about the state of the world. Of course I ask. Sometimes what's on his mind is the only hopeful thing I hear."

"Hopeful, huh?"

"Energy's a good thing, right? He can't stop talking about the possibilities."

She laughed, a gorgeous deep sound from her stomach that was somehow erotic. "That sounds like him, yeah."

This time I didn't know what direction she was heading. "Why don't you tell me where I'm wrong?"

"Yeah, okay." She put the gun down on the bar and took her shot, and slid the glass down the bar for me to refill. "So he told you about the pile under the stands."

"Bad name for it, but yeah."

"Sounds crazy, don't it? But it's true, it's real. They did it."

I refilled us both. When I put hers down close enough to reach she put her hand on the gun, almost as an afterthought, to make sure I didn't grab it.

In hindsight it probably would have been wiser to disarm her early—I'd passed on at least three opportunities—and go with my earlier instinct to run the hell out the back door before this got any worse.

"The first controlled nuclear chain reaction," she said, to her drink, which she then downed. "And he thinks it's keen."

"It's not keen?"

"It's the scariest goddamn thing in the world, Rocky no-last-name."

I am actually old enough to remember when we discovered fire. That's not half as impressive as it sounds because it wasn't like we didn't know what fire was already—I remember a lightning strike that caused a forest fire being the first time I saw it—we just didn't think of it as something we could do ourselves. The discovery came when we realized fire could be created, controlled, and extinguished when it was no longer needed, without having to wait for an electrical storm on a dry night.

Of course, once we got over the idea of using it for warmth and to make our food taste better, we started using it in less life-affirming ways.

"You're talking about a weapon," I said.

"On the nose. Except we both know you were already there, don't we?"

"No, I really never thought about it before now."

"Then you ain't as smart as he says."

"Al didn't think about it either, did he?"

"No, he don't get it. But he's not dumb, he's just not the right kind of smart. The French have a word for it. *Naïve*. See what he's working on is important, because he and those other fellas proved you could make a chain reaction in a lab, and control it. Maybe one day we can build things to use that energy like Al wants, but first we gotta survive what comes next. Because now these boys know their numbers are right the next thing they wanna do is figure out what happens when they release a *lot* of energy, all at once. Maybe enough to set the sky on fire and blow up the world, who knows? But that's another project, one he's never going to be involved in."

"Why's that?"

"He talks too much. Like when he talks to you, and you give up the stuff he's been saying to the enemy. Because I tell you, the only thing scarier than our boys having something like this is the Nazis having it."

There it was. I figured I'd hear something like that eventually, but I expected it to come from guys in suits, not a girl in heels and not much else. "Seems to me, of the two of us you look like a better suspect, Lucy Smith. He told me we can't talk any more, but I bet you can get anything you want."

"I already got everything from him I needed to, baby, don't you worry. He gave me you."

"Maybe I still don't understand what you're here for."

She reached into her pocket. "You may be right, Rocky. Maybe I *am* the kind of girl who'd Mata Hari poor Al, but I'm the one here with government credentials, so that takes me out of the running."

She held up a document and a badge. They both said FBI. And if you can believe it, her name really was down as Lucy Smith. I still didn't think it was her birth name, because you have to switch up names now and then when you don't die on schedule like everybody else.

"I understand now," I said, as regards the badge.

"Do you? Because here's what happened from where I'm sitting. Al and his friends down at the university had an idea for how to build their little reactor, and they worked out all kinds of complicated math to explain it. And then about a month ago a bar napkin with things only about two or three guys in the world understand turned up in the pocket of a German spy. That napkin was traced back to Al, and from him to this bar."

I was starting to get an inkling of how much trouble I was really in, and it was the kind of trouble *succubus with a gun* didn't completely cover. The notion of men in suits with papers to sign was sort of a vaguely threatening notion, but now I was facing an actual representative of the US government, and as far as she was concerned I was a spy. That was a huge problem, because I didn't exactly look like Joe American, not once you dug into my past a little bit. About all I had in my defense was that I *had* no past, and a real spy wouldn't have forgotten to make up something more concrete. I made a mental note then and there that if I was going to survive this, I would have to find a good forger.

"I'm surprised Al didn't get locked up," I said. "Isn't that what happens with this sort of thing?"

"Yeah sometimes, but scientists are hard to replace, and they don't think like the government does. These science guys, they figure something out and then they run and tell other scientists. It doesn't even matter most times whether that other scientist is American, British, German or Russian or what. He told the boys who came by before me that he knew better than to share the information with his 'colleagues' overseas. But he *didn't* know better'n to share it with the guys in the bar down the road."

"That's where you come in."

"That's right. My bosses decided it made more sense to send me to find out how that napkin ended up in the Kraut's pocket, rather than break the arm of a guy they needed to keep on thinking clearly. So I insert myself into Al's life and what do I find? A bartender with no last name, way too smart for what he does, asking my guy all kinds'a complicated questions. That same bartender has no legal record that I can find, works for pocket change and a roof over his head, doesn't pay any taxes, nothing. Nobody knows who he really is, how long he's been in town or what. And what do you know, he speaks German. And it gets worse from there."

"That sounds pretty bad already."

"Doesn't it, though?"

"Yeah. I'm beginning to suspect me too. But Al wrote a lot of things on a lot of napkins, pretty much anybody in the bar could have kept one."

"I talked to the guys in this bar all night, and I'm pretty positive none of them have the smarts to figure out what to do with those formulas. But you clean up the place, and you understood what he was explaining, and I'm thinking one of the mooks in this dive was your contact. Why don't you ask me why it gets worse?"

"Why does it get worse?"

"Because you resisted me."

"I'm… that wasn't easy."

"Well I appreciate that."

I couldn't figure out if she was insulted or something. I was basically one lull in the conversation from ripping her jacket off, but I wasn't about to say so. "I apologize, I guess, I mean…"

"No, no," she laughed. "My feelings aren't hurt. I'll be honest, you got me wound up like nobody's wound me in a long while. I'm gonna start ticking soon. But that ain't it. What I mean is, *nobody* resists me, not for this long. That's not normal, and it also ain't really possible."

"Maybe you're not my type."

"I'm everybody's type, baby. Even the Nancy boys give it up for me eventually. Plus I put a little something in the whiskey and the same stuff's in my lipstick. It should have you telling me everything from your birth name to the color of your Momma's hair. As much as you've had I should be able to get you barking like a dog if I want."

"Or just getting that jacket open and taking you right there in that chair." Yes, I was facing potential life imprisonment or death and this was what was on my mind. Draw your own conclusions.

"I didn't think I'd need the drug to get you to do that to me, but yeah, that too. So either you took an antidote pill beforehand like I did, or you have some kind of training I've never seen before. Both of those options mean you're bad business."

"Then we have some sort of problem, don't we?"

"*You* do, for sure. I got the gun, and there's a button in the pocket of this coat I can push and get a whole bunch of g-men down here lickety-split."

I was pretty sure that was an exaggeration, some kind of Dick Tracy gizmo that wasn't going to actually exist any time soon. But the rest of what she had to say was true enough.

"Maybe we can work out something that doesn't involve g-men ruining our night," I suggested. I was thinking my way out of this might have been to talk to her as one impossible person to another.

"Yeah, they do that. What do you have in mind? I probably won't believe anything you have to tell me and I'm leaning toward shooting you, just so we're on the level."

"It so happens drugs don't work on me."

"No kidding?"

"It's the truth. I also don't get sick."

"Well, you're a regular superman."

"Yeah, kind of. Let me ask you something: did you ever meet your father?"

She looked significantly taken aback. "What's that gotta do with anything?"

"Let me guess. You grew up in a well-to-do family, maybe even a happy one, except that your mom had a little fling on the side once and ended up with you. Nobody talks about it, but everyone knows when they look at you, because you don't look like anyone else in the family."

"You're about three seconds from losing some teeth, mister." She was no longer smiling or making any particular effort to look appealing. This had no negative effect on her appeal at all. "That ain't anybody's business and I wanna know what makes you think you know a thing about me."

"I know, because I know what you are. I know whatever your real name is it was given to you… fifty or sixty years ago, probably. Were you born here?"

"Yeah, I'm an American." She hesitated before continuing,

because this wasn't something you just spit out. She also had to decide whether to keep on being angry with me or to admit I was onto something. "It was round about 1890. But only me and five or six boys in the bureau know it, cuz I don't look much like an old lady."

"You don't look at all like an old lady."

"Yeah, thanks. So what the hell are *you*? You the same kind of thing?"

"No, I'm something else. There's only one of me."

The fundamentals of incubus/succubus reproduction are pretty simple. Succubi can't get pregnant regardless of whether they are mating with a human or an incubus. They don't want to have anything to do with incubi either way though, largely due to a massive, species-wide Daddy-issue thing. Basically, in order to make an incubus or a succubus, an adult incubus needs to impregnate a human woman. Since incubi hold no particular interest in sticking around and raising a family, what they do instead is seduce women in enviable situations. This means rich women, or women with rich husbands, or some combination of those two. That way the offspring are taken care of, and the incubus can be free to grift his way around to another advantageous arrangement.

Nobody liked incubi, including other incubi, who after all were fathered via the same arrangement. I'd met a few and thought they were raging jerks, but in their defense they almost had to be or the species would end up extinct. Unless that's a huge rationalization, in which case forgive me.

It made for a lot of unhappy childhoods, is my point. And if I were the "same kind of thing" as her it would have meant I was an incubus, and then she probably would have shot me.

"You're the only one, huh?" she said. "Until about two minutes ago I was pretty sure I was the only one of me, so how can you be so sure of that?"

Succubi also tend to steer clear of each other, mostly for territorial reasons, but usually there's some sort of mentoring program. I was surprised she'd never met another, but I didn't say so.

"I saw the only other immortal I knew about die in a fire about fifteen years ago. Beyond that, you're going to have to take my word."

"Yeah I don't think that's gonna happen. Immortal, huh?" Her bravado returned somewhat. I'd knocked her off-balance with the questions about her upbringing, but it wasn't enough. "What I think, I think maybe you met someone like me before and now you're trying to flim-flam your way out of trouble."

"Well I'm not your guy. I never kept any of those napkins, and I'm telling you everybody else in the bar heard the same stuff I did. Maybe one of them's playing dumb. I'm also a whole lot older than you are, which is why I don't have a last name or a legal record. I'm not an American because I'm older than this country. And the reason I know German, and Italian, and French and Spanish and damn near every other tongue you can name off the top of your head is that I was there when they became languages. But I *have* met your kind before all right, and I know your storyline because you all have the same one. I might even know more about you than you do about yourself."

Uncertainty flickered across her face again as she let all of that sink in. Then she pulled a cigarette case from one of her inside pockets and lit a new smoke for herself. It was something that involved putting the gun down on the bar first, so it felt almost like a decision on her part to take me seriously. I stepped behind the bar and had new shots poured for both of us before she had a chance to recognize that I'd gone where she told me not to.

"Let's pretend all that is true," she said. "Tell me something. You can't get sick and it sounds like you're saying you don't get any older than you're looking right now. Are you also bullet-proof?"

"That I'm not."

"Can you fly?"

"No."

"And you ain't working for nobody, nobody's working for you, and you have no idea what this business with the napkins is about?"

"That's what I'm saying."

We both heard the sound of a car driving up in the lot. It wasn't a tough thing to pick out because it was all gravel out there. The headlights went across the front of the bar from right to left as the driver parked, and then they went out.

Lucy slid off the stool and took two steps toward the door.

"Yeah, if all that's true then we got a problem," she said.

"Those aren't your g-men?"

"Nope. Thing is I did a lot of talking earlier to see if I could flush out your contacts. I figured they answered to you." There was a loud *click-click* sound near the front door. "Oh geez. Duck."

I dropped to the floor behind the bar at around the same time Lucy managed, in those heels, to spin around and vault over it, landing next to me smoothly and untouched by the hot lead that was by then tearing through the thin wall separating us from the parking lot. She even grabbed her gun on her way over. It was pretty damn sexy.

Me, I managed to save the whiskey bottle but that was about it.

"So these guys, they ain't with you?" she asked.

There was one person firing a Tommy gun into the front door, and a second one shooting through the wall next to the door. I could hear the place being turned into splintered remains around us, with about the only thing in our favor the fact that I'd put away the glassware and locked up most of the alcohol already. The liquor was kept in a wood cabinet above us, and while the wood wasn't keeping any bullets out it was keeping shattered glass in. More importantly, the bar we were hiding behind was the heaviest and thickest thing in the place and it was doing a fine job of keeping the bullets away from us. It was so sturdy I had a theory that the place was built around it.

"I don't even know what's going on," I shouted. Who's out there?"

"I'm guessing they're the guys that actually sold Al's notes. You got a phone back here?"

"Why don't you push your magic button?"

"Right, I made that up to keep you trying for the gun. How about that phone?"

I crawled over her and to the far end of the bar, reached up and pulled down the house phone. I handed it over.

"Try and call some real g-men, not someone you made up," I said.

She was still dialing when the shooting stopped. If I'd known any better at the time I'd have cursed how long it took to get a number completed on a rotary phone.

"Frankie," she whispered into the receiver. "Yeah, it's me. I'm at the place, and I'm pretty sure I got our guys but I'm gonna need a white horse or three… Yeah, I'm serious." She looked at me. "I never needed a rescue before, he's laughin'."

"You want me to tell him we're about to die? Maybe he'll believe me."

"Yeah, get some guys down here, before local P.D. finds our bodies… Never mind who's here with me, just do it."

She hung up. "We gotta buy about forty minutes, I think."

It was possible the local cops she was talking about would show up before that forty minutes, but that was unlikely. Jimmy's was still a mob bar, even if only just barely, and the cops knew better than to show up while the shooting was still going on. Better to turn up an hour or two later to see who didn't make it and sweep up the broken glass.

I heard the door get kicked open. "How do you feel about thirty seconds?" I asked her.

Someone had just walked into the bar, with at least one other someone behind them.

"Too bad you don't have a gun back here, huh?" she whispered.

"It'd have to be a bigger gun than the ones they have." I whispered back. "Who'd you get me tangled up with?" It probably wasn't all that necessary, the whispering, since the guys inside had been firing really loud guns for a little while. That'll wreck your hearing.

She shrugged. "I talked to a lot of fellas earlier, and I knew someone followed me here but I figured they were with you."

"Except they're not with me, so I can't exactly order them to stand down."

"I get that. If it helps, I think I might believe you now."

At the edge of the bar was a white dishtowel, which with a little work I was able to grab and wave in the air in sight of the armed guys. "Hey fellas, no guns back here, just me. I'm gonna stand, all right?"

No answer. I stood anyway, and saw two men I didn't recognize. Admittedly the lighting was now even worse due to all the dust and gun smoke kicking around the room, but I was pretty good with faces and names at the time, because that was half the job. These two had on nicer suits than most of the guys who came around the bar, and the guns weren't the sort of thing that showed up there too often either.

"What can I do for you fellas?" I asked. They both had their barrels trained on me but neither started shooting, which was nice. After a five count, the one nearest the door knocked on it, and two more men walked in. I only knew one of them.

"Rocky, I'm real sorry about all this."

"Hiya, Vinnie. Looks like you know some folks with guns."

Vinnie looked like he always did, which was to say he didn't look like much more than a bruiser of the sort you hired to shake down people smaller than him. He was someone I never really wanted to run into outside of Jimmy's, figuring if I did it was for a bad reason. We were still in Jimmy's, but this encounter certainly qualified.

The guy next to Vinnie, who I'd never seen before, took a good look around the place. "What a dump," he said. He was a squat little guy, the least physically impressive of the four of them, which made him most likely to be the guy in charge. He was balding, and had an unpleasant scar on the side of his face.

"It looked a lot nicer about five minutes ago," I said. "Who are you?"

"I'm nobody you need to know, except if I say so these guys here finish you off."

"Do you have a name?"

He eyeballed Vinnie, who shrugged.

"No," he said to me, "I don't have a name."

"This is my employer, Rock," Vin said. "That's all you need to know."

"Maybe you're right, Vin, and I don't need to know his name. But just maybe *he* needs to know whose bar he just shot all to hell."

This was a dangerous play on my part, but I didn't have many other options. My only secret weapon was the succubus with the pistol under the bar, and I didn't think she could shoot or screw us out of this. Maybe if there were fewer guys.

Vinnie's employer still looked annoyed about the state of the bar. "You aren't Jimmy?"

"No I told you," Vin said. "This is Rocky. I never met no Jimmy."

"Jimmy doesn't come around all that much, mister, except to collect the register and check on whose bar tab needs some personal attention. Couple of times a month he runs a poker game out back, but you're probably not invited seeing as you don't have a name and I don't recognize your mug. His last name's Ricca. Maybe that rings a bell or two."

It should have rung a whole orchestra of bells. Ricca was the surname of the family that ran the Chicago Outfit, which was the local syndicate.

Vinnie and his boss both went a little paler than they started out. "You saying this shop is owned by Jimmy Ricca?" the boss asked.

"That's what I'm saying. But I'm sure you fellas didn't mean to wreck his place. You can just call him up and apologize and I'm sure he'd understand."

The boss looked deeply displeased. "I think maybe we've got ourselves a big problem," he said. "Wouldn't you say, Vinnie?"

"Yeah…" Vinnie's expression made it clear he was pretty sure he was in a heap of trouble. I was nearly positive Vin knew who owned the bar, and just didn't think about it until right then.

"Tell you what," I said. "You four walk on out of here right now, I'll make up something and leave you out of it."

"You'd do that for us, Rocky?" Vinnie asked.

"Of course I would."

"No, no that's not gonna work," the boss said, shaking his head. "Vinnie might be a damn idiot, but he tells me he overheard you and some dame talking about going to the feds, and we're not okay with that. Granted, we could have perhaps approached the matter with more subtlety, but that don't change things all that much in my mind. So where are you hiding the girl, Mr. Rocky? And don't tell me she ran out the back because we were watching."

I looked down. It seemed inappropriate, having her stand wearing only that coat, like she was showing up at the door in a negligee. But she gave me a little nod, so I figured it was okay.

"You got her rattled with all the shooting. Can't blame her. Come on honey." I extended my hand for her to stand. She gave me a private eye-roll before getting to her feet.

"What's going on, Rocky? What do these fellas want?" She slid in with my arm around her like it was the most natural thing in the world. Felt good too, having her there.

Lucy gave them the doe-iest doe-eyes anybody had ever seen. You'd have sworn she was the most innocent girl on the face of the earth, regardless of how nearly naked she was. But it was clear nobody was buying the act. Problem was, most people—regardless of gender—would have been in hysterics after that show of gunfire, and she came off like we'd just met an encyclopedia salesman.

"I don't know, baby," I said. "I think these guys are just confused."

"She's the one," Vin said. "Asking too many questions."

"Well..." the boss said. He looked her up and down in a way that made me want to punch him in the jaw. "Ain't you a sight?"

"Aww, thanks, mister. But I don't know what you boys are talking about. I just stopped by here for a little nightcap with Rocky. What kinda questions you mean?"

"A nightcap, huh?" The boss eyed what she wasn't wearing.

"Maybe a little more than a nightcap, but what's it to ya? That's no reason to go around shooting up a place."

"No, it isn't. But you see miss, we procured some items from this establishment, and then sold those items and made a little money from them, and we'd rather nobody knew about that little arrangement. Vincent, who I think you met earlier this evening, helped with the procurement. He's a suspicious guy who doesn't want to go to jail for trying to make an honest buck, as I'm sure you understand, so when you started whispering in his ear he got to thinking maybe we had a problem. He heard a *similar* bunch of disturbing details just before running down the street and placing a call to me. Now we have a different kind of problem, because even if Vincent here was completely wrong about everything else, it turns out—according to your boyfriend here—I'm standing in a bar owned by the Outfit, with two witnesses what don't work for me that have seen my face."

He took a look at his two gunners. I'd been keeping an eye on them myself because it's never a bad idea to keep track of the guns in the room. Their expressions hadn't changed at all. I was pretty sure they were either stone deaf or didn't speak the language.

"I'm sorry, you seem like a classy dame and I'm sure this Rocky here is a stand-up guy, but my boys here are gonna have to shoot you. Then I figure we'll have to torch the whole place and work on our alibis. If Jimmy Ricca owns the dive it'll get chalked up as a hit on him, that's how I'm seein' this."

Something about me, and bars and Chicago always seem to add up to mobs, guns and fires eventually. It made me think I should choose a different city, provided I figured out a way to walk out of this one on my own, which was a tall order under the circumstances. I was pretty sure I wouldn't be able to convince Vinnie or his boss that I was immortal and didn't give a goddamn who he was.

Fortunately, Lucy took the information like it was nothing. She smiled and laughed like he'd just made the best joke she'd heard all year, and dammit if he didn't smile a little.

"You're funny!" she exclaimed. She stepped out from under my arm and leaned forward The boss had his hands on the bar, so she took one of them and started rubbing his wrist. I couldn't see the front of her from the angle I was at, but I knew exactly how much cleavage she was showing off when she did this.

"I'm serious, honey," he said, patting her hands. "Sorry it's gotta be this way."

"Ah, you! I tell ya what," she said, shooting him a comically perplexed expression that was adorable and not at all appropriate when contrasted with the news of her imminent demise. She reached behind the bar and revealed the half-empty bottle of whiskey we'd been draining all night. "As it turns out the only bottle your boys didn't shoot is the best one in the house. How 'bout you and Vinnie here join us for a shot and then we can talk about what to do about this little mess of ours. We got a little time, right Rock?"

"Yeah, plenty," I said, although what made anybody think I was an expert on this I couldn't say.

"There see? C'mon, you fellas have been all worried about this little secret of yours the whole night I bet you could use a stiff one."

⁓

A stiff one was exactly what they needed, and the drug in the alcohol was exactly what *we* needed. Ten minutes later Vinnie and his boss—whose name we quickly learned, was Echols—were feeling a lot better about everything in their lives. At Lucy's suggestion Echols ordered the two guys with the big guns to stand outside, which made relaxed the situation considerably. They would undoubtedly remain standing out there until her g-men backup arrived, and that was maybe bad news for the feds, but it wasn't my problem. My problem was either Vinnie and Echols, or Lucy. I couldn't be sure.

"Seems to me, you guys have a bigger concern than Jimmy Ricca," Lucy was saying, as she fed them their third or fourth shot apiece.

By this time the drug had settled in nicely and I was beginning to understand why she was so surprised when I didn't react to it. These hardened criminals had already confessed to selling the contents of the napkins, not knowing until later it was going to end up in the hands of the Germans. Once they learned this they did everything they could to erase any connection between them and the sale, which meant following the overly inquisitive Lucy and shooting up what they were afraid was a barroom full of federal agents. They felt awful about this, and agreed they had not acted particularly rationally, and now were panicking about the whole thing.

They were also ready to do whatever she said.

"What do you mean, sweetie?" Echols asked.

"You were wrong about the place being full of feds," she said. "But there was at least one." She put her credentials on the table. "Ain't that a kick in the head?"

Vinnie and Echols looked at it, thought about it for a while, and then started laughing. "Yeah," Vin said. "Yeah, that's a problem, huh?"

"Now we *really* have to kill both of you!" Echols said.

Lucy laughed. "No, no, no, you're thinking about it all *wrong*. I don't care about you boys, all I want is who you sold the napkins to. The Outfit don't have to be the wiser for it either way."

"But look what we did to this place!"

"I tell you what," Lucy said, a glimmer in her eye and a sidewise glance at me. "Word on the street is, Rocky here was into some stuff on the side."

Vinnie looked at me, wide-eyed. "*Was* he?"

"I didn't think so, no," I said. "I'm pretty sure I didn't have anything going on."

She threw me a wink. "Sure you did, Rock. You were in some stuff Jimmie didn't know about, and it turns out that stuff involved selling secrets to the Germans, and it's a shame how those secrets got you killed. And these fellas here, they're heroes for finding out and turning over the whole operation."

"Heroes!" Echols agreed.

"All they have to do is give me the name of everybody they know who touched those napkins. You know, since you don't actually know those names and these guys do."

"I'm not sure I like that story," I said.

"Yeah, I didn't think you would." She had her gun out again. Apparently she really did have a place in her sleeve to hide that thing. She pointed it at my head. "Sorry, Rocky. It's the only story everyone's gonna buy. Tough thing is, you gotta die for it to work out."

I was thinking she had skipped a couple of non-lethal options, and possibly also forgotten the part where I said I wasn't bulletproof. "These fellas will believe anything you say," I pointed out.

"Sure, you're right, but the FBI won't. You're a guy with no last name and no family, manning a bar that stole and sold state secrets. People get locked up for that much. It's better off for you this way."

"So you're gonna shoot me?" I was pretty sure I was missing something.

"Nah, not me. These boys are the ones that did it, right boys?"

"Sorry, Rock," Vinnie said. "You were a solid guy."

"Such a shame," Echols agreed.

I looked into Lucy's green eyes and caught her giving me another wink. Then I noticed the barrel of the gun wasn't actually pointed right at my head. It was aimed at the air to the right of me.

"I always figured it'd be a dame that got me in the end," I said. Because if you're going to go, why not go out saying something memorably cliché?

"Ain't that the best way?" she asked.

Then she fired.

I fell over, and lay on the floor for about ten seconds, while she reiterated that I was now deceased and furthermore, the two very drugged guys at the bar had done the deed themselves. While they were busy mourning my passing, I got up again. She pulled me around the corner.

"You got a back exit to this place, right?" she asked.

"I do."

"Good." She shoved something into my hand. "Take this and get outta here. Don't talk to anybody, don't let anybody see you, do nothing but head straight there, you got me?"

The thing in my hand was a key.

"I think I do."

"Good. I mean it, don't let anybody see you. Take the alleys and keep your head down. Oh, and have this." She kissed me, full-on, lips open, tender and fierce, and for about two seconds I forgot everything else including what I was supposed to be doing next.

"Now go," she said. Like I could run anywhere after that.

∼

The key went to a door belonging to a room in a hotel six blocks away, in just about the seediest part of the seedy part of town. The place made Jimmy's dive look like a four-star establishment. It could've taken me only a few minutes to get there but she said to stick to the alleys so I stuck to the alleys. More than once I had to park myself in a dark corner for a little while until I stopped hearing sirens. There ended up being a lot of sirens.

It was a crummy room. Small bed, one wood chair, a toilet that only flushed when it felt like it, and a lingering smell that was some unholy combination of mildew and vomit. About the only thing nice about the place was there wasn't anybody pointing a gun at me, which was a feature I could appreciate.

With nothing much to do—I was too wound up to sleep and anyway that didn't seem like a great plan—I sat on the chair and looked out at the alley through the one window. The drop was about three stories. I thought if I had to I could probably survive it. It wasn't a great escape plan, but it was something.

The delay was long enough for me to worry that I shouldn't even be there. I was waiting on a succubus who could shoot me, turn me in to the government as a spy, or screw me in a more literal sense, and the third option was the only one worth sticking around for. Could have been she just staged my death in order to help me get out of town, but so long as she had the US government behind her there was no way to be sure. I'd heard enough stories about agitators disappearing and whatnot to be concerned that the country's interests and mine didn't coincide.

It had to be four in the morning by the time Lucy let herself in.

"You alone?" She asked. There was a light from the hallway, so I couldn't see her face, but the figure and the voice and the gun in her hand was all I needed.

"Just me," I said. "Thanks for aiming a gun at me again, I was beginning to forget what that felt like."

"Just being careful." She kicked the door closed behind her and tossed a sack onto the bed. It made a jingle when it hit, which the bed didn't do when I'd sat on it earlier so I figured it was from the bag.

"What's that?"

"That's the money from the cash drawer. Place like that, I figured it'd have a safe but I couldn't find one."

"Nobody's crazy enough to steal from Jimmy," I said.

"Looks like *you* were."

I picked up the sack while Lucy put her gun away and took off the coat. I was disappointed to see she'd taken the time to put on some more clothing sometime over the course of the night because now she had on a skirt and a blouse. She looked like someone straight out of the secretary pool, if they had one of those in heaven.

To my unspoken observation she said, "Changed into 'em before the place was stormed by the feds. I got methods I'd as soon keep to myself, you understand."

"I do." It wasn't a lot of cash in the bag. "What's this for?"

"That ought to be enough to get you outta town. You gotta be in the wind, Rocky. You get that, right?"

"Explain it to me."

"Your story wasn't gonna fly with my people. They look far enough into you they're gonna have the same questions I had. You had to die."

She put one leg up on the bed and slid a hand up her thigh to unclip the garter holding her stocking in place. Then she began to slide the stocking down.

"I knew the first time I saw you, you were gonna get me killed. How'd it happen?" I asked.

"Your pal Vinnie and his buddy confessed to it. Sorry I had to fire the gun at your head like that, I've found this kind of persuasion works better if there's a show that goes with it."

She slid out of the shoe to get the stocking all the way off, then started on her second leg. I was having a little trouble keeping track of what she was saying on account of what she was doing.

"Once they were convinced I'd killed you, it wasn't all that hard to talk them into thinking they'd done it themselves. Now, they'll swear up and down they did it *earlier*, at the bar, brought your body to the lake and tossed it in, then went back to the bar looking for me. Oh and it turns out you were into some nasty stuff. It looks like Rocky isn't even your name."

"Those two guys with the big guns might have a thing or two to say about that story," I said. I was staying in the chair for the moment, happy to watch her take her clothes off for me.

"Yeah, funny thing tho. They were out front when the feds got to the scene, and I guess they both got a little trigger-happy. They were told to stand down, but whoops, they only spoke Polish. So they're dead now, looks like."

"You sent them outside on purpose."

She had taken care of the other stocking and now was slipping off her skirt as casually as if she was standing in her own bedroom alone, except I had to think nobody ever looked this good undressing without an audience.

"Could be. It's really hard to convince someone of something if you don't speak their language, no matter how much you drug 'em. Good thing my cavalry knew to expect gunplay, huh?"

"You might be too clever to trust."

"Look who's talking, Mr. no-name immortal man. Now, you wanna help me get out of this blouse or do I have to do all the work here?"

~

I left Chicago a week later in a midnight cab ride that took me to a train stop a few miles out of town. First I had to say goodbye to Lucy, which was two days of work all by itself. Once the gun was safely on the other side of the room and her clothes safely on the floor, she turned out to be much easier to get to know, and at least trust enough to appreciate properly. That appreciation took up five days, with breaks for food and so she could call her office. Her explanation for being out was that she was looking for my body, which was easily the most entertaining excuse I'd ever heard.

The money she gave me only took care of the cab ride and the train ticket, but that was okay because I had some money set aside—in the form of a duffel full of cash in a train station locker in Philly—and also some distant invested funds I didn't really touch, but was there in a pinch.

I didn't know it at the time but those investments were actually about to explode in value. One of the things Al told me that didn't make onto a napkin was about a company he was hoping to work for after his gig at the university ended. "It's called International Business Machines, Rocky," he had said. "I'm telling you, if you got any coin you should put some into it with them."

I followed his advice. I didn't remember doing it, but I did.

I don't know how things worked out for Al, but I did make Lucy promise to tell him the truth about her. I mean, about being a government agent, not the succubus thing. I think he probably didn't end up having anything to do with the Manhattan Project. That wasn't his kind of gig. Maybe he wound up at IBM like he wanted.

Lucy left me with about four different ways to contact her in the future, and made me promise to drop her a line once I'd settled on a new name. But as much as it was great to have a line on a succubus and a friend in the government, I didn't expect to ever look her up again. She was still trouble, and that wasn't going to change.

Turns out I was wrong. But that's a story for another time.

THE IMMORTAL CHRONICLES

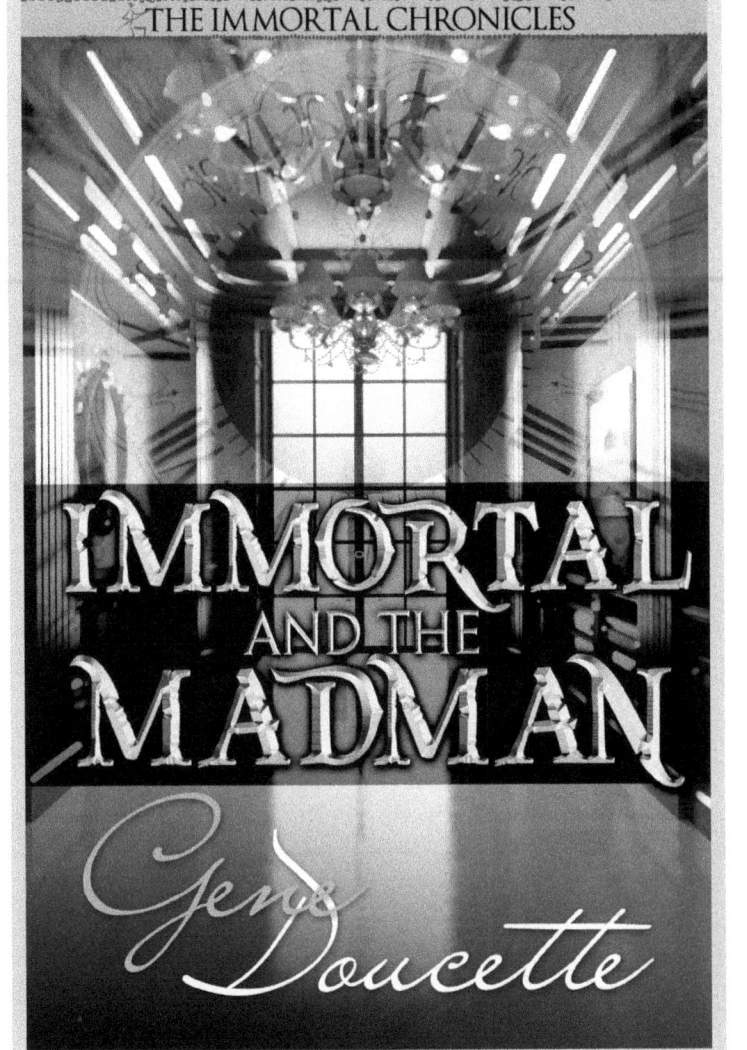

IMMORTAL AND THE MADMAN

Gene Doucette

IMMORTAL AND THE MADMAN

I go mad every now and again.

That's probably an outmoded way of describing what I'm talking about. I appreciate that there are truly insane people in the world who are suffering greatly because of some version of insanity, and I have never been *that* kind of mad.

I will explain.

Nowadays there's a thing called psychoanalysis, and whole sections of the medical world devoted to understanding and treating insanity, and it's all done rather respectfully and humanely, and that's fantastic. But for most of history we basically had *functionally crazy* or *batshit insane* and that was about all. There was no shortage of possible causes, from demonic possession—a personal favorite—to a huge range of supposed mental deficiencies that could be summarized as "being an outspoken woman."

There were different kinds of crazy is my larger point. Some kinds of madness resulted in the sufferer being unable to function within society at all, and other kinds were less obvious, and could even be described as a species of uncontrollable creativity.

Losing control of my mind is a real problem, because I

already live in a reality that's difficult to grasp for humans with ordinary lifespans. (That sentence by itself, written today while I am in full command of my faculties, could be enough to get me committed in the right circles.) Having lived a life that sounds like the rants of a lunatic is a real problem if I start to *actually* rant is what I'm saying. Losing my grip on things puts me in a great deal of danger.

The problem is, lucidity can be an act of will, and sometimes I lack that will.

I've always assumed that aside from a few quirks—I don't age, I don't get sick—I'm basically as much of an ordinary human as there is, and if that's true I'm working with the same kind of brain as everyone else. But since I don't die (or rather, since I haven't yet) that brain is sometimes working very hard to just keep everything straight.

To give a simple example, let's talk about pattern recognition. Seeing something and recognizing it as something you've seen *before* is a survival skill. For instance: I see a leopard. Last week, I saw a different leopard kill my friend, so even though this leopard is not the same one, I know not to pet it.

That the mind can compare a new object or animal or person to one from prior experience is a good thing. It jump-starts the fight-or-flight instinct, and it works exceptionally well for people who are drawing from ten or twenty years of experience on the planet. But then there's me, with the same kind of brain and the same kind of instincts, only I'm pulling from sixty thousand years of information.

If I'm not careful, I'll overreact to things that aren't important and miss something I should be paying attention to. I basically have to be on very good terms with that part of my brain, all the time.

There are times when I lose the capacity to do that.

I usually recognize when it's about to happen, and thank goodness. I have to self-monitor, because I don't often surround myself with people I can trust with my life and also with my secrets, so if I start to babble I'm generally on my own.

The first indication that something is amiss is when my heart starts racing, more or less randomly. It's what the body does in response to an apparent threat, and it's great when there actually *is* one, but when you're in a situation without any apparent danger it's scary as hell. As my heart rate increases and I start to sweat, I begin looking around for things that I can use as weapons and for weapons that are about to be used on me, in case I'm wrong about the danger thing and my instinct is accurate. Sometimes it is, and this is just worse because it means I can't ignore every instance.

Here's an example. I was in this tavern one evening in what I think was probably the mid fifteen-hundreds. It was winter, and there was ale, and a fireplace, and it was probably in the Austro-Germanic region or thereabouts. I'm pretty sure I was alone, but I'm not positive because around that period I traveled with a vampire named Eloise. Her reliability when it came to drinking alcohol and frequenting inns wasn't all that great, though, so she probably wasn't there.

Anyway, I was drinking—which is really one of the only two or three good reasons to be in a tavern—and in mid-conversation with someone when my heart rate sped up. It was sudden enough that I wondered if I was having an actual heart attack. I looked around the room expecting to find… something. Anything. A large cat, a python, a small army of Huns maybe. But there were only humans in there with me, and none of them looked particularly antagonistic or tribal or mob-like. And no Huns.

But it kept happening. I'd look around and calm down and get my bearings and remind myself I was among my own tribe in a safe enclosure and whatever instincts were telling me to defend myself were invalid, but I just couldn't stay relaxed.

After probably an hour of this I realized what was causing it was a combination of sound and shadows. A barmaid on the other side of the room had a high laugh, and there was a large man sitting near the fire casting a shadow on the wall to my right, and whenever the man moved and the maiden laughed in something like unison it brought me back to a time some fifty thousand years earlier, when there was a bird that made the same noise. It flew in from the direction of the sun to attack, and when you saw its shadow and heard its cry you knew to throw yourself onto the ground immediately, as this was the only defense in a time before we had things like arrows.

The bird no longer exists, so this isn't any kind of useful survival mechanism, but I'm sort of stuck with it now.

That panic attack in the tavern was the first sign I was heading for trouble. And it got worse. A couple of nights later I saw a man I mistook for an old friend. I greeted him as such, and spoke Etruscan to him for about ten minutes before I realized the person I thought I was talking to had been dead for a long time and this stranger was confused and a little terrified.

That was when I decided to go away for a while.

～

Fleeing for the countryside is my favorite solution. I mostly mean that literally, as in I would exit civilization and disappear into the nearest forest or mountainous region to hang out alone until I was pretty sure my head was okay enough not to endanger myself or other people. This was obviously a better solution back when there were forests. We don't really have those any more.

I know you're thinking we do, because you can see trees in satellite pictures and all, but you don't really know what you're talking about. When I say *forest* I mean the point at which the portion of the natural world that is in abeyance due to civilized man stops. The early American settlers called it Indian country and the Greeks called it the satyr woods, and while both are inaccurate—Indians had a civilization of their own, and so did satyrs after a fashion—it meant the same thing: wilderness. If you knew how to hunt and forage and build a shelter you could walk into these woods and live off the land for as long as you wanted, as long as you didn't mind being alone and not bathing very often. (That's all civilization—tribal, communal, national—really ever was: the opportunity to rely on someone else to keep you safe and find you food when you needed those things, in exchange for which you had to bathe more often.) There may be one or two places like that on the planet still, but I'm not sure where, and I *am* sure I would need a plane or two to get to them.

There is another version of *the countryside*, though, and it's the kind that wealthy people talk about.

This was always sort of true everywhere but I'm going to focus on England specifically, and the turn of the nineteenth century even more specifically, because that's where and when this story took place.

Back then if you and your family had enough wealth you could keep a place in the city and another place in the countryside, and that was all reasonable and normal. Residence in one estate or the other was mostly dictated by social and seasonal concerns, but that wasn't always the case. Sometimes the wealthy retired to their country estates because the strain of being civil was too much, and they had to get away to keep from acting too publicly crazy.

I think in a lot of ways this was similar to my problem. There were so many social rules and proprieties that frankly, if you didn't want to offend anyone important you had to pay constant attention, and it was exhausting. Or maybe I was the only one who saw it that way. I was, after all, an outsider. The *polite vs. not polite* rules of a society were always the hardest thing for me to internalize.

I had two or three close friends in this time, friends who were both reliable and pretty rich. Those are the sorts of people one should always strive to cultivate, especially if you yourself don't happen to be rich.

I was not rich then. I was well-to-do, but not rich. I was mostly living off the wealth I had personally acquired as a merchant some fifty years prior, which I attributed to my father and called my inheritance. There wasn't a whole lot of it left, but what there was of it took care of my nominal requirement of having coin on-hand to purchase things like food and drink and a roof. And those were the only things I concerned myself with right up until the day I started seeing dragons and dead people.

I'm not really clear on *exactly* what happened. I was at a ball, unless it was a dinner party or someone's birthday, or maybe a wedding. It was, at any rate, an excuse for wealthy people and people who knew wealthy people to get dressed up in whatever clothes were fashionable at the time and drink, dance, and act scandalous in ways that would sound immensely tame and boring to anyone not of that era.

I'd been having little problems here and there over the course of the month leading up to the evening in question, but nothing I couldn't handle. A racing heart here, an imaginary demon there, and sure, I mistook a carriage man for a Bantu tribesman and ended up speaking the wrong language for a little while, but I was sure I had it under control.

You tell yourself these things.

The night of the ball I was chatting up an old friend named Cornelius, and we were on the subject of hunting, and the guests were dancing in that annoyingly coordinated way they used to, when somehow I became convinced there was a dragon at the other end of the hall and my friend Cornelius was in fact my much, much older friend Gilgamesh (yes, that Gilgamesh) and we had to defend the room. So I charged right down the middle of the dancing line with my friend's decorative sword, and would likely have completely destroyed the three-tiered cake at the far end of the hall with it had I not been intercepted and tackled by two of Cornelius's men.

Later that evening I discovered myself resting comfortably in a leather chair in a lovely English study attached to the men's club not far from the scene of my social *faux pas*. I don't recall how I got there, how long it took, how many people were involved, or when the brandy ended up in my hand. What I do remember—probably the moment I became lucid again—was noticing Cornelius in a chair opposite me, sipping from his own glass and taking his time with a cigar. I couldn't tell you how long we'd been sitting there.

"How do you feel?" he asked once it was clear my senses had been regained. I don't know what indicators he used; perhaps my eyes just stopped wandering around the room.

"This is good brandy," I said. "Can I have some more?"

He made a gesture and a man came over from the other side of the room with the bottle, and refilled my snifter. Having people around to do that is why one strives to be rich.

"*Now* how do you feel?" he asked.

"I feel very well, thank you. Why?"

"Do you know who I am?"

"Of course, Cornelius."

"You called me by another name earlier this evening. I couldn't tell you what that name was. Nobody could understand what you were even speaking, but you became highly agitated as regards the baked confections."

He continued in this way to describe my actions, and only then did I recall what I *thought* had been going on. The gibberish he described me using was actually Akkadian. It's just as well nobody there understood it, insofar as a man in a formal suit waving a dull short sword and screaming about dragons would have only been worse, somehow, than one who was evidently speaking in tongues.

"I feel much better now," I said.

"I'm glad."

My friend was an aging patriarch of a decently well-off family. He had the physique of a man who had once been very active, which explained his tendency to attend formal events with a sword. Unless that was a symbol of some sort of military service. It was difficult for me to tell the difference, because I remember when people walked around with swords all the time, and that was still a true thing in certain parts of the world in this period. We had not yet reached the stage where guns were commonplace.

Cornelius wasn't a man to be trifled with, so when he fell into a long silence, sipping and smoking and watching me—perhaps to see if I was only pretending to be sane—I sat quietly and enjoyed my brandy and waited to hear what else he had to say. Clearly, there was more to be expected from him.

"Which war was it?" he asked.

"Which war?"

He coughed gently, which was for him a polite way of saying I should know exactly what he was talking about. "As you know, sir Reginald, I fought in the American war."

Reginald was the name I was using at this time. The 'sir' was entirely his invention.

"I do, yes."

"I was on the ground when we evacuated Boston. You strike me as too young to have seen battle there. And we both know you aren't truly a Britisher. But I also know what I saw this evening. You understand it took five men to subdue you? Two were combat-trained."

"Did I hurt anyone?"

"You didn't *kill* anyone, so let's celebrate that."

I noticed for the first time that we weren't fully alone. There was the butler with the brandy bottle, but this was the kind of place where the help wasn't factored into the head-count. The two men standing by the door, though, were definitely not a part of the staff. I wondered if they were the combat-trained men he was speaking of.

""Don't worry about them," Cornelius said, on noting where my gaze had drifted. "I made the necessary arrangements already. Nobody's going to clap you in iron and drag you off to the asylum so long as I'm here."

"Is that... was that an option?" Exactly *how* insane had I acted? I wondered.

"As I said, don't concern yourself. I've seen this sort of fatigue before. It's all right if you don't wish to tell me where you saw combat, I was merely curious. You are a complicated man, and I will allow you to keep your own counsel. But since I have put you in my charge for a time, I hope that even though you aren't willing to unburden yourself of your past with me, you *will* take my advice."

I looked at the men at the door again. "Your advice."

"I can't *keep* you here, or anywhere. You're not a prisoner. It's only that I've spoken for you, and if you manage to go mad again and start attacking noblemen while reciting that African tongue—or whatever in the *hell* that language was—it will reflect poorly on me. Your reputational risk has become mine, Reginald. I hope that you will take this into consideration when weighing your options."

"I understand," I said. "And thank you for speaking up for me. I'm sure I must have been a sight."

"I fear you also may have some... issues in a number of social circles just now, as fully half the court believes you possessed by demons. So. I have a place in the country. I've told you about it before, I think."

"You have, yes." It was a few dozen acres of land and something that sounded like a small palace. Cornelius was mostly to be found there when he wasn't in his apartments in the city. It was where his wife spent most of her time, if I recalled correctly.

"War isn't something we want the women to understand," Cornelius said, "but we can't pretend it isn't still inside of us either. Sometimes we need a place to go to face that war, in privacy, where nobody can be harmed. I speak from experience when I say these things. And so, when the need arises I have been known to collect wayward souls such as yourself and offer them the use of my estate, which is far too large for my family alone. My advice is to accept this offer. We have a carriage waiting."

~

I accepted the offer.

There were other options. I could have abandoned my station in life entirely and gone off somewhere alone, but the fact that I was on an island at the time—an island rapidly filling up with civilized people—made disappearing into any remaining wilds less feasible. It wasn't exactly a temperate zone either. If I let go and became completely unhinged, when winter came I'd probably end up hurting someone just in the interest of finding a warm place to stay. I also didn't know how close I was to becoming that completely unhinged person, so getting out of the city was probably a good thing.

Helping my decision was the fact that every time I looked at one of the two men at the door I swore I was looking at king Khufu of Kemet, an Egyptian pharaoh who had, needless to say, been dead for some time. I took heart in the fact that the other guy didn't look like anyone in particular. Hopefully that meant I was only about 50% insane.

Cornelius's mansion did not end up being nearly as countrified as I might have hoped, but it was quite large and quite private, taking up what had to be a sizable portion of the county of York. It was one of those vast structures that made one think of Versailles in terms of architectural ambition if not grandeur and pomp.

We arrived at the door of the estate by mid-afternoon the following day, having not bothered to rest or pack clothing. We literally exited the gentlemen's club, hopped in the carriage, and rode straight off without a break. He didn't say so, but the sense was that I had been legally remanded into his care with the understanding that he would be getting me out of London as quickly as possible.

My friend's penchant for collecting wayward souls was clearly no exaggeration on his part, as became evident the instant the carriage came to a stop before the main entrance. There was no way to get advance word to the house to expect us because we didn't delay in any way and there were no phones or telegrams back then, and carrier pigeons were no longer in style. The closest thing to advance word was the horn Cornelius's man sounded when we crossed the gates. Despite this, Cornelius's wife—Margritte, whom I'd met only twice—his youngest daughter Joanne, and five members of the household staff were all standing there when we arrived as if our appearance had been anticipated for days.

"Why Mr. Bates, it is *such* a pleasure to have you!" Margritte exclaimed, clutching my hands with the strength of a drowning woman. (I was using several surnames at this time, and Bates was one of them. The more money I had the more last names I found it necessary to collect.)

"It's lovely to see you again," I greeted back. "Thank you for opening up your home to me."

Margritte was a handsome woman for her age, the echo of a great youthful beauty still detectable. It was more obvious in her children—all daughters—who had inherited most of it. The eldest daughter, Mary, was the kind of beauty men told stories about. Appropriately enough, she was wed to a viscount.

Joanne was the least fortunate of the sisters, genetically. She was quite lovely, but not breathtakingly so, which in this family made her unattractive by dint of comparison. She was the only unmarried daughter left for Cornelius and Margritte, but if the rumors were to be believed, it was not due to lack of suitors.

This was my first time in her company, but our formal introduction would have to wait, for she nodded, turned, and went back inside without a word. It was a mild social rudeness everyone present chose to ignore.

There was a room prepared for me already, after a fashion. The estate had enough guest rooms to host a king and his retinue, so I was really just taking one of the many already-prepared bedrooms as my own. It was a whole lot better than any prison I might have otherwise been enjoying had someone not spoken for me, so I had no complaints.

I also had no clothes. I'd attended the evening's events in my finest suit, and fled London in that same suit, and everything else I owned was in an apartment for which I had the only key. Cornelius offered to send a man back for my things, and that was fine, but I had to tell this man what to fetch and where to find it, and so far I was having trouble arranging my thoughts around that task. The problem was I couldn't seem to visualize the flat in my mind, because whenever I tried I realized I was actually thinking about this little home I used to have in Italy about fifteen hundred years earlier. And when I was able to get that out of my mind the next three locations that came up were a Spanish villa, one of my homes in Carthage, and the top floor of a bordello in southwest India. Not only were all of those places utterly wrong, they ceased to exist long ago. (Except possibly the bordello.)

I could have sent his man along with the key and let him figure out where my clothing and so-on was, but the other problem was that I couldn't remember if I'd left anything nobody else should see and/or get their hands on. Two or three times in my life I've had things in my possession that were harmless to me but not to people with normal immune systems. Beyond that, I've been known to keep things that are just difficult to explain to people who don't know I'm extremely old. Like the occasional skull of a dead friend. (Long story.) And on top of *that* I kept company with creatures most humans just don't know about. What if I had a pixie in the apartment? I couldn't remember.

But I also couldn't wear the suit constantly, so Cornelius donated some clothing. He was (or so I thought at the time) the only one there with a decent amount to spare other than the women, and I was confused enough at the time that dressing in drag probably would have only made it worse. On the other hand, a dress might have fit better.

I didn't emerge from the room for close to twenty-four hours, during which time I mostly slept and tried to keep a grip on where and when I was. This wasn't all that easy. I had a set of windows overlooking the carriageway in front of the property, which was helpful because while carriages are as old as Rome, the designs have a generational flavor to them. Of greater pertinence was the existence of glass in the windows, for while glass as a creation had been around for centuries, we didn't get good enough at making it to put it in windows until comparatively recently. That helped keep me grounded. On the other hand, Margritte was French on her mother's side, and decorated her home—or if not the entire home then the room I was in—in a style that made a lot more sense in Paris, and not even the current Paris; the Paris of about a hundred years earlier. So when I was awake I wasn't sure if I was in England in the eighteen hundreds or Paris in the seventeen hundreds, and since the latter location meant I was probably in a good deal of trouble (very, very long story) I kept having mini panic attacks.

On emerging, I wandered around the mansion for quite a

while before discovering the veranda, which became my new favorite place in the world. It jutted out from the back of the house and led to a nicely manicured lawn that went on for a quarter of an acre before ending at a densely wooded area. It was a lovely view, the weather was perfect, and I felt a certain peace I couldn't seem to obtain in either the city or the room I'd consigned myself to.

As soon as I picked a chair at the edge of the railing, food and tea appeared on the small table beside me, and I realized the reason I had decided to leave the room was that I was extremely hungry.

I stayed in that seat for the rest of the afternoon, and then returned to it the following morning, and again the morning after that. Nobody approached me aside from the girl bringing food and tea, and I only left for long enough to avail myself of a chamber pot when there was a need.

I can't say I was surprised to have all that time alone. The way I was dressed suggested I'd recently lost a tremendous amount of weight and grown three inches taller. The pants were actually cinched with a curtain stay, since I couldn't find a belt that was tight enough to do the job. Not that anybody else knew this about the pants, since the shirt I had on was long and loose and hid the waist, but I knew. And none of that probably sounds all that terrible, but this was in a time when men wore suits to the breakfast table and women buried themselves under five layers of petticoats before they took tea. My clothes marked me as a person not to be approached, and I was still sane enough to be embarrassed by them.

It was for the best though, because while I seemed to have been able to arrest a total slide into madness—it was touch-and-go in the Parisian-themed bedroom—I couldn't completely stop myself from seeing things that weren't there.

I *had* succeeded in isolating the things I was seeing to the wooded area at the edge of the lawn. This was fantastic as it reduced the number of odds of my mistaking an actual human for something else significantly, and also made it easier for me to sleep at night. But at the same time I couldn't quite take my eyes off of those trees, at least not for the first few days. At first it was because I just didn't know when something horrible was going to sneak out of there so I wanted to be ready at all times, but that soon morphed into my trying to force myself to not see what I was seeing.

I knew what I saw wasn't real, but that awareness didn't appear to help. Every shadow was a predator of some kind: a dragon, an angry tribe of satyros, an ancestral species of cat, or something worse. Twice I thought I saw a unicorn, which I'm sure sounds lovely to everyone who never encountered a real one, but they're awful.

I even started seeing things I'd never witnessed. The satyrs used to worship a god called the Duh-ryadh, and this god was supposed to be the most terrifying thing in the forest. I had no reason to think it actually existed, except for the one time thousands of years ago on the Greek peninsula when I ended up fleeing from something that sounded very real and very large and really awful. Sitting on the veranda and staring into the woods, every time a tree moved in the wind I worried that this was the thing coming for me.

Considering my fallback plan if I couldn't get my head straight was to disappear into the wilderness, it was alarming how frightened I was by a few trees.

It was maybe my fourth or fifth day on the veranda before someone developed the courage to strike up a conversation. That person was Joanne, of all people. She hadn't even been interested in introducing herself upon my arrival, and so was just about the last person I expected to find in the chair next to mine.

"Papa goes hunting," she said, after a lengthy silence in which we took turns sampling cucumber sandwiches and sipping tea.

"Pardon?" My voice sounded weird to my ears, as I'd not used it for a little while. Her voice sounded very pleasant. She was also comelier than memory served, but that might have been because it didn't look as if she was making any particular effort to impress. She had her auburn hair down and wore a casual dress, and her face had no heavy makeup to it. Everyone in her family was a natural beauty, but somehow when she tried to make herself attractive she looked worse than when she made no effort at all.

"In the trees you can't seem to stop looking at," she said. "Papa goes hunting in there, on Sundays. Fox hunting, with the dogs. I'm certain if you asked he would happily bring you along."

"Ah," I said. "Thank you. Is Cornelius here?"

"Oh no, he's in the city for a time. He's not expected back for a month or more. Business, I'm told. As much as I'm told anything."

"I see."

In the uncomfortable silence that followed I went back to staring, while Joanne remained where she was and we made a game attempt at not feeling awkward.

She started and stopped two or three different sentences, before settling on one. "They want me to talk to you," she said. It was in a conspiratorial near-whisper. "But I don't know what to say."

I leaned forward. "They?"

She nodded over her shoulder. Behind us was a set of French doors that led to an indoor sitting room. As it was bright and sunny outside, the inner room appeared dark, but not so dark I couldn't see Margritte and another woman trying hard to pretend they weren't looking at us.

"I don't think I understand," I said.

I sort of did understand, but it was hardly polite to say so. At twenty-seven, Joanne was approaching spinsterhood. It was something of a minor family scandal that she had thus far failed to land an appropriate suitor, although it must also be said that as the youngest daughter she had the least pressure of any of them to marry. Cornelius and Margritte didn't need her to wed for political, social or financial reasons, so far as I knew. She should have been more or less free to marry for her own interests alone. That she'd not done so I took to mean she simply hadn't found the right man.

"Oh, sir, of course you must," she said.

"It would be my pleasure to enjoy your company for as long as you wish to extend it, but surely all concerned are aware of my current mental state."

"There *is* your unseemly preoccupation with the local flora. But you are hardly mad. I have met madmen, and you don't meet the qualifications."

"You are an expert?"

"I have become one. Papa has been tending to the... *exhausted*, shall we say... for some time."

Looking down the lawn, she pointed out another guest. "There, *that* is a madman." There were several tables and chairs set up on the manicured grass, and sitting at one such table was a man I'd seen a few times but not spoken to. (Not that I'd been speaking to anybody.)

"He's reading a book," I pointed out. "I fear your definition of madness is wanting."

"That depends on what he's reading, doesn't it? I agree right now he doesn't appear fearsome, but he is very much mad. Speak to him if you don't believe me."

"Perhaps I will."

There was a second guest on the lawn, one who had a vague sort of foreign quality that was difficult to pin down but impossible to ignore, even for me. "Is he also mad?" I asked.

"No, he's not mad, he's royal, which may be worse."

"Royal, you say?"

"So far as any of us here knows. He hasn't said, and neither has papa, but his demeanor is a telltale. We think he may be a prince, and we've heard him speaking in another tongue, but it's not one any of us can parse."

"Your mother, surely she knows."

"Oh yes, surely, but she's not sharing it. No, I mean *us* so to say myself or my maids. I am not, at any rate, to speak to him. It's just as well. He's much too young to be interesting. And I'm not entirely certain but I don't think he much cares for women as a whole."

I laughed, which no doubt pleased Margritte to hear.

"You can't speak to the prince or the madman on the lawn, and your third option is me, another madman, shabbily dressed and a comparative pauper. Surely there is a fourth option."

"As I said, Mr. Bates, I don't believe you mad, and I know perfectly well you're no pauper. You are also not option number three. Numbers one through seven or eight precede you, and do not include either of the men seated below."

"You're not shy for suitors, then."

"They are the only thing I don't lack excess of."

"And yet, under apparent duress, you're being pushed toward lunatics. I worry for the quality of your prior matches."

It was her turn to laugh, which was a lovely, infectious sound that was nearly good enough to distract me from the fact that I could see an imp named Silenus the Elder dancing at the edge of the woods with a bottle of wine and a goblet. He wasn't there, and I knew he wasn't there, but it had been seemingly an eternity since my last taste of wine—and an actual eternity since I'd tasted the ancient Greek permutation—which made me wish I were wrong about him not being there. Eventually, I was going to see something or someone I so preferred to think was actually there that I lacked the strength to convince myself otherwise.

I turned all of my attention to Joanne. Hopefully, she was real.

"It pains me to say so," she said, "but I fear my options have rolled downhill, not up. There were the younger, the wealthier, the better dressed certainly. Perhaps none so charming."

"I thank you, but I can't imagine how you could mistake anything I've evinced thus far as charm."

"Not charm, then. A levelness of character. You've not spoken to me as a woman."

"Haven't I?" In my thinking, this meant I'd insulted her somehow. "I apologize."

"No, no, you misunderstand. I mean you've not spoken down to me, or behaved as though it was my honor to be in your company. You are clearly a man with a congested mind and a deep reserve of private stories, but that only makes you more interesting. I might even enjoy pretending to be courted by you for a while. It would make mother so happy."

"Ours is to be an imaginary courtship, then?"

This was all very confusing, but not unpleasantly confusing. She was an attractive young woman, and if I were in playing the scoundrel and not the lunatic I might consider pursuing her, only not with marriage in mind. I'm not precisely in a good position to marry someone. The problem begins and ends with the part where I don't get any older, as this impacts my long-term relationships in a surprising number of ways.

"I hope that's all right," she said. "I've asked about, and the consolidated opinion regarding Mr. Reginald Bates is that he is not in the habit of eyeing women with any long-term perspective. And I'm afraid my assets will not be made available to you on a short-term basis, although I can arrange that for you with another if you find yourself with an urgent need."

This was quickly becoming the most unusual conversation I'd had with a maiden in a hundred years.

"Tell me, if we are to be honest with one another during this imaginary courtship, how it is that I have become the great hope for your parents in a claim for your hand?"

"I don't think they have *any* great hopes or expectations. They've only run through all the other possible combinations they could think of for lighting the necessary spark and appear to be reenacting their own courtship at this stage."

"How is that?"

"Oh it was a scandal, such as these things go. Papa was wounded in a minor skirmish with uncle Brandon—have you met uncle?"

"I don't know that I've had the pleasure."

"Yes, well, a scoundrel by all accounts. Brandon and papa were close friends at a young age, up until they had a dispute that coincided with too much ale and two swords too many. Papa was wounded, and it was mother that nursed him back to health. It's how they met."

"I understand. So now you are here—"

"—to nurse you back to health."

"I'm afraid I have no wounds to dress."

"We take what we can get. And you are far more tolerable than any of my prior madman suitors, for which I'm thankful. As for dressing your wounds, I don't believe I can be of any real use to you aside from conversationally, unless you'd like to tell me what exactly is so fascinating about a tree."

"It's not the trees," I said. "It's the shadows between them."

She looked at the woods. "Yes, I do see the shadows, but no more than that."

"That's the problem with shadows, isn't it? They keep secrets."

"Surely whatever secrets might be contained within that darkness is limited in scope, sir."

"Not in my experience."

As I said this, another dragon poked its head around one of the trees, winced in the face of the sunlight, and retreated.

It wasn't there.

My attention must have drifted obviously at the sight of the dragon, because it was at this point that Joanne stood.

"Well, I have overstayed," she said. "I will leave you to your shadows for now, but perhaps I can stop by again tomorrow?"

"I would like that."

I was being honest. Something about engaging her in conversation did a good deal to keep away the madness I could feel lurking at the edge of my vision.

"But before you go," I said, "I have one question I don't think I can leave unasked for a day."

She glanced into the darkened sitting room, where there actually *were* lurkers in the shadows. "Proceed, sir. Much longer and I'll be hearing nothing but stories of young women who appeared too desperate, but proceed."

I took her hand, so it looked as if this was perhaps an extended goodbye. "It's only the most obvious. Why have you *not* found a suitor by now?"

"Perhaps I am just exceedingly picky. That would be the consensus."

"You dismissed me as a viable candidate before we spoke a word with one another. More than picky, milady."

"'Milady'. Very courtly, Mr. Bates. I hope that you take no offense at this, and further that you don't relay it to anyone else, but I know what men want from a woman, and I know what women are supposed to want from a man, and I neither wish to give nor to receive those things."

"At all?"

"Not from a *man*, no."

~

I accidentally ended up speaking to the madman from the lawn later that evening.

It was after sunset, in the library. By coincidence I had gone there to get a book to read on the theory that if reading was helpful to a *genuine* lunatic, it would probably be of use to me as well. It was also pretty clear that staring at the trees wasn't doing me much good. Maybe disappearing into someone else's make-believe was a better idea than staying in my own.

The lighting in the library wasn't splendid, which was really true anyplace after sunset up until electricity but seemed especially true in this cavernous room. It made it difficult to see the titles on the spines—vast, leather-bound collections taking up whole walls—and also difficult to notice when someone else had entered.

He surprised me, in other words. It's a difficult thing to do when I have my head straight, but obviously less so when I'm in a condition. I turned around from a wall of philosophical treatises and there he was in the leather chair near the door.

"Oh!" I exclaimed. As one does. "You startled me."

He looked to be in his late-forties or maybe a bit older, but it was hard to tell because he also bore the look of someone who'd aged prematurely due to some sort of trauma. Though sitting, he seemed roughly my height, but was dangerously thin. If someone told me he'd been a prisoner until very recently, I would have believed them.

In response to my exclamation he neither moved nor spoke for a solid five or six seconds, which was legitimately creepy, especially to the guy who was already seeing things.

It was long enough of a pause for me to decide he either didn't want to talk or wasn't actually there, and I liked neither option. Or, he was deaf, but I imagined Joanne would have included that in her description, as that's an important thing to know about a person.

"Hello, I'm sorry," he said finally, startling me a second time. "I had to be sure you were finished."

"Finished looking for a book? No, I've just started. If you—"

"Talking. I can suggest a… oh you didn't ask that. You were going to but then you didn't, I see it's gone now."

I was deeply confused. "What's gone?" I asked. "I don't understand. I *was* going to ask about a recommendation. I saw you reading—"

"Reading."

He said the word at the same time I did, and then we both stopped speaking for a little while.

"I'm sorry," he said again. He was concentrating so mightily that he was breaking out in a sweat.

"I think you're a little confused," I said, which was an understatement. Sixty thousand years ago we knew the basics of conversation involved taking turns uttering things, and we were only grunting and pointing most of the time. He didn't seem to have even this much down.

"I am trying," he said, after another longish pause. "I am trying to have the conversation we are supposed to have without interrupting it and turning it into a conversation we almost had but didn't quite. I have had so many of those, but this one I have to get right."

"I see," I said, although I did not. "Well, I am Reginald Bates."

"Reginald Bates. Reginald Bates."

"Yes, you have it."

"I have it. Reginald Bates. Not your only name."

It was the only name anyone there knew me by, but he wasn't wrong. "That's the name I'm giving you," I said.

"Yes. I have only one. One name. You're going to kill me."

"What?"

"I'm sorry, I went ahead, I'm trying so hard not to, you were going to ask why it was important I got this conversation right, you were going to say it after I introduced myself, but then I went ahead and now we're out of order, yes we are, we're... but you are, or if not you... you'll be there, it might be you it's hard to see but you will have a sword."

I was thinking I owed Joanne an apology.

"Why would I kill you?" I asked. "We've only just met."

"Not now, not now you can do it later after and I'm ready not now. Forget I told you that, can you do that? I try and forget the future and it doesn't work but I can make it so it doesn't happen and then it's the future that forgets and not me. Can you forget that or is it too late?"

"It's too late."

"It's too late, I know."

"And you haven't introduced yourself yet."

He took a deep breath and steadied himself on the arm of the leather chair, as if the room were tipping dangerously to the side. "I'm John Corrigan," he managed to say. "And I look forward to dying."

"I told you," Joanne said the next day, after I described my encounter. I omitted the curious prediction of his death at my hands. "He's in awful shape. Should be in asylum but papa won't have it."

"Why is that?"

"Saved his life, so he says. Mr. Corrigan used to be a soldier, and I guess he did an important thing in an important battle and saved important people like my father. I don't really understand how. Papa can tell it better. Every time I hear the story it makes less sense."

From where we were sitting we could see Corrigan on the lawn, in his chair and reading the book he took out of the library the night before. It was possible he could hear us but gave no indication.

"I find that hard to imagine. He doesn't look like what I would call a great warrior." As I said this, at the edge of the trees, a goblin named Hsu appeared. He *was* a great warrior, until I saw him die eight hundred years earlier. I ignored him, and he disappeared again.

"Nor do you, sir, but I'm told it took a dozen men to secure you when the panic struck."

"Fair point. Although I was told it was no more than five." *Panic* was also not the most flattering description, but I let it go.

"As I said, the story makes less sense each time I hear it, but a summary would be that everyone was going one way, and he convinced some of them to go another way instead, and all who went with him survived."

"That seems less an act of heroism than prudence."

"It does, except to hear father explain, the way Mr. Corrigan brought them was tactical lunacy. I have not been to war and so can only pretend to understand that. Perhaps you should ask papa when he returns."

"I could also ask Mr. Corrigan."

"You can certainly try."

⁂

Later that afternoon I did try. I found my way off the veranda and onto the lawn, located a vacant chair, and put it down facing Mr. Corrigan at an angle that still afforded me a view of the woods. In the event they began marching toward me I would still be a witness to it.

I sat and looked at him, and waited. He was reading his book, but also not quite reading, as he was no doubt aware of my presence. Not speaking—and not planning to speak—appeared to be my best recourse given his difficulty with dialogue. Unfortunately, that also made it hard to have a conversation.

I wondered if he was a prophet.

I don't believe there's such a thing as psychic powers, much in the same way I firmly believe there is no such thing as magic. I've witnessed things that lacked a rational explanation and that were ascribed to magic contemporaneously, but eventually a non-magical explanation was reached. Sometimes it took a dozen generations before that explanation was made plain, and since

I'm the only one who can wait that long I could understand the strength of the magical argument, however ultimately misguided. I have likewise found that psychic abilities tend more often than not to be the product of a good series of guesses.

The closest thing to a real psychic I've ever come across was an oracle. *The* oracles, rather. The ones in Delphi. They had a limited ability to see future events, but that ability was tied to a drug-induced altered state that was controllable in the sense that once they recovered from the drug the ability went away. It was very difficult to attain that state and harder still to stay there, and the things they had to say were exceedingly cryptic as a consequence. That said, those cryptic statements *were* predictions of the future, and they were accurate. They were also unhelpful most of the time because interpreting the predictions correctly was just about impossible.

Oracles are still around, even if Delphi doesn't have any more of them. I've met one or two women—they always seem to be women—who have the ability, and there are probably a lot more than that. But since at minimum one needs to be immoderately stoned to make an oracular prediction, a lot of folks never discover that they have this talent.

Then there are prophets. Prophets are a lot like oracles in that they can also see the future, but they don't need to be in an altered state for it. That sounds great except for the most part they *can't stop* seeing that future, and this makes them mostly insane and largely ignored by the people who should be listening to them. Prophets tend to die young, because they're really hard to be around and don't have a problem telling important people when they're being assholes.

Prophets can be either gender. The lucky ones end up attached to an organization that values them—religious groups, mainly—and the very lucky ones get a scribe to follow them around and write everything they say. A few parts of the Bible were written like this.

John Corrigan *could* have been a prophet, but if so he was unlike any I'd ever met before. They don't tend to be lucid for long enough to be soldiers, for starters. Also, most prophets can't shut up for even a minute, which was the opposite of his problem. Finally, and most importantly, I had never heard an oracle or a prophet even attempt to predict his or her own future. They were very good at seeing everyone else's, but their own tended to be opaque.

But if he wasn't a prophet, I didn't know what the other options were. Aside from madman.

~

He was the one to finally break the silence. He did so by closing his book, giving me his full attention, and sitting still for another five or six seconds, as he had the night before.

"I'm sorry I startled you last evening," he said. "I get confused. It's worse at the end of the day."

"That's all right," I said. He was reacting to my words before they came out of my mouth, nodding affirmation. I decided to stick to simple declarative sentences for the moment. "Confused how? You see the future?"

He shifted in his chair. "I *experience* the future."

That was different. "Whose future? You can predict? Like a prophet?"

"All futures within my senses. I see it all at once, and I can't stop it. Your words, my words, they echo forward. Everything happens and will happen and is happening."

I waited for a while before responding, not so much because I wasn't sure what to say but because he seemed to need to hold conversations at this kind of pace.

"How far?" I asked.

"When I'm awake, as much as ten seconds. But it's worse when I sleep. It can be days when I sleep."

"Prophetic dreams?"

I'd heard of people having these, but never met one whose dreams were in any way accurate. They *remembered* them as accurate, sure, but that wasn't very reliable.

If someone says, "I dreamed that would happen" *after* the fact, I didn't put much stock into it. It's the ones who tell you before something happens that you want to pay attention to. But not once had I encountered a person who could make an accurate, sensible prediction based on a dream they'd had. Or, nothing more impressive than "I dreamed it was going to rain today and it is raining" which is about as useful as a sailor with a trick knee that can make the same prediction.

"Not dreams," he said, oddly. "I don't dream. I travel ahead."

Another pause. I wondered if I was the only one he'd ever really explained this to. I didn't know what made me think this, but it seemed right somehow. I was the person who could pick out the vampire or goblin or demon in a crowd; for whatever reason, the world's hidden circus had always been drawn to me. Why would John Corrigan be an exception?

"Why are you telling me this?" I asked.

"Because you believe me. You are seeing bugaboos and cockatrices in the shadows, and you are older than the world, and I know this because in one of our futures you tell me. That future is gone now, because my words have killed it."

"You believe a self-professed lunatic who claims he is older than the world?"

"Even if it is an invention of your psychosis, it is *your* invention, and not one I would have guessed on my own initiative. I choose to believe it, though. Madness, in my personal experience, is mostly the acceptance of a reality that is not commonly agreed-upon. Who are we to say which reality is valid?"

I am probably the world's first pragmatist, so in that sense I couldn't bring myself to agree completely on this point, but I could see where his perspective might bring him to such a conclusion. And as it related to me, his reasoning did deliver him to the right place.

"I see things that aren't there, and you live through futures that haven't happened. We are quite a pair, Mr. Corrigan."

"Indeed, Mr. Bates. But it is neither the futures that do not happen, nor the things not there, which should concern us. It's the future that does and the things which are."

John and I spent a lot of time together after that second conversation. It seemed my presence helped him cope with his apparently incurable malady, and I found his condition so fascinating I briefly forgot about my own. The shadows still lurked at the edge of vision, but I was getting better at ignoring them. It didn't make them go away, but I wasn't preparing to defend myself against phantasms quite so often.

"What is it you find so terrible in the dark corners," he asked me once, one evening when we both ended up back in the cavernous library.

I explained to him how it is for a man as old as I am to try and train himself not to react to his instinct. Prehistoric man—and it's worthwhile to keep in mind that I am really just a semi-civilized caveman—was much further down the food chain than the modern iteration, so a shadow representing a predator was a real concern. I had thought that this would be a difficult thing for a nineteenth century Englishman to understand. John proved me wrong.

"You've been to war?" he asked.

"Many times, yes." Usually by accident, almost never by choice. Again, excluding the caveman portion of my existence.

"With rifles?"

"No, not to this point."

Guns—I tended to call them *hand cannons* long after everyone else stopped calling them that—had been around for a little while by then, but it wasn't until recently that they had become common enough and reliable enough for use in warfare. The word *reliable* is relative, of course. These guns had to be loaded one shot at a time, were terribly inaccurate, obscenely loud, and could blow up in one's face just as easily as not. It wasn't until the repeating rifle came along some fifty or sixty years after this conversation with John that guns even made sense outside of light infantry. In other words, a hundred men with breech-loaded single shot rifles was a force to be reckoned with, but if you were one person with one gun you'd be better off getting a sword and learning how to use it.

"There is a terrible randomness to rifle combat," he said. "Skill, instinct, resources mean nothing. Musket-balls cannot be predicted. I saw men rushing a rifleman right in the line of his discharge arrive at their target undamaged, and other men felled by shot that came down seemingly from the sky. So, Reggie, if the base instincts you speak of are the same as that which is deep-rooted in us all, I know exactly what it is to have them fail."

"Remind me never to go back to war, then."

I had made the decision to avoid wars long before this moment, but at least in the past I could believe myself capable of outfighting most of the men trying to kill me. I can't defend myself against a random hail of lead, though.

"A rifle war is where you learn that God is fickle and indifferent."

"Unless you can see the future for yourself."

He nodded, and hesitated, and for a moment it seemed he was looking at his past instead of his constant future. "For most men, the only difference between standing in exactly the right place and exactly the wrong place is luck. For me, it was foreknowledge. But I also knew every man's death before it happened. I could only save a few. And sometimes, to save *myself*, I had to make certain someone else died in my stead. Tell me, in your life, have you ever had to make those kinds of decisions?"

"Many times."

"Then possibly… madness is what we both deserve."

∼

We spent a fair amount of time talking about what he might *be* as well. I explained to him what an oracle was and about the prophets I'd met, and that I didn't think he was either one of those things. But that left us in a bad place, because after that I was out of ideas.

"I don't know of any other species or types of people that can see the future, not as you describe it," I admitted. "You could be unique."

"I'm not. My father had it as well, as did his grandfather."

"Then it may be that the Corrigan *clan* is unique."

He called it a curse. It was hard to see him suffering and think of it any other way, especially when he described how he saw the world: people looking like fantastic pulsing snakes, their present selves at the back and their possible selves at the blurry front. Sound for him were never distinct events, but echoed through the future. Every conversation was a block of words, sometimes in no order at all.

He said when he was younger he could with some effort and training and concentration keep a hold on where the present was. But as he got older—especially after his war—it became harder and harder to keep that focus. By the time I'd met him he had given up even trying, and just let the fuzzy present and foggy future pass before him all at once.

In the abstract the idea of being able to see the immediate future sounded like an amazing talent. But this was a curse, all right.

Joanne was also enormously helpful to me, both as a companion and as a resource, especially when it came to finding my way through the mansion. She had an intimate familiarity with both the household staff and the less public methods by which one might navigate the building's interior.

It was always true that people with sufficient money to afford a household staff preferred that staff to be as invisible as absolutely possible. It was something very close to wishing there were such a thing as magic. *Look*, they might say, *dinner has appeared. And while we were eating, our beds were made and our chamber pots emptied. Truly, it is a miracle.*

To perform these daily miracles required a rather large number of servants. Sometimes it was possible to quantify the degree of wealth of a family by counting the number of servants seen as a ratio to the size of the staff that had to exist to maintain the house.

Cornelius and Margritte's household staff was nigh invisible except when needed, a feat partly accomplished by a series of servant passageways inside the walls. These passages led to every bedroom, and thanks to a number of staircases also led to all three of the kitchens and the servants' quarters in the basement.

I learned about the passageways in a somewhat unusual fashion.

I was preparing myself for bed at the time. In this era that meant exchanging one set of clothing for a slightly more comfortable set of clothing, something that still took a while to acclimate myself to given I could remember going whole centuries without any clothing whatsoever. (Thankfully, my madness hadn't reached the stage where I forgot about clothes.) I'd been in the mansion for a number of weeks by then and had clothing at my disposal that actually fit me rather well—not my own, but donated by John. He was, as I said, much thinner than I was, but his clothing was loose on him, and perfect for me.

I'd changed into bedclothes and was about to piss into the pot that was there for just that reason, when Joanne spoke.

"Good evening, Mr. Bates," she said, which was an utterly normal greeting and mostly how she said hello to me on every other occasion, except that this time she was saying it while standing against what I'd taken to be a solid wall in a bed chamber with an entrance on the opposite end of the room. Moments before I had been alone. To say that this caused me to jump was an understatement.

My surprise made her laugh. "I'm sorry, I forgot how my sudden appearance might resonate with your particular madness, sir."

"That's all right," I said. I would have made an effort to cover myself, but again, this was a time when clothing was so mandatory we all dressed from head to toe even when climbing into bed. I had no drawers on, but I had a nightgown and a robe, and socks just to make sure nobody caught a glimpse of my feet. "As long as you are actually here right now, I forgive you."

"Oh, I am."

"Can you tell me why? No, first tell me how, and then we will move forward from there to why."

To answer, she kicked the solid wall she was up against. It tilted in, revealing a small doorway I really should have known about.

"As to why," she said, "put on your slippers and come with me, I have a gift for you."

A few minutes later we stood on the other side of the wall. She was holding a lamp with a single candle that provided only the smallest amount of illumination. It was enough though, given our proximity in the close quarters, to enable me to take note that she was dressed in her bed-things as well. It should come as no surprise that this meant almost nothing in terms of what was or wasn't being revealed, as she was still clothed head-to-toe. But instead of an unholy number of layers there were only two or three, so it was possible to discern her basic womanly shape without accentuation or exaggeration. Her hips were where her actual hips might be expected to appear, and no garment tightened and pushed up her bosom to eye-level.

"The door latches from this side," she said, holding up the light to the very latch, "but for the most part nobody locks them. I can make it from one end of the mansion to the other without being seen by anybody."

"Is that important to you?"

"It can be, yes."

She noticed that my eyes weren't exactly on hers. They were, in fact, fixed firmly on her breasts. In the candlelight, the white cotton gown was nearly transparent.

This occasioned no comment, only a wry smile. "Come on, then. Follow me. Try and keep your voice down as we go, and watch your step."

The passageway was far narrower than any of the official public access ways in the building, and had more than a couple of unpleasantly low overhangs, most of which Joanne was able to point out before I ran into them. She missed one or two, but I discovered them just fine.

"I told you to watch where you were going," she said the second time I'd run my forehead against a support beam.

"You told me to watch where I was walking, not where my head was."

"You'd have noticed it if your eyes were looking somewhere other than my posterior, Mr. Bates."

"You are holding the only light. I have precious few other places to look."

After a few more minutes of this—bantering and walking both—we stopped at another bedroom door. She held a finger up to her mouth and made me lean closer.

"This is where the prince sleeps," she whispered.

"Is this what you've brought me to see?" I asked.

"No, no. But if *that's* what you're interested in, your friend Mr. Corrigan is just down there."

"Interested in what way do you mean? Why am I here?"

"No, I don't want to ruin the surprise. But I can tell you the prince is a heavy sleeper. If you were to look in sometime you could learn much more about him than I have been able to discern, I'd wager. You *are* more worldly."

"You mean for me to sneak through his things and find out if he's truly a prince, is this what you're suggesting?"

"I mean if you, of your own initiative and *starving* from curiosity, were to travel this route one evening and slip into his chambers for a short time, I'm quite positive none would hold blame for your actions."

"It staggers me that you have not yet found a husband, milady."

"You and my parents both. Come on."

A little further, down two flights of stairs and around a corner, the corridor widened and became a hallway with its own sconce lighting.

"The servants bunk here," she said.

I had lost all understanding of where we were in respect to the architecture of the building. We were underground, but under *what* I had no idea. "I trust they are not bunked one to a room."

"It's one or three or five, depending on status. There are gender divisions as well, as you can imagine. My parents are God-fearing people and all that."

We came to a stop at one particular door about halfway down. "Here's my present, then," she said.

"A door."

"The door opens to a room containing the gift. Her name is Miranda."

"My gift's name is Miranda?"

"You've begun to repeat everything I say, I do hope this is not the start of a new mental instability for you."

"I am not at all clear on what you're telling me, Joanne." I sort of was, but it wasn't the sort of conversation I expected to be having with her, in a darkened servant passageway or anywhere else. Really, the last time I'd had a conversation even approximately like this with a woman it involved that bordello in India.

"Reginald, you've been here for weeks, and I can tell you're getting better because yesterday afternoon you spent the *entire* conversation addressing my bosom rather than my face. I appreciate your attention, and I promise if I were inclined, I would have used the passageway to your room to partake in all manner of immodesties instead of our current course of action. I say this even after having seen you in that unfortunate dressing gown."

"I have a better one, but you didn't tell me you were coming."

"Again I remind you this is meant to be a surprise, and surprises are ruined by forewarning. Now it happens that I am friendly with the women who reside in this corridor. That familiarity has as much to do with my unwillingness to satisfy your needs personally as you think it does. And if you require me to be more specific, I can be."

"You have a friend on the staff."

"Two or three *very* enthusiastic friends. They are also talented and flexible, and one of them speaks French, which is *wonderful*."

The blood ran to her face. She wasn't blushing, she was becoming excited at the thought of her secret French mistress. It was adorable. I was unreasonably turned on by it.

She continued. "One of my friends happened to notice the attention you have been receiving from the fair Miranda. Don't hide your surprise, sir, I realize you were unaware of this. Between my bosom and John Corrigan's butchered lexicon I'm sure you had much too much on your mind to notice a scullery maid. But with her blossoming desire and your undeniably growing need, I saw opportunity. So now you understand."

"I think I might."

"Good, I was hoping I didn't have to go so far as to explain what you were supposed to *do* with her. I imagined you familiar with the basic machinery."

"Yes. But is she—"

"She's expecting you."

Joanne put her hand on the door, then hesitated.

"I'm trusting you are not a brute, Mr. Bates. She is very young and very pretty, and not very experienced. Don't ruin her, for God's sake."

"I will do my best."

"Good. I may wish for a turn myself one day."

If, some time in the future, scientists came up with a cure for madness, and that cure involved a tremendous amount of sex, I would believe it. I'm not saying the young maid Miranda had exactly what I needed to fix what ailed me, but it certainly helped. (It also may be argued in hindsight that what I suffered from was a form of melancholy, and when it comes to that condition I would *definitely* prescribe sex.)

She was, as Joanne said, very young. How young? I couldn't tell you, because I didn't ask. Young enough to attend college if she was a twenty-first century girl instead of a nineteenth century one, let's say. Probably.

She was also eager, and full of energy, and happy to slip into my room every night as soon as her duties were over. She was *so* energetic, I actually had to start asking her for nights off so I could get a proper amount of sleep.

Joanne was as delighted as anybody.

"When we're married we shall have to bring her with us!" she exclaimed one day. This was during one of our more brazen attempts to heal me of my condition. It involved my exiting the house and walking to the edge of the lawn with her and John Corrigan, where we laid out a blanket and ate a lunch out of a basket while I played a game of chicken with the forest floor that I was close enough to touch.

"Is our marriage on again?" I asked.

"That depends on who you ask. What do you say, Mr. Corrigan? Do we not make a good match?"

John smiled, nearly timing it correctly enough to not come off as creepy, but not quite. "Marriage is a wonderful thing," he said. "But not for the two of you, I think."

She gasped theatrically. "Then him we shouldn't ask. My mother, we could ask her. She is already preparing the ceremony."

"She isn't really, is she?"

"I'm afraid you may be forced to break my heart soon, Mr. Bates."

"You would mourn my departure?"

"Eternally."

John cleared his throat, which he had a tendency to do when looking for the present. We'd become conditioned to wait for words to follow, although Joanne probably didn't think of it as a sort of training.

"I suppose it's cruel," John said.

"Cruel?" Joanne asked. "How do you mean?"

It should be said that Joanne had grown somewhat accustomed to John's odd nature, and tolerated him as warmly as she could given he was my friend and she appeared to genuinely value me for some reason. But she never truly relaxed in his company, and tolerated his occasional moments of tactlessness with a demeanor that fell just shy of polite.

He looked at me to see if he had perhaps spoken before what he was responding to had been said aloud in the present. I nodded a tiny bit. We'd developed a familiarity with one another that made it easier on both of us. I occasionally needed him to remind me that something I was seeing wasn't there, while he needed me to keep track of the present.

"I mean that your mother only wants what's best, and if you do not have any genuine intentions on a marriage to *any* man, it would hurt her less to be told this, in the end. I'm sorry if I offend by saying so."

"I understand, Mr. Corrigan," she said, adding, "No offense taken," but in a tone of voice that suggested otherwise. "I understand well, but you see I've already told her this many times. She believes what I have is a temporary condition that will be cured by the *right* man, or perhaps the right application of his manhood. My proclivities are only a secret because she refuses to recognize them."

"Then I apologize," he said. "I speak only as a parent."

"Are you a father? I didn't know this." Joanne looked at me, but I didn't know either. "You've a wife?"

"I have a son, but no wife, if you understand my meaning. I fear the boy is growing without a father, to my eternal shame. I had hoped to regain my senses sufficiently to leave this place, find and speak to him before my grasp of the present slipped away again. He needs to understand our curse."

"Your curse?"

"He means," I said, "the peculiarity of his madness. Unique but inheritable, John?"

"That's it, yes."

Joanne patted him on the knee. "I'm sure you'll have a chance. You're getting better! We can all see that."

He smiled back, but there was nothing positive behind his eyes. He still had no expectation of leaving the mansion grounds alive. I hadn't discussed it with him since the night he'd made the prediction, but that prediction colored everything he said and did.

"Why don't we eat?" I suggested, as we were in great need of a subject change.

In the basket was a loaf of bread and some cheese, which I extracted. Beneath those was a bottle of wine, and three cups.

I don't know whose idea it was to keep me dry while recuperating, but it wasn't mine. I'd assumed it was a policy of the household. Whoever's it was—and it wasn't a terrible idea, let's be honest—this was the first wine I'd seen in months.

"Surprise!" Joanne said. "I snuck it from the cellar."

"You're a godsend. Maybe I *should* marry you."

I had the cork out and the wine poured in a matter of seconds, not drinking directly from the bottle only because that would have been unseemly.

"Cheers," John said, and we drank.

Across the lawn—we were some distance away but could still see and be seen—Joanne's mystery royal guest had taken his usual spot. He was facing us, but if he saw he didn't indicate.

"Maybe we should have invited him," I said.

"Oh, I'm sure the prince doesn't want our wine," Joanne said.

John looked at the man for an uncomfortably long time, as was his tendency. "He isn't a prince," he said. "He's a Saxony duke."

Joanne gasped. "How do you know?"

"He's going to tell me."

"You mean, John, that the duke *told* you who he was." I said, attempting to correct his temporal linguistic problem.

"Yes, Reggie. That's what I mean."

"When did he tell you this?" Joanne asked.

"Next week. He told me next week."

∼

*L*ater that same evening, Margritte paid me a visit.

I had just wished a good night to both of my luncheon companions and headed off to my own room when she manifested at the landing of the stairs. That's probably not the right word, but with the way the candlelight played with the shadows in this home, it feels correct. I didn't know she was there, and then she was.

I've probably not spent nearly enough time describing the layout of the mansion itself, but in my defense every time I went exploring I ended up getting lost and confused. I knew how to get to the library, the dining room, the sitting room and the veranda, and I was getting good at figuring out how the servant passages went, but that was about all. And if that sounds like a large portion of the home, well, it was a large home.

In addition to what I've already described, then, was the staircase in the center of the house. It was a vast, ornate, marble stair that headed straight up to a landing halfway, then to the left and the right side the steps branched off to two more landings before curling to the second floor. From the second was a more modest stairwell that led to the third, directly above the main set. This was the only way to get between the three floors if one weren't a servant.

My guest room was in the left wing on the second floor, only a few feet from the second level landing. The third floor, where I had never been, was where the chambers of the lady of the house could be found. For reference, John Corrigan's room was about halfway down on the same wing, and the duke of Saxony's quarters were (I believe) at the far end of the wing.

I had actually engaged in almost no discussions with Margritte since my arrival. We exchanged courtesies, but aside from her routine verification that I had everything I needed, we'd barely spoken.

"Mr. Bates!" She exclaimed, as if our encounter was entirely by chance, which I doubted. "I'm *so* glad I caught you!"

I was tired and buzzy from the wine, and thinking about the naked body of maid Miranda, which I expected to get my fill of shortly. "Evening to you, Missus," I greeted back, my hand on the doorknob. If I could get inside I could save myself from a lengthy chat, but Margritte moved too quickly.

"I wanted to tell you how very happy we all are with your progress. You seem to be very much more yourself of late than when you arrived. Do you agree?"

"Oh yes," I said, and it was true. I no longer entertained thoughts of abandoning civilization, and I hadn't had a real panic episode in a few weeks. I'd reached a pleasant midpoint, with two friends whose company I greatly enjoyed and all the sex I could ask for. About the only thing that could ruin it—or so I thought at the time—was my hostess's irrational belief that I was mere days away from asking for her youngest daughter's hand.

This was where I thought the conversation was leading, which was why getting away from her and safely into my room was at the forefront of my mind. What she had to say instead *did* ruin everything, but not in the way anybody could have anticipated.

"I'm so very glad. Now, you don't need to answer this immediately, but next week we are having a *small* social event."

"Oh!" I said, legitimately surprised. "What sort of event?"

For a home this large the absence of any full-on parties was actually unusual. Margritte had guests all the time, for the day and sometimes for a night or two, but they tended to be visiting family matrons and their brood. It was never a formal thing, so I had no obligation to converse or even extend courtesies, and as a consequence was never formally introduced. The same understanding was extended to the other two long-term guests, so far as I could tell.

"We're going to have a dinner party. Our *foreign* friend is taking our leave, you see, and I thought it only fitting that we send him off properly. It will be small, I promise. A few guests, all of us, and his retinue, once they arrive. Cornelius as well, if he can get away."

"I see."

"Now, I *completely* understand if the prospect is too daunting for you just now. Your last party was eventful, I'm told."

I laughed. "It was at that. I would be happy to attend, Margritte. Thank you for taking the time to speak to me personally."

"Of course! Now I must find our dear Mr. Corrigan and see if he is up to it."

∼

I was going to be overdressed.

I'd arrived at the mansion in my finest suit, which could have meant that a party was the one thing for which I had adequate clothing, except that this was a dinner meant for one's second- or third-finest, and those were still in my place in London. But the other option was to borrow one of John's spares, and while his leisure clothing fit me well enough to get by, real suits are tailored to the man, and I was the wrong man.

The choice, then, was to look *too* good, or not good at all. I went with the former.

"You should wear that every day," Miranda said.

This was the night before the party. I was trying on the suit because it occurred to me I should make sure it still looked okay. I wasn't worried that I had gained or lost significant weight and therefore no longer fit into it, because my basic physique has remained effectively the same for my entire life. The concern was that the suit had perhaps suffered a malady while being cleaned and pressed.

"I look presentable?" I did a slow turn. The room had only one mirror, and it was a small one. Miranda's gaze was much more encompassing, and I trusted her enough to be critical if something was amiss.

"I don't know how *anyone* could resist you dressed like that."

"You're a naked girl in my bed. I respect your opinion, but let's accept that there may be a bias. Are there no spots or blemishes or tears?"

"None that I can see. Would you like some? I can rip it off of you."

"That would be deeply counter-productive."

"Then you had best take it off on your own, sir."

"As you say."

Despite her youth, Miranda had become more brazen with each encounter. In my company she'd gone from shyly curious to modestly insistent, to actively directing our coital escapades in order to get what she wanted and how she wanted it. I may not have been her first lover—the evidence suggested I was not, but she could also have been an active rider of horses—but it was obvious already that for this beautiful young maid I was going to be only one of many. I almost pitied whoever came after me.

I undressed slowly, not out of any particular showmanship but because clothing back then was incredibly difficult to get into and out of.

"I spoke to him once," Miranda said.

"Who? The duke?"

"Is that what he is? He's *very* young. He'd be cute except for that nose."

"I can't say I ever noticed."

"It's a large nose. And his hair looks greasy."

"But you spoke to him."

"I did! His usual girl, Bethany, she had a touch of the queasy. Missy thinks she got herself with child, but I think it's Missy's cooking what did it. It was sudden, and we didn't have nobody else to bring him his tea, so I had to. Put on my best and went out and I gave him his tea, and that's when I first saw you, sir. Sitting in your corner all full of thoughts."

"What did you say to him?"

"I said, 'your tea, sir'. Just like that."

"How clever."

"Oh shut up. At least I spoke to him, that's more than most can say. I think he's lonely. I don't know why you lot aren't supposed to speak to him, but I wonder if he even knows it. I bet he sits there every day wondering why you and Mr. Corrigan and Miss Joanne don't go and talk to him. I bet it makes him sad."

"Did he say anything back?"

"He did, he said 'thank you'. And then he looked at me and saw I wasn't Bethany, and he said, 'you are new.' And I said, 'she's sick', and then I left."

"That was all?"

"I didn't want to get in trouble!"

"No, I guess not."

"He has a funny accent. I don't think he speaks much English."

I was down to my drawers and the suit was back on hangers. I sat on the edge of the bed. "German, probably. Or Hungarian."

"I don't know, I never heard it before. Why do you think they don't want anyone speaking to him?"

"I've learned not to wonder overly much about things like that," I said. "My assumption is it's either for his protection or for ours."

"That's very wise." She sat up and crawled to the foot of the bed, not at all concerned that the sheets had slipped away and fully revealed her. "Can I help you out of those drawers, sir?"

"Yes, that would be very kind of you."

～

The mansion had three distinct dining areas, not counting the kitchen tables where the staff ate. With the exception of the basket lunch, my meals had mostly been taken on the veranda, where they were brought to me and no socializing was expected, but like the kitchen tables, the veranda also didn't count as a dining space.

The sitting room from which the veranda sprang was one, as it was also called the tearoom. Then there was the dining room, an informal space where regular guests and family ate or were expected to. I dined there once or twice a week and otherwise begged off.

The third space was the banquet hall. This was an enormous room directly off the main hall—where the stairs and the front entrance were—that took up about half of the right wing of the mansion. A vast rectangular table occupied the center of the room that could seat anywhere between twenty and forty people depending on how many partitions were added to it and how many chairs were on-hand. This was where the evening's festivities were to take place.

For this party, in addition to myself, John Corrigan and the guest of honor—whose exact name we never did learn—several of Margritte's local neighbors were also in attendance. With Joanne and her mother, this brought the head count up to fifteen, not counting the nearly equal number of servants ringing the wall near the hidden door to the kitchen. The table, though, was set for almost twice that many.

"The extra chairs are for papa," Joanne said, sliding her gloved hand under my arm. She was wearing the kind of elegant dress nobody has any more, which is sort of a shame. In hindsight, corsets seem inhumane, but at the time I was pretty pleased with what they did to the female form. Taking them *off* the female form was a real pain, I'll admit. "He's bringing guests as well. And our foreign friend's companions, when they arrive, will also join us. I don't know how many of them will be coming, but we're expecting at least four."

"I was hoping this would be over with early," I said, specifically commenting on the fact that we were not eating yet, which meant there was no telling how far away I was from escaping the evening. "How long before they arrive?"

"Oh, relax. When we're married you will have to do this all the time."

"That's another excellent reason to avoid marriage."

She shot me a look, but it was more mischievous than unhappy. "All right, no parties then. But we get to share Miranda."

On the other side of the room, John had just entered. Between him and us was a clogged floor full of guests who knew enough not to take their seats at the table as yet, which meant standing and drinking wine and noshing on food brought around by the staff, and most of all, *mingling*.

I hated mingling when I was sane. Insane I found it intolerable. But I didn't have it nearly as bad as my friend. With his condition, a crowd of people was nearly as nightmarish for John as combat.

It was fascinating, then, watching him navigate the crowded room. While his expression was that of a man whose head was on the verge of bursting, he moved with astonishing grace. Because of his constant future-sight he could pre-react to events, which put him at a distinct advantage in a crowd where he had no interest in holding a conversation. People would turn to greet him and find he wasn't there, or he was but another person had come between them. Incidental contact—which often triggered at least a nominal exchange of niceties—was avoided at the last second. He moved like a dancer, but a dancer whose feet were causing him agony.

Joanne noticed too. "He is an odd one, your Mr. Corrigan. I

still can't put my finger on how, but there is something. *You know what it is, don't you?*"

"I do, but I don't know if I could put it in a way you would accept."

"Well that *is* cryptic. Hello, John, you look dashing this evening."

"Miss Joanne," he greeted, having just reached us. "You look lovely."

"Charmed," she smiled, curtsying with only the slightest exaggeration. "Shall we socialize?"

"Oh, I don't think so," I said.

"Yes, really, I'm perfectly all right over here," John agreed. *Over here* was near one of the front-facing, floor-to-ceiling windows that made up an entire wall of the banquet room. Specifically, we were in the far corner of the room and not at all close to the main thrust of the party. Margritte was in the middle of that thrust, playing hostess, and if she looked displeased by the decision her two madmen had made to remain out of the crowd, it didn't show.

Joanne was not at all okay with it, though. "You two! This is our *one* night to actually speak to the man and you'd rather hide in the dark. Oh, there he is! Come on, then."

I looked at John, who appeared genuinely panicked at the notion of diving back into the center of that many people. I knew if I went he would have to follow.

"We'll need a moment or two," I said.

"Ahh, you." Joanne pulled her hand out from under my arm. "All right, if you won't go to him, I will bring him to you."

She disappeared into the social morass, braver than either of us for doing so.

"I'm surprised you came, John," I said. "I'm sure Margritte would have accepted your regrets."

"I considered it. But no, I had to come."

"*Had* to? She insisted?"

"No, she didn't at all. I fear I accepted before she formally invited me, which must have been alarming. Yes I had to come. Tonight is important because... oh." He stopped himself, which he did sometimes when realizing he'd gone too far ahead. I said what I was supposed to say next. It was less complicated that way.

"Why is that?" I asked.

"Tonight is when he tells us he is a duke, of course."

"Of course. You know, John, I never did tell you how old I was, and yet you act as if we had that conversation. You didn't need to be here to learn his title. I take it something else is going to happen tonight?"

"Yes, something else is going happen tonight." His answer ran over my question. If anyone had been listening it would have sounded like we were running through a rehearsed script. "I want you to promise me something, Reggie."

"What shall I promise?"

"If I tell you to do something, do it immediately, without question. Do you trust me enough to do that?"

"I think I do, yes. But I'd like to know what you mean."

I couldn't imagine a dinner party circumstance in which it might be vitally important to accept the instructions of a future-seeing lunatic. Perhaps, I thought, I was at risk of being scalded by tea later.

But then Joanne had returned with the foreign guest on her arm, and I never got an answer. "Gentlemen!" she said. "It turns out our esteemed guest is a *duke*!"

John and I feigned surprise, greeted him, and introduced ourselves.

As Miranda observed, the duke was very young, much younger than I'd taken him for from a distance. Younger than twenty, surely. A prominent nose and long black hair, he was not a terrifically attractive young man, but handsome enough for a person with royal lineage to get by okay. That is to say, money makes everyone a little bit more handsome.

I didn't know why he was being hidden away in Cornelius's estate—I never really *would* learn—but I knew enough about hereditary monarchies to imagine ten or twelve plausible reasons. Most of those reasons had to do with valid or invalid claims to a throne somewhere, an unsavory by-product of a system that inevitably put the lives of very young people in grave danger entirely because of their blood.

But then, every political system has its flaws.

I also knew enough not to ask him for details. Even if he knew why, I had no reason to expect him to tell me.

"It is… a pleasure to make… to meet you both," he said in halting English.

"It's our pleasure as well," I greeted back, shaking his hand. Then, perhaps foolishly, I tried out some German. *"We are all sorry to see you go."*

His face registered genuine alarm. He understood the language I was using, clearly, but for some reason it wasn't okay that I knew how to speak it.

"I am sorry, I don't understand," he said back, but in Hungarian rather than German.

I nodded. "My mistake, sir."

John stepped between us. "I feel as if we are old friends, my lord, even though this is our first conversation."

The duke smiled and shook John's hand while Joanne pulled me away. "What did you just *say*?"

"I greeted him, that's all. I know a little German."

"No wonder you're hiding in the corner, you are *terrible* at this. Why German?"

"Saxony."

She sighed. "*I* didn't say Saxon duke, did I? It was your friend Mr. Corrigan who told us that, and Lord even knows where he got that. Honestly, Mr. Bates. I may have to break off this fake engagement if you don't develop some tact."

"I can apologize again."

"No, don't bother. Let me deal with this."

She reinserted herself into what had to have been an excruciating conversation between a man who can barely hold one and a man who can barely speak the language.

"Has anyone ever told you the history of this mansion, sir?" she asked the duke, taking his arm.

The intent was to lead him away from us and, presumably, to the host-friendly arms of her mother, and I'm sure that's what would have happened if the team of riders hadn't arrived at the front door at just that moment. Everyone in the hall was aware of this because the main carriageway was what the windows overlooked, and because there were enough riders to make a substantial amount of noise.

"Is that Cornelius?" I asked. The curtains where sheer white, but it was difficult to make out much of what was going on outside because we were in a lit room and the front was largely unlit.

"Too many horses," Joanne said. "And father sounds a horn when he crosses the gates. We'd have heard of his coming minutes ago. This must be our duke's retinue, yes?"

"I think it must be. Except that was a lot more than the four men you were expecting."

A moment later, the doorman was walking two of the horse riders into the room. They weren't dressed in the finery one typically associated with an event such as this, wearing riding leathers and looking like the kind of dirty and sweaty one gets when pushing a mount hard through the countryside.

"Excuse me, misses and misters," the first man said, somewhat loudly. His accent was unmistakably not English, and also not the one our duke was using. I was nearly positive it was French. "I must apologize, both for my late arrival and for my enormous rudeness, but I am afraid your guest of honor must leave immediately. It is... an emergency. Utterly unforeseen."

Both men had swords on their belts, and they weren't the decorative kind. The second man had his hand on his hilt. When I saw this, my heart rate went up. It could have been another panic attack, but I didn't think so. I thought I was reacting entirely correctly to the start of a bad situation.

"Just so I'm clear," I said to Joanne. "There *are* two men with swords standing in the vestibule, is that correct?"

"Yes. Do you think you're imagining this?"

"I wanted to check. I failed to do that at the last party I attended."

Margritte, ever the hostess, wasn't picking up on the nuances of the situation the way I was. Neither was Joanne or anyone else there, all except for John. And when the guy who can see the future is reacting the same way you are to something, it's a good bet your instinct is on the nose. Considering how bad my instinct had been of late, it was almost gratifying to see him as concerned as I was.

"What a shame!" Margritte said. "Surely, sir, we can wait until my husband arrives. He so wanted to see our young guest off properly."

"I am sorry, madam, it really cannot be helped," the man said. Looking right at the duke he added, "If he does not come with me *immediately* I am afraid there will be *many* deaths. Surely he would not want that."

"Oh!" Margritte exclaimed. "That *is* an emergency. Well then, I will extend your apologies to my husband, Mr...?"

"Sinclair, madam." His words were all for the lady of the household but his eyes were all for the duke.

"Yes, of course, Mr. Sinclair."

"Such an emergency, I will go with you, of course," the duke said. His voice was thin and his words trembled on their way past his lips. "Straight away. Of course."

I turned to ask John to check at the window for an idea of the kind of force that had arrived with Sinclair, but he was already doing that. Whether he heard me ask him in the future or had decided to do it on his own, it hardly mattered.

I stepped next to the duke and put my hand on his arm. *"Sir, are these the men you were expecting?"* I asked, in Hungarian.

He looked at me. He was surprised to hear Hungarian, and he looked afraid, but the fear wasn't for me. *"They are not. But it is all right. There will be a ransom and that is all."*

He shook his arm out of my grasp and started across the room. The guests—all tittering and muttering—stepped aside for him.

"What's going on?" Joanne asked. It was obvious to her only that John and I were alarmed. Before I could answer, John had left the window to stand in the middle of the room, putting himself directly between Sinclair and the duke.

"You have to get all of these people out," I said to Joanne. "Through the kitchen, get them into the servant passages. They should be safe in the walls until your father arrives."

"I don't understand."

"You will in a moment. Hurry!"

"I don't believe the duke should go with you, Mr. Sinclair," John said.

Margritte was appropriately scandalized. "Why Mr. Corrigan! Please, don't…"

Then Sinclair drew his sword. The guests gasped almost as one, and backed away as quickly as they could from the man with the weapon at the front of the room. All except for John Corrigan, who continued to walk toward the danger.

I remembered the last thing Cornelius said to me that night so long ago in the study in London: *War isn't something we want the women to understand.* Now somebody's war had found those women, and John and I were the only soldiers around to do anything about it.

The time for madness was over, whether or not we were ready.

"I do not know who you might be, sir," Sinclair said. "But I know what an unarmed man looks like. I wish not to draw your blood before these fine people, but I shall."

"Do not do this!" the duke shouted. "I will go with him!" He was ready to run to Sinclair.

I held him back. I didn't know what John's gambit was, exactly, but if he thought it was worse to let our foreign friend go quietly I was ready to support that claim.

"Here I am, then," John said, spreading his arms wide. "Get through me and then you may have your prize."

Sinclair shrugged. "Very well."

He lunged forward at the exposed chest of the man before him. An instant before the blade struck true, John leaned and turned his torso until parallel with the weapon. The women in the room gasped, one screamed, and all of them backed further away. I realized I had been holding my breath.

"Joanne!" I barked. She nodded, and ran to the kitchen door. Collected there were several of the servants, whom she began to engage in quiet conversation. She was going to need their help.

The Frenchman—I was nearly positive now we were dealing with the French—nearly fell over, so startled was he to have missed. He muttered a curse and swung again, and found nothing but air.

After the third failed attempt to drop John Corrigan, the man behind Sinclair ran out of the room. I doubted it was cowardice.

"John," I said. "How many?"

"I counted twelve horses," he said.

Joanne returned to my side, having left the ushering of the guests to the staff. I was still holding the duke, who had stopped trying to struggle free and was now approximately as mystified by what was happening as Sinclair.

"Joanne, get him out too," I said.

"You're only two men!" She exclaimed. "You can't hold them off alone, come with us!"

"You're right. To attempt it would be madness. But don't worry, we're already madmen. We can do this. Trust me."

She looked into my eyes, beautiful and angry and defiant, probing—I guess—for some kind of weakness of resolve.

"All right, fine!" she said, finally, grabbing the duke's arm. "Come with me, my lord. Don't argue, or I'll put you over my knee."

"I don't... understand. Knee?" he stammered, as she dragged him off.

Meanwhile, Mr. Sinclair was still trying as hard as he could to damage Mr. Corrigan, and failing utterly. It would have been easier to pin water with a fork.

"Stand still!" Sinclair shouted. He fell back and lowered his sword, dumbfounded at having missed so spectacularly so often.

"Why would he do that, when as you've already pointed out, he doesn't have a weapon?" I asked.

"And who might you be?"

"I'm nobody of import," I said.

I glanced once more over my shoulder. Joanne and the duke had gotten out, and so had all of the guests. "I'm only another unarmed man you will have to kill in order to take your ransom."

"Ransom? This is not for ransom. That boy is leverage, do you have any idea who I represent?"

"No. Don't really care. John, do you care?"

"I am fully unconcerned."

"There you are. Neither of us cares. What we do care about is that the young man you've come for is a guest of this house, and as the lord of the manor is absent we will have to hold you off at least until he arrives. Which should be soon, I believe."

About 90% of this was bravado on my part, and the other 10% was just my trying to stall. I hadn't been in an actual fight for a few years, and the last time I picked up a sword it was to defend a lot of people against an imaginary dragon. I had every reason to think my skills were still intact, but my familiarity with reality was self-evidently horrible.

"The master of this house is going to find a building full of dead women and children if you foolish men do not stand aside and hand him over!" Sinclair said.

I looked behind us at the empty room. "Alas, it appears we have no duke to hand over."

Sinclair laughed, in part because he was genuinely amused by what I had to say, but mostly because as I was saying it eleven men were entering his side of the banquet area, turning a two-on-one swordfight into a two-on-twelve situation that was unpleasantly different.

"We shall find him," he said. "It won't take long." He stepped back, and to his men said, "The boy went through the servant door. Rush these fools and let's be on our way."

The banquet hall, as I said, was large, but not quite wide enough to allow for twelve men with swords to attack us at once. There was plenty of room for six at a time, though, and given we had no weapons, that six should have been perfectly sufficient.

"John, I could really use a sword," I said. "Can you get one for me?"

"Stay *exactly* where you are," he said.

I was only a few paces behind him, and to his left. Any frontal assault would reach me only seconds after reaching him, but he told me to stay where I was so I did, even when three men came charging directly at me. This was something of an act of faith on my part, to put it mildly. If I stepped back they could either surround John or just continue past us to the servant door. But staying where I was with nothing in my defense but harsh language wasn't going to work well either. It might have been different if any of the men appeared wanting when it came to basic swordsmanship, but I didn't see any weaknesses on first sight.

While I tried to work out all of my possible defensive options that didn't include losing a limb, John lunged forward to meet the first man on his side, ducking under a clumsy overhand, spinning around and driving his elbow into the man's throat. While the man gasped for air, John slammed his forearm across the swordsman's wrist, which jarred loose the sword. As the blade fell to the floor, John stepped away from the now-crumpling attacker and kicked the weapon in exactly the right way, catching the flat of the blade just past the cross-guard. It flew over the heads of the men who were seconds from removing many parts of my body. I caught it mid-air with enough time to parry the first attack.

"Thank you, John!" I shouted.

"You're welcome."

I went to work fighting off the three men, which even with a sword was not at all an easy thing. They had some skills, and while I had quite a few talents of my own I couldn't see what they were going to do before they did it like my friend could.

I was holding my own, in other words, but that was about all. John was doing something else completely. It seemed that being able to see a short way into the future, while making it extremely difficult to hold a conversation, really was an extraordinarily good talent in combat.

After dropping the man whose sword I was using he danced his way around the next three men confronting him, had managed to get two of them to mortally wound each other, and still hadn't bothered to get a sword for himself. He was always right where they wanted him to be up until they reached him, and then he was somewhere else. It wasn't even that he was moving quickly, only that when he did move, it was in the exact right way, every single time. Sometimes it seemed as if he wasn't even looking at them. He was looking at where they were going to be, or at something else entirely. Two or three times, he was looking at me.

"Reggie, on my mark," he said at one point.

"On your mark what?" I asked. I was getting pinned by the men on me and didn't have time to catch any more things he felt like throwing my way.

"Drop! Now!"

I fell to my knees. A sword swing that would have been a killing blow whistled just above my head. It was a fourth man I didn't know was there, and he would have done me in. Instead his blow killed one of the other men and left his underside exposed, so when I stood again it was with my sword slid under his ribcage.

"Thanks again, John," I said, pulling out my sword. To the men before me I asked, "Now who's next?"

The fighting continued, to the enormous frustration of the attacking parties—including no doubt Mr. Sinclair, although I couldn't see him. I had the two men at my feet, and John had three, plus one wounded man that was mostly just getting in the way of everyone else. We'd likely ruined the floor with blood, none of which was ours. We had also damaged a few of the chairs, and the table had a knife sticking out of it for some reason. I didn't know where it had come from, but I wasn't watching John all that closely, for obvious reasons. Maybe someone had tried to use it on him.

The most important detail, aside from neither of us dying, was that nobody had gotten past.

"Enough!" came a shout from the back of the hallway. The men in front of us fell back. I was nearly exhausted, and thankful to whomever had decided to call a halt to the attack. But then the men parted and I saw Sinclair in the center of the main hall, holding a crossbow.

A crossbow was bad, yet if it was going to come down to projectile weaponry I was a little glad not to see a rifle in his hands. As I said before, guns didn't make a whole lot of sense unless you had a lot of them and an infantry, but they still represented a new and mysterious threat. I could understand a crossbow; I'd been seeing them for centuries. Guns were smelly and terrifying. Also, firing one indoors was a great way to deafen everybody there.

In short, I was glad Sinclair had stuck with something reliable with which to murder us.

"Reginald," John said, very calmly. "You're going to have to stand behind me now, please."

"John, that's—"

"I'm aware of the capabilities of a crossbow, thank you. Please."

I stepped to my right, which put Corrigan between the weapon and I. Sinclair found this amusing.

"You are going to catch the bolts now?" Sinclair asked.

John leaned over and picked up one of the swords on the floor. "Not precisely."

Sinclair sighed and lowered the crossbow. "Sir," he said. "I say this with all honesty. You are a fine soldier, and clearly an honorable man. I'm *not* an honorable man, and so if you forced I will drop you with this, and then I will kill the man behind you, and anyone else who is feeling honorable this evening, and then I will get who I came here for. I would much prefer it if you stepped aside and let me do this thing."

"I'm happy that you would prefer to not kill us, Monsieur Sinclair. I would remind you that your departure would also accomplish this feat."

"You won't stand down, then?"

"I'm afraid I cannot."

"Very well."

Sinclair fired.

When you're in the line of fire of a crossbow, prudence dictates ducking or hiding behind a thick object. I had no thick objects to hide behind; only John, and he could avoid every other kind of attack—including, if his war stories were to be believed, one from a gun. I thought it was likely, then, that if the crossbow bolt found any home, the home would be inside of me.

All of which is to say my eyes were closed when the next thing happened, because I expected to die.

I didn't die. I heard a metal-on-metal sound, and when I opened my eyes John had his sword raised and the bolt was stuck in the wall on the other side of the room.

Looking at the faces of the Frenchmen I saw fear for the first time. Apparently, John Corrigan had deflected a crossbow bolt from a few feet away with the flat of a sword blade. If he could do *that*, I'm sure they were thinking, what else could he do?

"Impossible!" Sinclair shouted.

It was a repeating crossbow, so he had a second shot, which he took. This time I kept my eyes open, but it happened almost too fast to comprehend. The bolt was due to strike John in the chest and would have landed true, but at the last second his sword—a blur—swiped up and across his body. Redirected, the second shot landed in the wall right next to the first.

The men with Sinclair looked legitimately spooked—I heard the word *witch*—and I had hopes that this performance might be enough to persuade them to leave.

I also heard a gasp from an unexpected part of the room.

It was Joanne. She had snuck through the kitchen door just in time to witness John's last trick and now was just standing there, agape, apparently unaware that she had put herself in tremendous danger.

John heard her too. He turned, stared for a couple of seconds, and then looked at me.

"What is it?" I asked.

He just smiled, a sad but relieved smile. "It will be okay, my friend."

"What will? I don't understand."

But then I almost did, because Sinclair had reloaded his crossbow.

"Yield," the Frenchman said calmly.

"I cannot," John said.

"Very well."

Sinclair fired again, but he wasn't aiming for John at all this time. He was shooting at Joanne.

John knew it. He jumped to his right and whipped the sword down in just such a way as to intercept the bolt before it could pass. It landed in the floor well short of her.

But in doing so John exposed himself. Sinclair had fired twice rapidly, with his second shot cleverly targeting the space John had to occupy if he was going to intercept the first.

The crossbow bolt made a sick, soft sound when it struck John in the stomach. Immediately he fell over, clutching what was without question a mortal wound. Joanne let out a scream that was overwhelmed by the cheer that went up on the other end of the room, and she ran to the side of our fallen friend. I would have done the same but there was the small matter of the seven blackguards John had left me alone to deal with.

Gamely, I stepped into the middle of the room and waved my sword around defiantly. There was literally no way for me to do this alone because at least two people were needed to keep anyone from the kitchen door, but there wasn't anyone else left and I wasn't really in a position to run away at this point.

"All right," I said. "Let's go."

"For God's sake, Reginald, enough!" Joanne shouted.

I didn't know what Joanne expected me to do. If she thought these men were going to let everybody live after all of this she was terribly mistaken, especially after we'd dropped five of them. Possibly, the fact that John was dying in her lap had impaired her judgment.

Sinclair shook his head. "This house is overrun with honorable men," he said. "Kill him and let's get on with it."

The one John had wounded was still closest, because the fool hadn't figured out he was a tremendous liability and fallen back.

I'd intended to start with him, as a shield and as a means to knock over the others, maybe clutter up the space a bit and make it difficult to stand. Anything that kept the seven of them from launching a coordinated attack, especially since I didn't have John looking into my future and telling me when to duck.

It wasn't much of a plan, but it was all I had. And it would have worked only until they figured out they could just go around me.

But before anyone could get close enough to launch an assault or do much of anything else, a distant horn sounded from outside.

"What *now*?" Sinclair asked, to nobody in particular. He was really not having a good night.

"That's my father, brigand!" Joanne said. "And his men. The horn means they've reached the gate and will be on you in minutes."

"I thank you for the warning." To his men he shouted, "Regroup! We take the fight outside!"

Joanne laughed. "There isn't going to be a *fight*! My father travels with half an army, you idiot. Why do you think your prized duke was staying here? No sane man would cross this household. If you think the two you already faced were a handful, wait until you see what the rest of them can do."

The men with Sinclair looked extremely uncertain about this entire endeavor, and I couldn't really blame them. These were some species of mercenary, and one thing that has always been true of a company of mercenaries is that they are only really comfortable when the odds are overwhelmingly in their favor. They have no interest in a hard fight and no motivation except money. They also aren't particularly interested in causes.

Sinclair had a cause. I had no idea what it was, but he clearly had one. So he made every effort to convince the men he had left to rally and organize, but all it took was one of them to decide they were done for all to follow. The six men were gone before he could even finish handing out instructions.

All of which was a good thing, because Joanne was bluffing. Cornelius traveled with a couple of soldiers at most, but the rest of his party consisted of guests from London, and not the battle-tested variety of guest. Cornelius's men along with the aging patriarch might well have turned the course of the battle, but it would have been a battle and not a rout.

Sinclair, the only man to remain, was still coming to grips with the idea that he had lost the night.

"I took on three of yours alone," I said, holding up my sword. "You're welcome to try me by yourself."

"I might take those odds, sir, but no," Sinclair said. "I would ask only the name of the man I killed. I feel as if his is a name I would do well to never forget."

"His name is John Corrigan."

"Corrigan. The greatest soldier I've ever seen."

I had seen better, but none of the ones I could think of were also human. That said, I was pretty sure John could have given even a vampire a pretty hard time.

We both caught the sound of Cornelius's carriage rearing to a stop. "You'd better flee, if that's your intent," I said.

Sinclair bowed. "Until next time." Then he ran out the front door.

I thought about giving chase. Running him down wouldn't have been all that difficult. The property was large, and there were at least five spare horses roaming around outside. Plus Cornelius and his men, once notified, would certainly have been up to the task.

I didn't much like the idea of a chase that led me to those woods, however. More importantly, as soon as Sinclair left I remembered my friend was dying behind me, and decided I didn't much care about anything else.

Joanne had John's head cradled in her lap.

"How is he?" I asked.

"I don't know. Not well, I think. I feel as if I should pull this out, but also if I do so it will both ease his pain and hasten his departure."

I knelt down next to him. His breathing was shallow but his eyes were still alert and focused. His hand found mine, and squeezed with some strength.

"I told you..." he muttered, "I told you it would be all right."

"It's not all right at all. You're dying."

"I am. And I've been waiting for it. I'm glad it's here. I need two favors from you, Reggie."

"Anything."

"I need you to find my son. Find my son and tell him who I was and who he might be. He needs to understand... if he has the curse, he needs to understand."

"Yes, of course."

"I can't see," John said. "I can see nothing beyond this night so I don't know if you'll find him or not. I hope you do."

"I can spend a lifetime looking. He'll be found, I promise."

"Good. Good."

He drifted off and his eyes fluttered, and I thought we'd lost him for a moment, but they snapped to attention again.

"The second favor, Reggie," he said. "Pull out the bolt."

The bolt had landed just at the bottom of his ribcage. From the sound of his breathing it had taken out one of his lungs, and there was no telling how much other internal damage had been done. The blood beneath him was dark and thick. But still I had hope that he could survive this.

"You'll bleed to death if I do that, John," I said. "We can find a doctor. I'm sure there's one. We can wait."

"I will bleed out the second you remove it," he agreed. "But I'll die either way. I told you, I can't see past tonight. You know what that means. Nothing you can do will change that."

"You're certain."

"Reginald, don't," Joanne said softly, through a mask of tears.

"Didn't I tell you this day would come?" John said.

"Yes. But you're a madman. We both are. So why should I believe you?"

He smiled. "Sometimes madmen are the best kinds of people."

~

We buried John on the grounds. Nobody had any idea about family or other friends that might warrant notification of his passing, and since that was the case we also didn't know where else it made sense to bury him. I thought the location was appropriate because as little as I knew him I did think while he was at the estate he was happy.

The men who were supposed to arrive for the duke did eventually make it there, but a day later than expected. Whatever skullduggery Sinclair was involved in included delaying their arrival through some means I didn't really bother to hear the details on. I was also extremely uninterested as to *why* anyone would go through the trouble to kidnap the young man John gave his life to protect. It was the machinations of royalty, and I wanted no part of it.

The young duke was from a background of some wealth, however, and I *was* interested in that. He felt it important to award the men who had protected him, and seeing as how my savings had been dwindling for years I wasn't about to turn down a heavy purse. (Two purses, actually. The second was to go to John Corrigan's son, whom I'd already promised to find.) He also made me promise to seek him out if I ever needed assistance or a reference or anything else at all. I shook his hand and made the promise, never expecting to need any such thing from him. About this, I ended up being wrong.

~

"What was John's secret?" Joanne asked after our makeshift funeral service. We were in my room. I was wearing my fine suit again and staring out the window at the carriageway as my ride was being prepared below.

It was a few hours before I was due to depart for London. I wasn't returning to the London day-to-day life I had led, but I didn't let anybody know this, exactly. My madness appeared to have finally abated—after needing all the clarity I could muster to defend myself it seemed my mind had figured out some things—but it felt like it was time to move on. I had John's family to find, and plenty of reasons to reinvent myself as someone who hadn't gone insane in front of wealthy and influential people.

"How do you mean?" I asked.

"I saw how he moved. He could barely speak most times, but his motions were… It was like I was watching a play but he was the only one who recalled the rehearsals. Up until the end. Reggie, did he trade his life for mine?"

"It wasn't your actions that caused his death. It was the man with the crossbow."

"I appreciate that. But had I not returned, he would have prevailed, I think. Even against that army. So what was his secret?"

"He saw the future," I said. "You can believe that or not believe it, but that was how he could do what he did."

"Oh thank goodness!" she gasped. "I wanted no part of magic or devils. Nor was I prepared to accept that sort of explanation. But this… no, this I can believe, after what I've seen."

"I don't think either the sacred or the profane had any role in his curse. He also said he saw no future beyond the night he died, so don't blame yourself. If it hadn't been you returning it would have been something else."

"I imagine that depends on how one feels on the subject of predestination," she said.

"He could change the future. He told me so. But his own death appears to have been fixed."

She nodded. "So that was John Corrigan's dying secret. What is *yours?*"

I turned away from the window. Joanne was seated on the edge of the bed, still in her mourner's clothing, only without a veil. She looked very small and sad just then.

"I have no dying secret."

"You understand me."

"I do. And that's my answer. My secret is in not dying. I don't grow old."

She arched an eyebrow, a trace of her former mirth returning. "Really. That's quite a trick. I just remembered I'm speaking to a self-professed lunatic."

"Can we correspond?"

She laughed. "Reginald Bates, honestly!"

"Is that a yes or a no? I can't tell."

"Mr. Bates, if you asked for my hand, right now I might give it, because save for one important particular way, I believe I actually love you. But you will not, because when you leave here I *also* believe the name you are using might cease to exist. Knowing this, if you fail to write me letters and provide for me a way to respond, I swear by all that God has made that I will hunt you down, in this life or the next."

"That's a yes?"

"That is a damned yes, sir."

"All right, then. Some time in the future, after we have corresponded for many a year and you have had the great adventures I hope for you, we'll meet again. And when I still look as I do now, you can tell me how mad I truly am."

"Perhaps by then *I* will have gone mad, and will not know the difference."

"My hope is that never happens. Your wits are far too great to lose."

"Now I shall be forced to blush."

She stood, and we hugged, and kissed one another gently. And then it was time for me to depart.

~

Joanne never did marry. Margritte evidently considered me the last, best hope to find her daughter a husband who could cure her of her sexual preference. After my departure—I'm told, as we did correspond regularly—Joanne and her mother reached a degree of acceptance that was far ahead of its time, socially speaking. And later, when an outbreak of dysentery in the city of London claimed the lives of her older sisters, Joanne suddenly found herself the eldest heir to Cornelius's estate and guardian of her nieces and nephews.

When we met again, years later, she had become a formidable social and economic force, especially given her gender and the age in which she lived. The story of that meeting is one for another time.

It took me over six years to find John Corrigan's son. The boy's name was David, by then a grown to a man of twenty. Having never met John and not known why that was the case, David likely would have had nothing to do with me at all but for the gold I brought.

I told him everything I knew about his father, including the curse, and while he seemed very polite about the whole thing I got the sense that he took me for a madman. Maybe I was.

David didn't have the curse, though. That much was obvious.

I left thinking John's special abilities had died with him, and his family's curse was over. I turned out to be wrong. The curse lived on in another Corrigan, but I wouldn't discover this until many years later.

But that too is a story for another time.

AFTERWORD

Read **Fixer,** also by Gene Doucette
for more on that Corrigan family curse

THE IMMORTAL CHRONICLES

Yuletide IMMORTAL

Gene Doucette

YULETIDE IMMORTAL

The first time I met Santa was in a bar.

I appreciate that this is a true statement about a lot of the people I've met in my life, especially the most recent portion, by which I mean the last hundred years or so. I spent most of the twentieth century in North America, in bars, clubs, restaurants, and so on. Any place that served alcohol. I also appreciate that this was not always a stupendous plan given for a solid decade there weren't any places to legally purchase and imbibe alcohol in the United States, but at the same time Prohibition was going on Europe was a crap place to be thanks to the fallout from the War to End All Wars and plus, I was too lazy to get up and go somewhere else.

Still, by 1955 you'd think I would have figured out there were easier places to get drunk. Aside from prohibition, by mid-century I had also survived a nightclub fire and a mob hit in two different bars a decade apart, which is the sort of track record that can make a guy consider—if not drinking in a less violent country—abstinence or drinking alone.

The problem is I've been alive for a really long time—going on sixty-thousand years—and a whole lot of that has involved solo drinking. Generally if in a culture where I'm welcome, regardless of how dangerous that culture can turn out to be occasionally, I'd rather share a pint with some people than be alone with a bottle.

Which, again, is how I met Santa.

I was occupying a barstool in the Village in lower Manhattan at the time. It was December, of course—one does not meet Santa in August—and as I said the year was 1955.

I don't like New York City all that much. I'm not sure why. I mean, there are times when it's just the right kind of controlled hedonism, but there's also a certain tribal rudeness to the inhabitants that I could never appreciate from the perspective of a fellow tribe-member. I think it's probably also a lovely place to be if one has a lot of money, but for the century in question when I was there it was either as a common laborer or a modestly well-off tourist. I never got to enjoy it as a fabulously wealthy gadabout. Maybe if I had I'd have appreciated it more.

Anyway. Santa. He showed up as I was on my third or fourth pint of really crummy tap beer and engaged with a few of the locals on the subject of the new bridge opening up that month, and how this would or would not signal the end of civilization as we knew it.

I'm not really kidding. There were four other patrons in on the conversation plus the bartender, and they collectively seemed to think the Tappan Zee Bridge would be bringing all manner of aliens into the city.

This is a common affliction, historically, in which change is viewed as a negative regardless of what kind of change it is. I remember having similar arguments over pre-sliced bread, cars, and Roman aqueducts. Although in fairness I agreed with the argument against cars. I still think they were a bad idea.

"We have enough undesirables in this neighborhood already, thank you kindly," the bartender was saying. He was a square-jawed Irishman named O'Shea, running an Irish pub full of other

Irishmen. I was the only theoretical 'undesirable' in the room, but thankfully nobody had bothered to make that point as yet. "What do you think, Santa?"

He was speaking to the fellow to my right. I was aware the seat had just become occupied but hadn't turned to look until then.

And... it was Santa. By that I mean it was a portly gentleman with a long, grey-white beard, a dark red suit with white trim, wire-framed glasses and a balding head. His cheeks were rosy either from the cold or the exertion of hoisting himself up on the barstool. He was not particularly tall.

"What's the rumpus?" Santa asked, as a pint was placed in front of him.

"This fella here don't agree with us," O'Shea said, meaning me. He then went on to describe the social ills sure to befall the neighborhood in the coming years thanks to a modest traffic improvement. He managed to roll the dismantling of the Third Avenue El into his dissertation, despite that being an event everyone there could agree was good.

Santa took all of this in, nodding patiently. He turned to me. "Who might you be, sir?"

"Stanley," I said. It was a name I had just started trying on. It matched the identification in my pocket (along with the surname Jones) I'd only recently purchased from a very good counterfeiter not too far from were I was sitting. I had picked neither name.

It was around this era that I realized the world was going to be a whole lot more complicated if I didn't have multiple documents identifying me as a member of whatever country I was in, on-hand, all the time. That meant finding someone who could make me multiple people so as to provide the sort of versatility I needed. That was what led me to an old Russian in an unsavory pawn shop in an unsavory part of town.

This was actually why I was *in* New York. I just hadn't worked up the energy yet to leave.

"It's a delight to meet you, Stanley," Santa said.

"And you are?" I asked.

He laughed, and clapped me on the shoulder. "You're a funny one!" Then he took a long drink of his beer and ignored the question.

"So what *do* you think, Santa?" O'Shea asked.

Santa put down his beer and looked around the room, which was already beginning to crowd around him in anticipation. "Well, gents, I'm afraid I will have to go against you on this one, and agree with our new friend Stanley."

This prompted an exaggerated outcry, as if the bar had a bet going and he'd just lost it for them.

"I will explain," Santa said, holding up a hand, "with a story."

He cleared his throat and began. "I heard tell of a village not so far from here and not so long ago. The village was almost *entirely* isolated, with a mountain face behind them and a thick forest in front. On a third side, a rushing river and swamp land. The only way in and out was down the raging river or through the dangerous woods, but the people didn't much care, for they *had* all they needed. The ground was fertile, the crops plentiful, and the animals healthy.

"One day a man from the nearest village, on the other side of the forest, arrived in the town with a peculiar offer. If the villagers were to help him widen the road through the woods, it would make passage easier and safer for all of them, and then commerce could flow more freely, to the benefit of all. Or, so the man claimed."

As Santa told this story more men from the edges of the bar started drifting over. I got the sense that this was not the first time they had been treated to a story from this person. I also got the sense that he was not a person at all.

"The village elders presented the idea to the people. Almost as one they answered: *No!* For they had no *need* of anything outside the town. All this would do, they said, is invite people from that other village to relocate, and none of them had any use for outsiders. Strangers! People not like them. Like Stanley, here."

"Hey, leave me out of this."

"Isolation, they said, was better! Isolation was to their benefit! And so the elders—taking the concerns of the local citizens under consideration, of course—discussed the matter in private, and do you know what they decided?"

The bar responded with a number of guesses ranging from *no* to *never*.

"They decided *Yes!* Yes, they would help build out that road."

The men in the room practically rioted at this news.

"And after it was done, the people of the town, the ones who insisted that a better path would only lead to ruin? Why, those people *saw all their worst fears come true*! Strange men and women began *appearing* in the village! People never encountered before! People with odd languages and strange accents and bizarre skin color. People not at all like them! And they were angry with the elders for allowing such a thing to happen."

"There you go," O'Shea said, pointing at me, either because he thought Santa had proven the bar correct or because I was now representing the dangerous strangers in this imaginary village. I didn't like the second option. I've been that stranger quite a few times, and am allergic to lynch mobs.

"*Until!*" Santa said, slapping the bar emphatically. "The rains came! It rained and poured, for days, a *great storm* that caused the river to swell above the banks and into the swampland. It rained so hard that Noah—if he were there—would have said, 'My *goodness* but this is a lot of rain!' And then *more* water came down off the mountains in great waves and the river rose again, out of the swamps and into the town. And the villagers *looked* at the rising floodwater, and did not know what to do.

"But also in that town were families who had come from a land beside the ocean. They knew flooding, and how to stem the waters, and they showed the rest of the village what to do. And for a while it worked! But the water kept rising, and so another people stepped forward. *We can build boats* they offered. And so they did, but by then the river water was too treacherous to risk, and so another group stood and said, *we will send word to the other village.*

"And soon people came down the newly widened road, with carriages and wagons and horses and men, and the strangers from the next town helped all the men and women and children from the village *out* of the town before they were drowned by the flood waters. An entire village—every single family—saved by the road they *swore* would bring about their demise."

This brought actual applause.

"Ah, but that is not all, my friends!" Santa said. "For when the waters receded and the villagers returned, they found two men in the center of town sitting in a dinghy and drinking beer. And when they asked the two men why they didn't also evacuate, they looked at one another and then at the questioners, and said, *but it was just a wee bit 'o rain.*"

Laughter, more applause, and then someone bought Santa his next drink, and nobody tried to tie me up and set me on fire. I have few requirements for an effectively told story, but that's one of them.

Later, after things quieted down, I asked Santa, "Did you just tell an immigration parable and end it with a bad Irish joke? Or am I a lot drunker than I thought?"

Santa smiled. "It wasn't so bad a joke as that. It suffered only from not being particularly funny, but I've found any story of sufficient length can be made into a joke with a little brogue tacked on the end. Especially given the audience. Even the Bard knew you have to throw some low humor in for the folks on the floor."

I laughed. I knew my Shakespeare pretty well—because I knew Shakespeare pretty well—and he actually did say that.

"Maybe so, but I doubt anyone here will be recalling the parable part of that story."

"I don't know that I agree with you, Stanley. In my experience, stories told well stick with a person, even if with details forgotten. Wisdom is like sunshine. It leaves behind evidence of exposure. Perhaps next month, when this crowd starts rattling sabers over the next Negro emancipation or suffrage motion or Filipino war, something of what I said tonight will show itself in their reasoning."

"Or just the next public transportation improvement."

"It doesn't take much to excite a crowd, does it?"

"It does not," I agreed. I held up my pint. "Well, cheers."

"Cheers!"

"Now tell me how an imp such as yourself ended up in the Village, calling himself Santa."

He nearly choked on his mouthful, swallowed, then laughed uproariously. "An imp, you say! My boy, it's been years since anyone called me that."

"It's been years since I've met one."

"Really. How *many* years, would you say?"

"At least a thousand."

He laughed again. "O'Shea, I'd like to forward my next round to Stanley here. He and I have a lot to talk about."

∼

*I*mps can be a lot of fun when you know ahead of time what you're dealing with. They are professional fabulists, by which I mean they tell fantastic stories that have an unfortunate tendency to be untrue. That's fine so long as you're ready for it. Problems with imps arise from the fact that they won't tip you off when they've stopped being fully honest.

In the abstract, a guy who doesn't distinguish *true* from *factually accurate* is mostly harmless, unless that guy also happens to command a lot of attention because he's a gifted storyteller. One such imp was a fellow named Silenus, who nearly got me killed many times over because of the tales he was telling about me, specifically. Those tales gave the impression I was a god—my name at the time was Dionysos so you've probably heard a few of them—and then everyone in Greece wanted to take a poke at the god. It was awkward.

Imps also have longer-than-average lifespans, although I don't know exactly how long because another annoying thing is that the men of a line of imps all tend to look very much alike. (The women don't. I don't know why this is.) This is tremendously confusing for an immortal. I'm really used to people dying off in a predictable timeframe, and have been known to use generations as a sort of crude clock, but with the Silenii, I usually couldn't tell if I was talking to Silenus the elder, the younger, or the third, because they all looked the same when they reached adulthood. Yet the amount of time that elapsed between my meeting the first Silenus and the third—I never met anyone from the line after the third—was more than six hundred years. I could have asked how long their lifespans were, but asking an imp a question like that means never knowing if the answer you've gotten is correct.

They can also drink. Aside from iffrits—and women—imps are probably my favorite sort of drinking companion. The reason I don't spend more time with them may be partly due to imps being very rare, but more likely because whenever I spend a lot of time with one I end up in danger for some reason.

~

"You're *how* old?" he asked. This was a little while later, after we compared stories about how we'd ended up in this particular pub, and also after two more rounds apiece. We had relocated to a table away from the bar. It was in a corner against the storeroom wall, where we were pretty sure nobody would overhear.

"Old enough so I couldn't say for sure how old I am."

"And you knew the Silenii? I'm deeply impressed, my friend. They're an old line. Died off, I'm pretty certain. The last Silenus I ever heard tell of was a victim of the inquisition purges."

Of all the creatures on the planet—other than perhaps vampires—imps are probably the most likely to take me at my word when I tell them I'm immortal. It goes back to the whole question of truth versus fact. To an imp, my truth is that I'm an immortal man, and that's good enough for them to believe it too. As I said, this sort of thing can blow up in your face quickly if you aren't careful.

"Those must have been difficult times for an imp," I said.

"Oh, it was! In Europe especially! For a thousand years you couldn't tell a single good story without it involving Jesus somehow. The clever ones figured out ways, but the Silenii... they were too proud, if you must know. Pride and stubbornness and inflexibility of mind are a dangerous combination. It's a pity, they had so many stories."

Another thing about imp lineage is the elders teach the young all of the same tales, so a line of imps is an unbroken chain of oral history. The stories mutate over time, as they have to, but generally at the discretion of the teller. It's been said the mind of an imp is the mind of his ancestors, and implicit in that definition is that any change made by any generation to any story is sanctioned by the historic originator of that story. It's a bit too mystical of an interpretation for me, but I could understand the appeal, especially for the imp who's changing a story.

What Santa meant, then, was when the Silenii died off so did their stories, because they belonged to nobody else. I wasn't terribly broken up about this since, again, I was in a whole bunch of those stories.

Something occurred to me. "Does that mean the whole Santa thing is a survival technique?"

"You could say so! And, as good stories involving Jesus go, it's not so terrible."

By the way, asking him if he was the "real" Santa would have been useless, for the same reason he had no problem with my immortality. And if the whole Santa thing began as an imp family story, he had a better claim on the title than anybody else around. If he said he was *the* Santa, I would have had a time disputing it.

This was not to say Santa is real, in the sense that there was anyone—imp or otherwise—living at the North Pole and delivering toys. But that was exactly the kind of fantastic tale I'd come to expect from his kind.

"What are you doing in New York?" I asked.

"Oh, I've lived here for years. Nobody needs Santa year-round, of course, but I keep busy. How about you? What's an immortal man doing in the city? Should I take your presence here as proof this is indeed the greatest city on Earth?"

"I'm sure you have a story or two to back up that claim."

"Oh, I *do*! Would you like to hear one?"

"Not right now. And that's not why. I guess the question is, what's an immortal man doing anywhere? This seemed like a good place to stop over and have a drink for a while. I don't have more of a story than that."

This was true, but really more accurately described my time in the whole country. And more generally, my approach to life.

Emotionally speaking, the twentieth century was not a good time for me. I suffered a loss twenty years in, and spend most of the next eighty years or so in mourning, which in my case meant trying to maintain a high degree of non-sobriety. When I ran into Santa I was only thirty years in on that eighty-year jag, and pretty bitter.

If it isn't already obvious, I tend to handle my problems by drinking more than I really should.

"Where *wouldn't* an immortal man go?" Santa said. "I don't have the gift of *your* longevity, but I'm thankful every day to have been granted an extended time on Earth. Think of all the stories I would miss otherwise!"

I smiled. Imps are always looking for a better story. It's what drives them. I never had anything so simple to live for. "Is that what Santa is doing in New York? Collecting stories?"

"Why not? This is my favorite time of year, Stanley. I spend my days at Gimbel's, listening to the stories of children and making them happy, and my evenings in bars like this."

"Listening to the stories of drunks."

"And making them happy. You know, a child and a drunkard share a similar fondness for unconventional storytelling. Ask a sober soul to tell you a story, and they'll furrow their brow and work through the steps of the thing. First this happened, then that, and then most reasonably, of course, the other thing happened as a consequence of it all. They're terribly, terribly boring most of the time. But a child's perspective is untethered by the rational. And a drunkard, well… they will just speak, and whatever words come out of their mouths only so often pass an internal inspection."

"The honesty of the irrational."

"You have it, yes."

"It's been said the only honest man in a king's court is the jester."

Santa laughed. "That's marvelous! What a story *that* must make!"

"Sorry, it's just an observation. It doesn't come with a story."

"Well. I shall have to compose one. Or you will. I'm sure you have a storyteller inside of you somewhere. An immortal man… the tales you must have!"

I *do* have a jester story, but it doesn't have a happy ending and I didn't feel like telling it. A lot of my stories—and he wasn't wrong in assuming I have quite a few—end in ways that make them either not worth retelling, or retelling only in the interest of depressing or frightening those assembled. I am an aggregator of cautionary tales.

I didn't often share them, though, at least not at the time Santa and I were talking. I had found that keeping my own counsel was the best strategy for survival. That said, there have been a few periods in history where I wrote some of my life out, mostly in situations where nobody could take me seriously. Epic poetry, once it was invented, was a decent outlet, although I wasn't what anybody would call a decent poet. Fiction prose writing, as a form, has also proven to be decent cover for my autobiographical writings.

Telling stories aloud was a skill I excelled at once too, a millennium ago, when traveling storytelling was in vogue. But that was only rarely about my own life, unless there was drink involved. As Santa had already observed, men talk more freely when plied with alcohol. I'm certainly not an exception.

"I think," Santa said, "you should come to Gimbel's with me tomorrow."

He said it in a way that indicated this was already a settled decision.

"Why would I do that? Do you need someone to dress up as an elf? I think I may be too tall."

There are real elves, incidentally. They're nearly indistinguishable from humans in every way, including height. However, the child-sized elves of the Santa mythology are *not* real.

"You can be a helper! No costume needed, just dress normally. If any of the staff asks, I can explain you're there from the agency to… I don't know, to inspect matters or some such thing."

"There's an agency?"

"They think there is. I'm the only one who shows up, but they believe I'm part of a team of Santas that all look alike. The store has another agency on call if I'm unavailable."

"Well, Santa *is* supposed to always look the same, isn't he?"

"Tell that to Macy's! So what do you say?"
"I can't think of a single reason to do this."
"Excellent! Then I'll see you in the store. I begin at 10."

∽

The 1950's were a little odd. With hindsight it's possible to look on the era and see things that appear entirely normal and familiar from a modern perspective, but in the moment those things were new and innovative. And odd.

It was in the fifties that Americans figured out living in cities can suck, and the suburbs became a thing. That was only possible because of affordable cars and more widely available public transportation, two new realities that featured prominently in the disagreement in the bar. Not discussed at the bar but also a relatively new thing: everyone suddenly had a television. This was in part because TV reached the same level of affordability, need and utility that made radio mandatory some thirty years earlier, and partly because the whole country seemed to be enjoying an immoderate level of affluence, with no new war to spend it on.

Americans needed to spend all of that new money, and television had advertisements for products that they could spend their money on, so all they needed to know was where to go to get the things being advertised.

Thus: department stores. People would get in their new cars and drive from their new suburban homes over the new bridges built for them, to go to the nearest department store and buy the new things they saw featured on their new televisions.

I am generally an enormous fan of innovation. Legitimately new things are exceedingly rare, and when I come across them I am more often than not dazzled. The wheel, for instance, was a fantastic idea. So were toilets, and so was television, and more recently, the Internet.

But department stores aren't new innovations. They're more annoying versions of the street bazaar, which is a very, very old idea.

I like street bazaars. Sure, they're noisy and smelly and crowded, but they're also held outside, which is nice. And I know how they work. I probably have more experience as a consumer than any man alive, so I know how to find a bargain and how to negotiate one. But department stores are not designed for someone with my talents in mind. Specifically, when I went into one for the first time—I believe I was purchasing a shirt—I attempted to haggle.

Haggling is a wonderful thing that nobody does any more unless they're buying a car. When I asked the salesman what the price of the shirt was and he told me, I naturally assumed the price was too high, and then counter-offered a price I thought was much too low. What should have happened was that he—after a lengthy discursion on the subject of the remarkable quality of the shirt, no doubt—would give me a lower price. I would then insult the shirt and the salesman's mother, and counter with a slightly higher offer.

Eventually, we would arrive at a price we were both willing to accept, I would give him the coins and get the shirt, and that would be that. I'd walk away feeling I had gotten a good bargain, and the merchant would feel satisfied that he had made a sale that preserved a decent profit margin.

This is how the world is supposed to work.

But in the department store—this strange indoor bazaar, just as crowded only now enclosed in a suffocating fluorescent nightmare—the price of the shirt was the price of the shirt. The salesman had no say in the price, because he didn't own the shirt and had no authority to negotiate. He also had no idea what was happening when I counter-offered, and I had to leave the store before security got involved. I also had to buy the shirt.

This is a terrible arrangement. I'm sure it's nice for the

conflict-averse—not everyone enjoys haggling as much as I do—but as far as I'm concerned a non-negotiable cost is the same thing as accepting the outrageous initially-quoted price in a street bazaar. Instead of me—the consumer who is looking to purchase X number of shirts with Y number of coins—having some direct say in the value of shirts, the only pressure the seller feels is from the other guy selling similar shirts down the street. I realize both shirt sellers should have an economic interest in outselling each other, but I don't know if the two guys selling shirts aren't also working together to determine a minimum shirt value of some kind.

Anyway, I like haggling, and I'm good at it, and it's a skill I wish I could use more often.

Also, if that hasn't been made clear yet, I don't like department stores, so I was at a loss to explain why I went to Gimbel's the following morning to meet up with Santa. Maybe it was that I had nothing better to do, although this sort of described the entire millennium. It could also have been the Christmas miracle of waking up without a hangover, or just the novelty of discovering an imp in New York City calling himself Santa.

Whatever it was, I put on my suit, the shirt I paid too much for, and a tie, and headed downtown. (This did not mean I dressed up. Everyone wore a suit and a tie unless they were at the beach or on their way from the bed to the bathroom. We didn't get t-shirts until the sixties.) Santa wasn't surprised to see me.

"There you are, Stanley!" He greeted, waving me forward. His throne was on the second floor of the store, in the back, at the end of a series of decorative arrow signs. The signs directed shoppers—mothers with children in this case—down a non-straight path to the Father Christmas corner, passing nearly every perfume counter, kitchen appliance, cleaning product and toy the store had to offer. By the time I reached him I smelled like flowers and was thinking about buying a vacuum cleaner.

Santa was between kids. A modest line of mothers with their

children had formed twenty feet away, behind a "Line starts here" sign and some velvet ropes. There weren't any elfish helpers and the chair he was in was essentially a lounge chair from the furniture department with a few bows attached. It didn't look like anybody much bothered to make it look like the North Pole. I didn't even see a photographer.

"There's a chair..." Santa said, looking around behind him. A closed lawn chair was propped up on the wall behind him. I grabbed it and sat down. "Did you have any trouble finding your way?" he asked.

"You are literally the only person in this building that it's impossible to not know the location of," I said.

Well, I guess that's true, isn't it? Come on, smile: it's Christmas!" He turned to the line. "Who's ready for Santa?"

I spent the whole day there, as apparently I really did have nothing else to do. We talked between children, who were content to wait for a while to see him even when there wasn't anybody on his lap. The pace was surprisingly honorable and stately, and something one doesn't see now. Although nowadays there are Santas are all over the place, which probably has something to do with it. People tend to have more respect for the unique.

"How long have you been calling yourself Santa?" I asked him during one break between kids.

"Oh, always, although the name itself is new to my generation. My father was one of the Father Christmases, and I have an uncle and two cousins who went by Sinterklaas. There are even a couple of Yule Goats in the family. My great grandfather was Jodin Longbeard. One of the first of the Santa line."

"But you're all Santas now."

"Of course, just like your friends the Silenii."

"I don't know that I would call them friends."

"If you are who you claim, Silenus actually worshipped you, so perhaps you're correct. Friend is not an adequate word."

That wasn't what I meant, but I didn't have an interest in pressing the point. My history with Silenus and his sons was complicated by a number of factors, including the perhaps accidental founding of a religious cult. It's a long story, and I didn't want to get into it with Santa, not in the middle of another religious cult's holiday. But then he was calling up the next child and I didn't have to elaborate.

"Ho ho! What's your name, young man?"

The degree of patience and genuine interest Santa had in the things the children said was honestly impressive, especially to someone like me. I am resolutely terrible with kids, partly because I spend almost no time around them. This is for a number of reasons, the first being that I can't have them, so far as I know. This became a topic of conversation as well, in a roundabout sort of way.

"Why am I here?"

"Aren't you enjoying yourself?" Santa asked.

"I neither am nor am not. I'm mostly puzzled by all of this."

He laughed. "Puzzled, you say!"

He called up another child and went through his routine, which consisted of asking about the child's day, life, and wishes for Christmas. Whether those wishes were capitalistic or aspirational didn't much matter. The *have you been good this year* question never came up. Maybe the Macy's Santa was more concerned with good versus evil, but this one mostly assumed the best.

"Why puzzled?" he asked as soon as the boy jumped down on his own.

"Maybe puzzled is the wrong word," I said. "I've been alive for a lot of different traditional festivals and celebrations, all with their peculiarities. Right now I feel like I'm watching the birth of a new tradition."

"People have been celebrating gift-giving holidays for century upon century. Perhaps as far back as Saint Nicholas himself."

"Was he one of you?"

"Oh, oh no, I don't think so. Not of my line, at least."

A little girl came up with a long story about a doll she had to have and a second one on the perils of her brother's hand-me-down tricycle, and how chocolate ice cream is good but nobody in the whole entire world likes strawberry.

"The celebration of a saint's day isn't new," I agreed, once the girl had left. "Neither were the old harvest celebrations, or Yule day. But this seems unconnected to all of that."

"You become far too analytical when sober. Relax and enjoy the spirit of the holiday, I say."

"What spirit is that?"

"Look around! Happy children, happy adults, people spending time with family and giving each other things… it's jollity at its finest!"

"I see advantageously leveraged commerce preying on buyers who already have all they need in order to survive."

He shot me a look. "You're trying to be sour intentionally."

"Probably. I'm usually drinking by now."

"Well if you're looking for an answer to the question, this is why you're here. You need to be more connected to the world! Especially during Christmas."

"What kind of connection did you have in mind?"

He called another little girl up. This one also said she wanted a doll, and then told Santa about a boy named Billy who pulled her hair in school. She wanted to make it very clear that Billy had not been nice, and should therefore not get what he wants for Christmas. She was just the right kind of annoying to make me glad I wasn't often around children. I was sympathetic to Billy's urge to pull her hair, certainly.

"Oh I don't know," Santa said. "Get involved! Do something nice for someone, just for the holidays. Give a gift to a person deserving of a gift. You have no children, I gather."

"I have no family at all."

"Then find someone else. Just one person, but one nobody has on their list. One person in need of that one gift they can't get for themselves."

Mostly, this sounded like a good way to get a girl into bed, but this seemed like a terrible place to say that aloud.

"How would I know where to find this one person?"

"I don't know, Stanley. But I know you aren't looking for them right now. So this is my charge to you, Santa to Santa's helper. Find that someone. You have only seven days until Christmas."

"I'll think about it."

"It will cheer you up!"

"Who said I needed cheering up?"

"You're an immortal man, of course you need cheering. Especially with no family to call your own."

"How about you?" I asked. "Where's your family of Santas?"

"This is our busy time, obviously."

"Yes, but any sons for you?"

I didn't know how old he was and hadn't asked, but I got the sense he was nearing the end of his career. It was the way he winced a little every time he leaned down to lift the next kid onto his knee. It seemed a reasonable assumption that he had a son learning to follow him, or who was already an adult Santa somewhere else.

He faltered for just a second. "It's a good story," he said. "I'll tell you some other time."

Then he called out for the next child.

Santa broke for lunch at just past noon. Lunch was a couple of sandwiches in the store's commissary, and soda pop.

"So what do you do?" Santa asked. "For money, I mean? I gather you don't hold down a job or you wouldn't have been able to spend the day here."

"Day's not over yet," I said, eyeing my sandwich with some suspicion. The food was provided for the staff by the store, and was just exactly edible enough to keep me from leaving the premises for a burger, yet inedible enough to guarantee I would never willingly take a job that involved deliberately consuming such a thing in the future.

"I'm between jobs," I said. "I was a bartender for a while, though. Good, steady gig, twenty years back."

"Are you rich?"

"I don't know. I might be. I'm not sure what the definition of rich is."

I wasn't really kidding. I had money sitting in a Swiss account. At the time of this conversation the account was nearly a hundred years old, yet the bank was still taking my calls. Or they did the last time I contacted them, which was in 1952. That year, I had them wire funds to the nearest financial institution in the name I was using at the time, and then I took out the funds as cash. It was evidently a lot of cash, because the bank took a while to get all of it to me and because I'd been living off of it ever since.

I had no idea what the overall balance in the Swiss account was. I only knew every sum I had asked for up to that point had been sent, no questions asked. One day I would have to get a full accounting, but I find it very difficult to do math and also to drink a lot. Plus, again, monetary figures don't mean all that much to me. If you've ever gone to a foreign country that uses a base cash value that isn't 1:1 with the currency of your own country, you've experienced something like this. With me, that's all currencies all the time.

"The definition of rich," Santa said, "is never having to worry about where your next meal is coming from or where you're going to sleep."

"That's a pretty low standard."

"And being happy."

"Now you've gone off in the opposite direction."

"One can measure wealth in friendships, no?"

"I believe it's possible to measure wealth in terms of influence and power, but I'm reasonably sure that isn't what you're talking about."

"It isn't, but it's close. A calculation that isn't based on money is what I'm aiming for. Right here is where my riches are, in the smiles I get from these children, and the joy I feel when I hear their stories."

"Well, you're an imp. You live for stories, don't you?"

"I do indeed. I do indeed."

"And the roof over your head?"

"The roof is in an uptown penthouse. My riches are also very monetarily real."

Things picked up in the afternoon. The line got longer and the time between each child a little shorter, possibly because Santa was thinking about the same beer I was. Mercifully, at six PM someone closed the back of the line. That should have compelled him to perhaps hurry things along, but of course it didn't. He didn't get to that final child until nearly seven.

"And what's your name, young man?" Santa asked of the aforementioned final child, lifting the kid onto his knees. He'd done this a hundred times already, and was perhaps not as frail from age as I'd taken him to be. If I had to do that all day I'd probably have dropped two or three children by now.

"Davey," the boy said. He looked about ten. He was dressed in old clothing that was a little too big for him. I had always taken ill-fitting clothing as a sign of poverty, but having occupied a seat next to Santa for a full day I could now say that a large portion of the mother-child population of New York City wore clothes that didn't really fit. If it was an indicator of poverty, the new affluence I'd been hearing about hadn't reached clothing yet. Or perhaps all the tailors in New York had died due to some kind of tailor-plague.

"And what can Santa do for you Davey? Do you have a special thing in mind for Christmas this year?"

The boy nodded, and looked around. "Yeah but not for me. For my ma... I want you to get something for her."

There was nobody else in line. All day long kids had been coming up with one or both parents beside them, or standing within line-of-sight.

"That's very nice of you, Davey. Is she not here?" Santa asked, conspiratorially.

"Nu-unh," Davey said. Implied was that she was shopping in another part of the store, only because the notion that he had come all the way downtown alone was far-fetched. It was not unusual to see unattended children playing in public—far less common today—but this was in the middle of the city, after dark, in a place without a swing set.

"Ah, it's a secret, then!" Santa said. He was also looking around for her. "Well you must tell Santa before she comes back."

Davey smiled. "Yeah... a secret."

"So what can we get your mother for Christmas, Davey?"

"A flower vase," the boy said.

"A *vase*? What an interesting idea!"

"Not *just* a vase, right? Not none of the stuff they have here. A special vase."

Santa looked at me. There was a sparkle in his eyes that I understood to mean he could tell he was approaching a good story.

"And what makes this *particular* vase special, Davey?"

Davey's eyes fell. He looked embarrassed. "I got sick."

"You were sick?"

"Uh-huh, last Christmas. And ma, she didn't have the money to pay for doctors so she hocked it. And it was her favorite thing. She used to tell me, Mr. Santa, about how when she came here from the old country, how she kept this vase wrapped up in all her clothes so it wouldn't get broke. It's been in the family a real long time. She called it a... airy something."

"Heirloom?"

"Yeah, that's it. We don't got a lot of those, not like other families. You know, not like the ones with money. We had just that one. And she had to sell it because of me, so... that's what I want for Christmas."

"Well! That's a very special wish, Davey! Santa is going to have to put a special elf on this one." He was looking at me, and I can't even tell you how much I wished, in this moment, that I was already down the street at the bar. "Can you describe the vase for Santa?"

"Yeah it's kinda like, blue with white flowers."

"That's good! But that describes a *lot* of vases, Davey. Can you tell me something *very* special about it?"

"Like what pawn shop she brought it to," I said. "That would be helpful."

"Oh, yeah, mister, I know that!"

If there was any justice in the world, the pawn shop he named next would have been the same one owned by my friend and passport counterfeiter. It wasn't. This one was in a different part of town.

"So," Santa said, "a blue vase with white flowers in the Bowery pawn shop. Now, I am sure a clever child such as yourself knows the address where you and your mother live?"

"Sure, but... don't you already know where I live, Santa?"

"We-ell, of course *I* do, but you know how difficult special elf helpers can be!"

Dinner was steak at a restaurant down the street. Santa talked me into a proper meal, which was probably a good idea as I have attempted to subsist on beer and pretzels a number of times and it always ends badly, and after a day spent in a department store I was just about ready to have that kind of evening. He only suggested this as a way to keep me sober long enough to convince me to help out this kid, but it was still a good idea.

Santa, in case you ever wondered, likes his steak rare.

"I know just where the shop is," he was saying between bites.

"I do too, but that doesn't mean I'm going there."

He laughed. "Of course you are! Why wouldn't you? Aren't you curious?"

"Not really. You go. Tell me about it when it's over. Better yet, write me a letter, I don't even know why I'm still in this town."

"We'll go together. And you haven't left because you have no place else to go."

"That's… actually, that's true. But only because I never have any place to go. It doesn't mean I *won't* go. I'll find someplace I like better, which is everywhere. Europe, maybe. New York is already proving more annoying than it's worth."

Santa laughed again, although I really wasn't kidding. "It's going to snow for Christmas this year, I can feel it! Have you ever seen this city in the snow?"

"I'm sure it's lovely," I said. He was surprisingly enthusiastic about seasonal events for someone his age. I've seen more snow than any man alive. I've seen glaciers. Snow isn't much of a thing, and he was more qualified to recognize this than most people.

"It *is*! How can you not be excited by snow?"

"I know it's easier to track a mammoth when there's snow, that's about all."

He grumbled. I may have been wearing him down. "At least stay in the city until after the holidays, Stanley."

"And help you find this kid's mom's family heirloom, I know. It's been a year, what makes you think the vase is still there?"

"Of *course* it is."

I drunk deeply from the beer I'd ordered to go with the steak. It was the cheap, domestically bottled species of beer, marginally worse than the stuff on tap at the bar down the street. America makes lousy beer, but at a time when we weren't on great terms with Germany it wasn't a shock that there was nothing better to be had. This was another good reason to consider returning to Europe. Either that or switch to aged scotch, which is harder to screw up.

I needed *something*, because Santa's relentless positivity was just brutal.

"I know I'm going to regret asking this," I said, "but why are you so sure the vase is still there?"

"It makes for a better story."

"Ah, of course."

"In my experience, the better stories always end up coming true."

From the perspective of an imp this was undoubtedly the case, but only because imps are notorious for ignoring inconvenient facts and inventing better ones in the service of a good story.

"You also realize you aren't actually Santa, right?"

He looked wounded. "Of course I am!"

"All right, you sort of are, in the sense that nobody else has as good a claim on it, outside of your family. That's not what I mean. You can't slide down a chimney, no matter what the stories say. Not that there's going to be a chimney involved, because that kid gave us an address in an apartment building. With no supernatural assistance, how are you going to get the vase under the tree?"

"I can give it to little Davey," Santa said with a shrug. "Or rather, you can. This is *your* redemption, not mine. I'm perfectly happy this time of year, you're the grumpy Methuselah in need of Christmas spirit."

"Methuselah only lived to about seventy-five," I said. "And I seriously doubt this will have any impact on my mood. It may worsen it."

We started looking the next day.

Pawnshops, it should be noted, were much more common in the fifties than they are today, so it wasn't a surprise that although we were notified as to which shop the vase had been pawned, we still went to the wrong one.

"It's not here," I said quietly. We were in an uncomfortably small storefront surrounded by the detritus of modern consumerism, which is just the sort of place to make one feel worse about Christmas at a time when one is supposed to feel better about it. That Santa was standing in the middle of it as well made the whole tableau not a little bit ironic. If I'd thought about it at the time, I'd have taken his picture. I didn't own a camera, but the place had four to choose from.

"Then we must be in the wrong place," he said, with unwarranted conviction. "We'll try the next block."

"We're going to check every pawner in the city, aren't we?"

"That would only improve the story!"

I sighed. "Don't you have to be somewhere?"

He didn't, though. Theoretically, this should have been the only busy time of the year for him, and yet he clearly considered helping me achieve some manner of temporary positivity more important than talking to kids all day. Sour as I was, I felt a certain obligation to tag along. Plus, it was a little too early to start drinking.

The second shop was considerably seedier. You had to already know it was a pawnshop beforehand, because there was no signage identifying it as such, only a window display of sun-damaged clothing and trinkets that would have looked more impressive were it not for the layer of dust.

It wasn't the sort of place I would have expected to find a valuable family heirloom. Maybe off-market heroin, or a kidney. But there it was.

"I wonder, sir, if I could have a look at that blue flower vase up there," Santa asked.

The proprietor was an enormous man of northern Italian descent. He appeared disinterested in courting our business.

"This?" he said. He didn't touch it; he pointed. "Very valuable. You want?"

"I was hoping to examine it first. My comrade and I, we are looking for a particular vase, and that appears to be the exact one. Subject to examination, of course."

I put my hand on Santa's shoulder. "You're going to impoverish both of us if you go at it like that," I whispered.

"As I say, very valuable. Very rare." The shop man's broken English was not so broken he couldn't smell a markup.

"Money isn't a concern, Stanley," Santa said, thankfully not loudly enough for the guy behind the counter to hear.

"Just... let me handle this." To the large Italian I said, *"That vase is shit. My friend is nearly blind and cannot see this for himself."*

He was somewhat surprised insofar as I had said this in his native tongue. But not *too* surprised.

"It is a work of art! The most valuable thing here. I can barely stand to even part with it. You have eyes, make an offer."

"It's a ceramic pile of dung, but my friend thinks otherwise. If you don't let him examine it for himself we will take our money elsewhere."

"Fine." He pulled the vase off the shelf and put it on the counter. *"It is one-of-a-kind, try not to breathe on it."*

Santa, not fluent in Italian, immediately touched it, picking it up and rolling it around in his hands. "This is what Davey described," he said to me, his back to the proprietor.

"Yeah, I think you're right."

"How much does he want for it?"

"I'll let you know."

I took the vase and put it back on the counter.

"A wretched piece of junk," I said. *"I'd sooner cut off my hand and shove flowers in the stump than use this miserable excuse for pottery, but my friend is deranged enough to think otherwise. It's not worth the spit from my mouth, but I'll offer two pennies for it because I am feeling generous."*

~

An hour later I'd acquired the vase for what I considered an acceptable price, and made another friend in the pawnshop business. He threatened to murder me with his bare hands three times, and invited me for dinner twice.

"I told you, price wasn't a real concern," Santa insisted as we left. "I don't know why you had to go through with all of that."

"It's difficult to explain."

"But such a hassle!"

It was more fun than I'd had in weeks, actually. I was tempted to go find another shop so I could haggle with someone else over a random object for a few more hours. But that wasn't going to happen. Instead, we were headed across town to a skid row apartment near Chatham Square. While the pawnshop was only a few blocks from the Broadway of Gimbel's, the economic distance was appreciable. The economic disparity between the pawnshop neighborhood and the apartment of Mrs. Davey's-Mom was even more extreme.

That said, I rather liked the bowery. I enjoyed the bars there, certainly, and I didn't have as big a problem with vagrants that the more well-to-do New Yorkers did. A lot of times I was one of those vagrants. (Not this time, though. I was currently living in moderate extravagance, having found a hotel off Bleecker that offered private bathrooms. If that sounds to you like a standard amenity for a long-term hotel, you're mistaken.)

With the vase wrapped up in a rag and stuffed into a satchel, we pushed our way into what appeared to be the correct row house, then counted flights until we'd reached what should have been the proper door. Davey never gave us a last name or an apartment number, so all we had was "third floor, fifth door to the right of the stairs" to go on. This might have been because it never occurred to Santa to ask for it—or he didn't want to, given he should have already known it, being Santa—but it also didn't look like the apartments *had* numbers.

"Why don't we just leave it here?" I asked, once we reached the door. The hallway smelled like boiled cabbage and feet, the lighting was mainly of the bare electrical bulb variety, and it was narrow enough to make it difficult for us to walk down the hall beside one another. I was feeling a touch claustrophobic, and I don't feel that way often.

Santa shook his head. "No, that's no good at all, Stanley. Then it wouldn't be much of a gift. There's no magic in it."

"There's no magic, period, and it's time little Davey figured that out," I said.

Santa just shook his head, and knocked on the door.

A large, squat woman in an apron answered. I was guessing Polish descent.

"Yeh," she said. "What do you want?"

Santa pulled off the hunter's cap he'd been wearing, as a gesture to her womanhood. I had no hat to doff. "Yes, ma'am! I'm sorry to bother you, and I am sure this is going to sound like an odd question, but if there is a young man here who goes by the name of Davey, I have something I'd like to give him. If it will not be too much trouble."

She squinted. "Davey? Not nobody here by that name."

"Ehhh, then a small boy. Yea high, eight or ten years of age, no more."

She still looked puzzled.

"Miss, is your son home?" I asked.

"My son?"

"Yes, ma'am," Santa said. "We have something for him."

"No, he's not. My son died. Near a year ago. What is it you brought?"

Santa was temporarily dumbfounded, but the woman was eyeing the bag with the vase so I took it from his hands as he sputtered to think of something to say.

"There's been some confusion," I said. "We're so very sorry for your loss."

"Thank you, sir. As I say, though, it's been a year. The sorrys were plenty last Christmas. What kind of confusion do you say?"

"We're only here to give you this, and then we'll leave you be." I elbowed Santa. "Right?"

"Yes! Little Davey… or *someone* wanted you to have this."

I pulled the vase from the bag and handed it over. The woman's eyes widened when she saw it.

"Oh, Lord." She let out a little cry, and took it from me as one might take a baby. "My mother's, oh I never thought I'd see it again."

"Merry Christmas, madam," Santa said.

He was tearing up at this little reunion, and if I'm being completely honest I was feeling pretty good too. I got to experience a tiny bit of the joy my friend had been trying to fill me with, and I admit I sort of liked it.

For about five seconds.

"Are you the ones that took it, then?" the woman asked.

∽

I learned a number of things very quickly.

First, the vase had not been hocked by this woman, or by anyone else in the household. It had been stolen, one year earlier, on the occasion of her son's wake. Evidently a large procession of locals had passed through the apartment to pay respects, and one of them decided to take a precious example of Polish ceramics on their way out.

Second, the woman's husband and brother-in-law were both longshoremen, neither currently at their jobs, both sitting in the kitchen up until she began shouting for them. Both were also very large and not at all interested in hearing our side of any story we wished to tell.

Third, Santa can run a lot faster than his stature might suggest.

We were running and hiding for about an hour, through a neighborhood that was entirely capable of not being friendly, given we weren't dressed like people who belonged there and were being called thieves loudly by large men.

We didn't stop looking over our shoulders until we were back at the Irish pub again.

Then things really got out of hand.

"It was a ghost!" Santa said. "That poor boy's spirit visited us to get his mother's vase back! It's a Christmas miracle!"

We were the only ones in the pub, as it was just past noon. O'Shea was there, stocking the bar and filling up our pints, but thankfully nobody else was, because Santa sounded insane.

"It wasn't a ghost," I said, for probably the third or fourth time.

"There's *no other explanation!*"

"Yes there is, we just haven't found it yet."

"Then there's no *better* one!"

"Whether it's better or not, there's an explanation that doesn't involve ghosts. Look, it makes for a fantastic story. It does. But if there is anybody on Earth who can attest to the fact that there is no such thing as ghosts, it's me. I've seen more people die than you've seen alive, and I'm telling you, they don't exist. They certainly don't manifest in department stores to ask strangers for favors."

"A *miracle*, I tell you. A little boy's sad spirit couldn't be freed from this world until his mother was made whole again. Admittedly, it works *much* better if she'd actually pawned it to buy little Davey his medicine, but even so…"

"…Even so, you'll be telling it that way from now on, I'm sure. You should also leave out the part where we were nearly beaten to death. And the part where her son's name wasn't even Davey."

"Stanley, you disappoint me. You've been given a gift and yet you are just as grouchy as ever."

"I have a talent for preferring reality to whimsy, Santa. It may mean I'm more prone to seeing the worst in everything, but my way has a better survival rate."

"Fine. Then tell me a better story."

"I'm working on it."

I didn't have anything better. But this is the thing about supposedly supernatural events, and why it's always a good idea to wait until a more complete explanation comes along: magic is never the best option.

I have the luxury of being alive for long enough to see the things we used to call magic explained in ways that don't require magic. Magnets, for instance, would have been considered magic up until recently. The same thing could be said about gunpowder, or a solar eclipse, or slow-acting poisons, or Greek fire. The supernatural is always going to be a placeholder explanation until a better one comes along.

∼

We stayed at the bar the entire day. Santa got jollier and jollier as time went by, perhaps not coincidentally at the same rate his beer stein got refilled. I heard him tell the story of little Davey and the magic flower vase at least fifteen times, with each version a tiny bit different from the one before. It was like that game where people take turns telling a story, until by last person there's no resemblance to the original tale. Except in this case only one person was telling it.

Imps, as I've said, are primarily known as gifted storytellers. I've known this for a few thousand years, but this was probably the first time I'd seen one of their stories evolve right in front of me. I won't go through all the iterations of Davey's story for you, but let's just say by the end of the night Davey had turned into a little girl, I was an angel, and the vase had become a locket. Also, this event somehow occurred at night in a snowstorm on Christmas Eve, which was still a week away.

None of this did a thing for my mood, which as Santa repeatedly noted had not improved.

I'm unaccustomed to being around someone for long enough to have my mental state the subject of conversation. I'm also not tremendously self-reflective, so I wouldn't have thought my apparent depression was notable until there was someone else attempting to cure me of it. The thing is, I've been known to be depressed for entire centuries, and I usually plan ahead. Depression was why most of my money—however much I had—was a phone call away instead of sitting in a steamer trunk somewhere, because when you're expecting to be on a hundred-year lousy-mood drinking bender it's always a good idea to lock up your valuables first. It was also why while I had decided on this occasion to live in a hotel, I picked one close to an area where, if I passed out someplace public, I wouldn't draw any particular attention.

That I live a lot of my life in a dark mood is my point, and I don't really notice until someone else points it out, and then it becomes barely tolerable until I either stop spending time around that person or forget about it. Only very rarely am I cheered up and out of this mood. And when that happens a woman is usually involved.

"Stanley, I don't know what to do for you," Santa said, much later on in the evening. He'd bought one or two rounds for the now quite ample collection of patrons, it was past ten in the evening, and we were both substantially drunker. "This was a good day! Yet a cloud remains over your head."

"Yes, well I don't believe in ghosts."

"Never mind that! Did you see the look on the mother when she laid eyes on that vase? How can that not warm your heart?"

"It did at first, but that feeling was quickly driven out by the immediate threat on my life. I don't often associate impending death with a sense of joy and oneness with humanity. Although *surviving* impending death can sometimes feel that way for a few minutes."

"Aaah!" He clapped me on the shoulder. "I'm not giving up on you yet. The secret to happiness in this life is bringing joy to others. That's true whether you're Santa, a small boy, or Lazarus himself."

"Like how you're bringing me so much joy right now?"

"I'm doing a better job of it than you are."

And so it went for the rest of the evening. Santa would go off and tell another newcomer this fantastic story of his, and periodically return to the corner I was sitting in to try and convince me I was actually happy, and then he would go back to making everyone else happy for a while. He was incredibly good at this as far as most of the bar was concerned. I just couldn't bring myself to see things the same way.

It's probably true that once one has lived through as much history as I have, cynicism is the default outlook. I appreciated that Santa was always expecting the happy ending and the good outcome and all of that, because as old as he was, he'd still come of age in a modern world where violence is largely an exception rather than an expectation. In his understanding of things, the sad part of any story always has a happy counterpart, or if not happy at least bittersweet. That was why he preferred to focus on the reuniting of the heirloom with the family, while I couldn't ignore the part where their son died at Christmas.

I've been told before, by a number of people, that my attitude toward death and tragedy is casual and indifferent, almost callously so. I never thought that was true. I think what comes off as indifference is only a lack of surprise. I expect tragedy, in the same way Santa expects his good story with a happy ending. When I'm right—and I often am—I'm the least surprised person in the room.

~

When in a gloomy mood it usually helps to be around other people who also happen to be gloomy, which is one of the appeals of dive bars like this particular pub, but since Santa was livening up the place I had little in the way of like moods to latch onto, so I mostly stayed in the corner and watched the room.

Watching humanity at a remove is a normal state of being for me as well, and probably began as a survival technique. It was what I was doing when I noticed something peculiar about O'Shea.

It was a Saturday night, so the taps were busy all evening. A few ran dry on O'Shea, and when that happened he did this weird thing where he stomped his foot hard, twice. A few minutes later he'd lean down beneath the bar as if talking to it, and maybe he was, because a minute or two after *that*, the tap wasn't dry any more.

He had a few people working for him—two barmaids and a

guy who dealt with dirty dishes—but nobody else went behind the bar that I could see. He also never addressed anybody regarding the dry taps. I was assuming the kegs were in the basement since he didn't roll anything out under the bar, and the stomping was an obvious attempt to communicate to someone beneath our feet, but a foot-stomp didn't really convey all of the necessary information, such as which keg needed work. So that had to have been what he was doing when he leaned over and spoke to someone small enough to fit in the cabinet.

I leaned over the bar and took a peek at the underside of it, but the only interesting thing was that there was nothing interesting to see: stored boxes and glassware and the closed cabinet door, but that was all.

So when O'Shea was on the other side of the bar, I stomped on the floor myself.

A few seconds later the cabinet door opened, from the inside. This O'Shea *did* notice. He leaned over and whispered something I couldn't hear over the racket in the barroom, and then slid the door closed again.

I didn't get a look at who was on the other side of that door, but I had a good idea who it *might* be.

~

"Tell me again why we're standing out here?"

Santa was confused. We'd gone from opening the bar to closing it, and now instead of wandering off to our respective beds we were standing in an alley.

This was, for wont of a better term, the bar's piss alley. There was a bathroom to be found inside O'Shea's, but it was a terrifying place with only one toilet that few had seen. It was difficult to tell, on most nights, if it was occupied or if the owner had just never unlocked the door. Either way, it made more sense to continue past the bathroom door to the rear exit and take a leak in the alley instead. This worked fine for everyone, by which I mean basically no women went to the pub on anything like a regular basis.

It was not where one lingered, and certainly not at the end of a day of drinking when one's body is very much interested in shutting down.

"I told you," I said, "we're ghost-hunting. Now keep your voice down or this won't work."

We were in the shadows. Other than the bulb above the bar's exit the only light came from the streetlamps, and those had a diminished impact in the narrow alley, so there were plenty of shadows to choose from. We were halfway down the wall, could see the back door clearly, and were pretty sure we couldn't also be seen from that door. It was actually only the second-best hiding place, with the best being behind a Dumpster. But the trash really smelled.

"Are you practicing divination?" he asked. "I'm growing concerned that madness might be an aspect of your extreme age, Stanley."

"No, this isn't madness. Trust me. It *is* a guess, but a decent one." Not that he was wrong to suggest this; I do go mad now and then.

"How exactly will we know when your guess is officially incorrect? I'd like to get some rest or I'll fall asleep on my throne tomorrow."

"You can sleep after Christmas. The bar turns off the light when everyone's out, that's how we'll know I'm wrong."

"How do you know *that?*"

"I fell asleep back here one night," I said. This wasn't really true, but it sounded good.

"But how..."

"Shh!"

The back door, which was mostly left open during business hours, had been closed since the bar shut down. But now someone inside had opened it, and a few seconds later that someone was revealed as little Davey.

Santa gasped.

The kid looked more or less the same as he'd appeared in the store. Different clothing, but clearly the same child. And definitely corporeal, unless we also believe ghosts cast shadows.

The kid looked down along both ends of the alley—failing to spot us—then reached inside and turned the light off. As our eyes adjusted we could hear the door being closed and latched. The next time I was able to see him it was in the faint light coming from the street lamp at the far corner of the alley. He was walking away from us.

Santa was ready to leap forward and probably embrace Davey. I was more inclined toward strangulation, myself. But neither of us much moved because it turned out another man was in the alley, on the other side of the Dumpster, who was also there to intercept the boy.

The ensuing conversation between them didn't look friendly. We couldn't hear what was being discussed, but when the guy grabbed Davey by the shoulder in a way that looked painful, it was clear this was no social chat.

Santa toddled down the alley, not in any way sober at the time or formidable on any occasion, but also not about to let someone beat up a child in front of him.

"Here now, what are you doing with that boy?"

Startled, the man turned, but didn't let go of the kid. "This is none of your business, go on."

I expected to recognize him from the bar, only because at this time of the night the only people lingering in the area were patrons. But I had never seen him before. He was large and sloop-shouldered, but in the light there wasn't much more to see. I couldn't tell how he was dressed or anything useful like that.

"I'll do just that the moment you unhand the child," Santa said.

"Walk away, mister."

I stepped into the light. "How about if you walk away instead?" I said.

The man held onto Davey for another beat or two, possibly considering whether it was worth his trouble to deal with two full-sized people in addition to the half-sized one already in his grip. Then he let go, his palms in the air.

"All right, fellas, he's all yours." To Davey, he said, "Me and you, we aren't finished."

He walked out of the alley in a direction that didn't require also walking past us.

As soon as he was gone, Davey turned to look at his rescuers for the first time, and the thanks that was sure to follow died on his lips.

"Aw, geez, *you guys?* This night just gets better and better."

~

The all-night diner may be the greatest invention of the Twentieth century. I realize the list of inventions to choose from is very long indeed, and I may be overstating my point somewhat, but it's a reasonable conclusion to draw if one happens to be awake at one in the morning and in need of food and a place that's warm and dry. This is especially true for someone who only occasionally has a place to call home.

The ready availability of unspoiled food is really something taken for granted by most people nowadays, at least in the West. I don't mean that as a commentary on First World vs. Third World economics at all, only that it's incredibly difficult to grasp how much of one's day has to be devoted to obtaining food when the option of purchasing it in a store is taken away. I was a farmer on several occasions, and spent most of my waking hours either tending to the food I was growing for myself or eating that food. I had no time to *do* anything else.

If you want to know why the great works of art and philosophy and science and history and religious thought were performed by the wealthy classes of the world, it was because they were the only ones with the requisite leisure time.

We were in one such diner as Davey attempted to defend himself.

"Aw c'mon, guys, it was just a joke," he said, between bites of food. Santa thought it would be best to ply the young man with the bribe of a full stomach, which was a better idea than mine, which was to pick him up by the scruff of the neck and drag him someplace where the lighting was worse. Admittedly, my approach didn't differ much from the one of the fellow in the alley, but moral equivocation wasn't something I had the patience for at this point in the evening.

"If you would just explain yourself, that would be most satisfying," Santa said.

"I can explain it," I said. "He heard us talking in the bar and decided it would be fun to play a little prank."

The kid nodded. "Yeah, pretty much. I can hear most everything under that floor, you know. And the walls are thin too."

Santa continued to look befuddled. "But you knew so much about the boy and the vase and—"

"Because he stole the vase himself," I said. "Would have worked better if you'd used the dead boy's name."

"I know! Trouble was, never knew that kid's name. Never met him. When he was alive I mean. I saw the stiff when I nicked the jar."

"You *stole* from the dead?" Santa said.

"Naw, I stole from his family. Plus I felt bad about it, okay? But then I heard you guys. You think you're Santa Claus, and this guy thinks he's on his thousandth birthday, and both'a you were looking for someone to make happy so I figured, I know someone who could use some'a that. Right?"

I had no reason to think there was anything remotely altruistic about his intentions, but my friend was swallowing it whole.

"Why didn't you just tell us the truth?" I asked.

"How many reasons you want, champ? You'd be askin' about my parents in a hot minute, and next thing I'm getting walked down to Our Lady of the Wooden Rulers so you can feel better about yourselves. Everybody who sees a kid on the street looks for the easiest story they can find to get out of worryin' about him, and I gave you one."

"And so instead of the truth you told the story that would best convince us to return the ill-gotten family heirloom," Santa said.

"Yeah. That sounds right, sure. You guys seemed wacky enough to fall for it, so yeah."

"I'd stick with the ghost story if I were you, Santa" I said. "When you retell this one."

"Oh no, you're wrong, my friend. This is a *much* better story. A little thief, haunted by the memory of his crime, concocts a brilliant solution!" He shoved a forkful of food into his mouth. "Nearly perfect. All it's missing is the right ending."

"Geez," the kid said, looking at me. "He always like this?"

"More or less."

"Head injury or something?"

"It's in his nature." To Santa I asked, "What kind of ending did you have in mind?"

"Orphan stories can only have one kind, Stanley. The boy must be reunited with his family or adopted into a loving household."

"No thanks, buddy," Davey said.

"But you *are* an orphan."

"No, I'm a freakin' Martian. The sisters said they found me on the steps of the place, that's all I know. If you're lookin' for me to shed a tear about how nobody loved me and I'm all alone and all that, you better just keep lookin'. I got past it a long time ago."

This was a rather worldly statement from a boy his age, but living on your own does have a maturing effect on a person.

"Surely there's more we can do!" Santa said. "We can't just let you walk off on your own, you're a child!"

"I'm doin' all right, mister. This food's great though. Real nice of you. But look, I got a steady job. That basement under O'Shea's place, I'm the only one short enough to stand upright down there, so that's some real security, until, you know, until I get bigger. And I got places I can sleep in the winter. I got friends."

"Does that include the guy shaking you down earlier?" I asked.

"Oh, him?" His eyes darted to the window, and the street beyond, as if he was actively searching for the person in question. "You boys don't want to get involved in that."

"If he means you harm, we certainly do!" Santa said.

"Nah, nah, I got that under control." He didn't say it like someone who was at all confident that this was the truth.

"Look kid, you may as well tell Santa here everything or he'll have to come up with his own happy ending."

"I'm certain the nuns at your orphanage are worried terribly about you, Davey," Santa said.

"Right, fine. But it's not a story for little kids, right? It's a gambling thing."

"You owe him money?" I asked.

"Kinda. The guy he works for thinks I owe *him* money. We don't agree about that. What do you fellas know about horse racing?"

Santa and I looked at one another. "I think the question, young man, is what could *you* possibly know about it?" Santa asked.

"More than you'd think from lookin' at me," Davey said. It was a sentence that defined him more accurately than anything I'd heard up to that point. He had just the right combination of knowledge and intelligence to be dangerous, and his age made it easy to forget that fact.

"So here's the deal," he continued. "Down at the track the

jockeys all know each other, right? They ride for the horse owners and only make coin when they win, so they got lotsa incentive to win, but they're also real friendly with each other most'a the time. And they look out for each other, right? So now and again, like if one of those boys are about to get canned or they're hard up for a purse, they'll get together and throw a race. Not all the time, just here and there, mostly on weekdays when the action ain't that much in the first place."

"They'll decide who is going to win ahead of time?" Santa asked, for clarification.

"Exactly. Or place or show. Anything with a purse, just for a pal. So it helps to be in the room with the jockeys when they all decide to throw one. That's where I come in."

"You're secretly a jockey?" I asked.

"Naw, I hate horses. I could be though, maybe. No, I'm in the room only they don't know it."

"Hiding."

"Yeah. Thing about being this size, there's lotsa places I can fit. So my friend in the alley, he works for a guy who likes to place big bets on those horse races, but he likes to make those bets when it ain't really gambling, right? He likes it when he already knows how it's gonna play out, I'm saying. So for a little of his action I been spying on the jocks and tipping him off whenever there was a sure thing. And it was workin' beautiful for a long time. That was until a few weeks back, when one of my sure things broke his leg on the back stretch. *Now* the guy is sayin' I owe him the money he lost on the horse."

"Why that's ridiculous!" Santa said.

"Sure it is. But he won't leave me alone about it until I cough up money it's pretty obvious I don't have. I even offered to earn it back with more sure things, but he doesn't want to hear it. Which is a shame, because I've got a good one in a few days and he's gone deaf. That's what we were really arguing about. Me and the guy in the alley, I mean. He came to tell me it was a no-go. It's a pickle, right? I got this one-in-a-million set-up, just *perfect*, and I don't have the money to take advantage. And if I did, they don't let kids bet on the horses anyways. If I did, though, I'd have the money for Vito and then some."

"His name is Vito?" I asked.

"Yeah. Heard of him?"

It was a pretty common name in certain parts of the city, so it was hard to say. However, were I to make a list of people not to enter into a business agreement with, *people named Vito* would be near the top.

"Does he have a last name?"

"Probably. I don't know it though. Everyone just calls him Vito. Why, you thinkin' of paying him a visit? I wouldn't. Me, he threatens. You, he'd prob'ly just kill. Or have one of his guys do it. He's that kind'a person."

"What's this sure thing?" Santa asked.

"Why? It doesn't matter."

"Indulge me. I've never heard of a sure thing before in gambling."

"That's because it doesn't exist," I said.

"Hey, now that's unfair. Sure, I'm in a bind because of a horse with a broken leg, but how often does that happen? I can name every single one of my other sure picks for you if you want, you go back and look 'em up in the papers. You'll see."

He turned back to Santa. "So there's a jockey by the name of Beautiful Pete. Used to be a big deal for a while on the circuit, but he had this problem. Women liked him too much, see, and that got him into jams, and some'a them jams were big enough that Pete needed help getting out of 'em. But Pete won regular, and that made all the difference because even if he was stuck under contract with the same guy that whole time, and the guy had to keep greasin' wheels to get him out of trouble, he made more money than he cost. Pete also never made it as big as he could'a, because nobody wanted to take on such a wild card, even if he was one hell of a jock."

"There's a point in this where you explain what it has to do with your sure thing, isn't there?" I asked. I was already signaling the diner's one employee that I was in need of more coffee. In another hour I was going to be sober enough to start drinking again.

"Beautiful Pete *is* the sure thing, mister. See, all that was a long time ago, now he's a lot older and he's not winning so many races, but his boss won't let him off the hook, right? Pete wants to retire, but because of all the trouble he got into over the years he's got a bunch of back-pay owed to him that he can't get out of the guy. Like, the boss, he's taking revenge on Pete for being such a pain the ass. So I heard, at least."

"You've heard a lot."

"The jockeys like me. Most times I don't even gotta hide any more, they just forget I'm in the room. Anyway, so Pete's on his last tour one way or another. The last race he's gonna be in is this Thursday at the Aqueduct. Then the whole team heads South for the Mexico circuit and he ain't planning on being a part of that. But first, he needs to win *one* race. That was the deal he made with the boss, right? He wins the race, straight-up, he gets his back-pay, everybody's happy. But—and this is the best part—to stick it to him one last time, his boss is making him ride the worst nag in the stable. I mean, this horse hasn't won a race one time. The jocks nicknamed her 'glue factory', that's how bad she is. But since it's Pete's last trip around the track, everyone's gonna lie down for him regardless. He could run that race on foot and cross the tape first, you understand? But riding glue factory, that's even better."

"I'm not sure I *do* understand," Santa said.

"The nag's never won," I said. "So the odds will be long."

"*Exactly.* So this is my dilemma. I got a horse that's gonna pay back on eighty to one, and no money to put on it, and a debt to clear that I don't even really owe to the one guy I used to trust to make these kinds'a bets for me."

"That is quite a dilemma," I said. "What's the actual name of this sure thing of yours? I assume the horse doesn't race under the name *glue factory*."

Davey laughed. "Yeah, right, like I'm givin' that up. Listen fellas, I gotta take off. I got until Thursday to find someone to make that bet, and time's wastin'. Thanks for the food though." He got up. "Also, sorry about the thing with the vase."

"Do you have a place to stay?" Santa asked. "Because if you want…"

"No, no, this is what I was saying. Everyone meets a kid like me, they wanna save me, but I don't need saving, even from Santa Claus and whoever his friend thinks he is. Don't worry about me, I'm fine."

"But still…" Santa was looking at me, expecting some sort of volunteerism on my part, but I wasn't sure how much of what the kid had said was worth believing. Even the part about living alone on the streets. I was pretty positive none of it was fully true, but I was much more cynical than my friend and, really, more cynical than most other representatives of the human race, so it was difficult to tell if I was reacting appropriately.

I did know, on some basic tribal level, that having discovered a ten-year old living on the street—assuming, again, this was true—I held some sort of responsibility for his wellbeing, just by virtue of being an adult. But I'd known a whole lot of street urchins in my life and he seemed considerably better adjusted than most of them. My impression was, he would be no better with my assistance than without it, and likely had a long and admirable life of crime to look forward to whether or not I interfered.

Santa was coming from a different place, though. He wanted a way to keep Davey around that didn't involve coercion, and could only think of one.

"If someone were to place that bet for you," Santa said, "How much would it have to be? Just hypothetically?"

"Hypothetically?" Davey said, smiling. He returned to the table. "Hypothetically, how much money are you looking to make?"

―

"It's a scam," I said for perhaps the fiftieth or sixtieth time. It was my new mantra, replacing *there's no such thing as ghosts*, and I expected to be just as right about this one.

Four days had passed since Santa had struck the deal with little Davey, which was as follows: on Thursday afternoon, they would meet at the track and enter together, at which time Davey would give Santa the name of the horse and he would place the bet for both of them.

Only after the horse won would Davey give Santa his share, which was said to be in the neighborhood of a thousand dollars. I considered it highly unlikely he actually had that much money, but since he wouldn't get his cut of the winnings without first proving he had the cash, the angle escaped me. For his part, Santa was putting five thousand dollars on the horse. He could spare it, and was likely planning to split the winnings equally regardless of how much of the bet was his and how much was Davey's. Santa was that kind of guy.

The name of the horse remained unknown up until a half hour before the race, Davey claimed, in order to protect his investment. This was a little silly, because if Santa was in any way dishonest he could just keep all the winnings, regardless of when the name was revealed. But that was how they'd worked it out.

I was cut entirely out of the proceedings, which was fine. Gambling is one of the oldest and worst inventions in history, and I grew tired of it a few thousand years ago. That was why, the day before the race, I was still telling Santa he was being scammed.

"Stanley, you have no faith in human beings, even young human beings. I think we have firmly established that by now."

We were at a bar again, but not O'Shea's. Since discovering the subject of our conversations could well be listening in, we'd taken to frequenting the next-nearest Irish pub down the street.

"I've earned this distrust honestly, over many centuries."

"So you have. But you've lost the capacity to be pleasantly surprised by humanity as well. You've lost hope."

"I thought you were going to find it for me."

"I was, but you may be a lost cause. Besides, we've been over this. Davey has nothing possible to gain."

This was the biggest problem with the scam argument. Santa was taking his own money and walking it up to the window himself and placing the bet. If he lost, he lost, but the kid wasn't going to gain anything from that loss, not unless he also owned the track.

"Maybe it's another prank," I said. "Like with the vase. He wasn't getting anything out of that either."

"Of course he was! He cleared his own conscience."

"Because he didn't have the money to buy it back himself? I'm not sure he has a conscience."

Santa growled into his beer. "Any other man, Stanley, I'd tell them an appropriate story and they would feel better about themselves."

"You're the one who thought I needed cheering. I never asked for that."

"Of course you do! It's Christmas! Everyone should be happy at Christmas!"

Christmas is a pretty new holiday, really, at least as far as how it's celebrated now. It was on the calendar for a long time, but only recently became the kind of big deal that involved otherwise-total strangers demanding cheer. That said, there were always events like it: harvest festivals, royal birthdays, religious anniversaries, and so on. One or two made me legitimately happy when I participated. For instance, anything involving sex as an act of celebration I am entirely in favor of. But that's not the sort of thing one expects out of Christmas. This is a holiday for family and friends and happy memories of childhood, and I don't have any of those things. I can't celebrate it the way other people do, in other words.

Interestingly, neither could Santa, which made his general sense of optimism and default state of happiness perplexing enough to continue to be around. As much as he was trying to figure out how to get some Christmas spirit into me, I was figuring out where he even found the energy to have it himself. Granted, questioning why Santa Claus was happy in December was a strange place to find myself, but this Santa was real, he was actually an imp, and he was stuck with the same bunch of humans as I was for the other eleven months. On Christmas Day this Santa wasn't going to be resting from delivering toys to all the little girls and boys. He was going to be sitting at home alone, watching a parade on television and drinking, just like I was. And then it wouldn't matter how many kids he made smile.

I appreciate that this is a terribly depressing way to look at life, but it's where I was at the time.

I didn't say any of those things to Santa, both because I wasn't drunk enough and because I was pretty sure I already had said some version of it to him in the past week. He was not compelled by my thesis.

"By your reasoning, if I want to be happy I have to make someone else happy, right?" I asked.

"Yes, after a fashion." Unspoken was the hint of a very long discussion on the topic of selfishness and the act of bringing joy to other people for the sake of their joy rather than for oneself. It was a profoundly annoying conversation we'd already had few days earlier and I never wanted to have again.

"Then I'll make *you* happy for Christmas," I said.

"I'm already going to be happy. Make Davey happy instead."

"He seems pretty happy. But you aren't going to be happy if I'm not happy, so I'll be happy and that will make you happy and we'll both be happy. How's that?"

He growled again. "It's hard to believe you've lived this long."

~

The first time I watched horse racing I couldn't understand why everyone was going in the same direction and the riders weren't armed. This initial confusion has colored my understanding of the sport ever since, to the extent that I still don't really get the appeal. Gambling, certainly, is a major factor, and as I've said I'm not overly fond of gambling, or at least not the kind that relies on almost pure chance. (I do sometimes like poker.) Beyond that, watching large animals run around an oval a couple of times just doesn't strike me as overly productive unless one is trying to discern the best quality breeding stock, which I'm told is not the point.

Still, there I was, at the track a couple of days before Christmas, waiting for Santa to make a bet on a horse to make a little boy's dreams come true. It was one of the stranger holiday scenarios I've ever been involved in—excluding certain Sumerian fertility events I won't go into here—but it wasn't all that terrible, because there was beer at the track.

Santa met up with Davey at the entrance. I wasn't privy to their conversation, as I'd been told already that my negativity might somehow influence the proceedings in some way, which I'm told more often than you might imagine. The name of the horse was exchanged, though, and a few minutes later Santa was placing a bet on *Bacchus Doubtful* to win. It was an incredibly appropriate horse name under the circumstances.

Santa was in an annoyingly good mood.

"It's been *years* since I was at the track, Stanley! Can't you feel the excitement?"

"I'm trying to."

"If this doesn't get your pulse racing, nothing will!"

In my experience a racing pulse meant a predator was nearby, so I couldn't really understand why that was considered a valid form of entertainment, but in fairness I was in a crappy mood.

I was more interested in scanning the crowd than checking out the racing, anyway. Searching crowds is an old habit of mine, and probably fundamentally a survival mechanism I'd internalized and stopped thinking about. I think I do it because it's always helpful to know if there are any non-humans hanging around worth keeping tabs on. I find it's hard to relax in a large group until I've done this two or three times.

It wasn't a large crowd though, so it took only a few seconds. I didn't see any demons or goblins or anyone else easily identifiable from a distance, but I did come across an unexpected and familiar human.

"Hey, when's our race?" I asked.

"Not for another forty minutes. Should we get more beer?"

"You go ahead. I just saw an old friend, I want to say hello."

He treated me to a raised eyebrow, because generally speaking all my old friends are dead, and he knew that. "Well don't be too long or you'll miss it," he said.

The person I saw wasn't actually a friend, and likely had no idea who I was. I only had a dim notion of his identity, but I was pretty sure we shared a common associate. It was the guy who'd threatened Davey in the alley. It had been dark in that alley, but I was sure I was right about this. There was a certain sloped-shoulder quality about the way he stood that was hard to mistake.

I'd seen him pacing in the back of another section. My intent was to talk to him and maybe assess how much of the kid's story was fact-based, but before I got to where I'd spotted him he had slipped under the grandstand. Suddenly I was tailing a stranger with likely mob ties. This is almost never a good idea.

I located him again a couple of minutes later, beneath the stands and in the middle of a conversation with Davey. I didn't know whether or not to be surprised by this.

I couldn't get close enough to hear their exchange, but it concluded with him paying the kid some cash. Then the guy walked off, shaking his head, while the boy stayed where he was and counted the money.

"How much did you get?" I asked.

Davey looked up, surprised, but maybe not all that surprised. "Two hundred. Not bad, right?"

"Not bad. What were you betting on?"

"Funny story. You'll love it."

"I bet."

"That's my buddy Larry. He's a degenerate, gambles on everything. Met him a couple of years ago, I swear he hasn't won a bet with me once, but he keeps tryin'. I don't even have the money to put down, he don't care."

"Not a mob enforcer, then."

"Nah. Sells mops for his father-in-law. Totally harmless. Apologized three times for grabbin' me in the alley even when I asked him to as soon as I clocked you fellas on the other end. He's not real smart about a lot of things, though, like what makes the numbers on horses go up and down. I bet him two hundred bucks the odds on the worst horse at the Aqueduct would drop by at least twenty today, and since he don't know those odds are tied to the action he has no clue how he just lost."

"You're right, that's not very smart."

"He'll get you a deal on a mop though."

"Right, I'll remember that. When did you make the bet?"

"Couple days ago, after I lined up your buddy to put down the five large."

"And I take it there's nobody here named Beautiful Pete."

"Nope. Like I said though, good story, huh?"

"Very good, yes."

"I'm told I got a gift. Anyway, he looks like he's got plenty, your friend. Plus all that North Pole money I'm sure just keeps on rollin' in, right? And hey, it made him happy to help me out so, no-harm."

I didn't think I had it in me to explain to him that disappointing Santa at Christmas is definitely not without harm.

"I pick up an extra two hundred from my dumb friend," he continued, "and your buddy up there sleeps at night because he did what he could to help out the poor little orphan. Merry Christmas to everyone."

"Sure. Until you don't show up after the race."

He laughed. "Why would I show up? Like you said, there's no Beautiful Pete here, and the jockeys ain't gaming the results. If they were, I'd be as much in the dark as anybody, cuz I never met any of them. The only thing I told the truth about was the horse. He's been bringin' up the rear at this track forever. Maybe your Santa buddy will be a little confused about why his sure thing lost, but I'm not gonna be there with an explanation. I'm out. If you're worried, you can make up something yourself so he feels better."

He walked past me. I reconsidered my original impulse to strangle him, and wondered if anyone would notice if I did.

"Hey," I said. "You know if you'd asked he probably would have just given you the five grand."

He laughed. "Yeah, but where's the fun in that?"

~

I didn't dream up an explanation for Santa. I couldn't think of one, and the idea that I even had to was suddenly very unpleasant. This would have been a good time to discover the same gift for gab that Davey had, or a talent for turning a bad ending into a good one like Santa did, but that wasn't going to happen.

Santa and I had been going back and forth for more than a week on the subject of Christmas, and happiness, and hope, but it was really more an argument over whether people were worth doing nice things for or not. Whether people were good, or bad. I was sure, based on a much larger pool of experience, that people will always disappoint eventually, while his much more positive outlook was one that had humanity acting nicely towards one another in stories with happy endings, where everyone ended up okay and getting what they wanted out of life.

There was no way to take his perspective seriously, but a part of me really wished the world actually worked that way. It would make it much easier to live in.

I could have gone back up into the stands and told him what I'd learned about the cherubic little scam artist he thought he was helping out. I could have proven I was right and he was wrong, in other words. It was the only story I knew how to tell. And when *Bacchus Doubtful* lost for the umpteenth time, the point would have been driven home.

But I couldn't do it. I've done enough awful things in my life already and I didn't want to add "ruining Christmas for Santa Claus" to that list.

Instead, I chickened out and left him at the track.

This was probably not the best way to handle the situation, but it was the way I went with. Honestly, dropping and running to cope with a problem is one of my more popular solutions. It works particularly well when people in town decide I'm a witch, but also for those uncomfortable times when I've cuckolded someone more powerful than I realized, or when I've inadvertently insulted a king, or when someone asks me to marry them, and so on. I outlive everybody, so acting like a total bastard and running away until everyone I've angered or disappointed has died is a legitimately viable option.

This was what I was telling myself as I packed up my room. The hotel, as I said, was not memorable or particularly clean, but it did have a dedicated private bathroom I much appreciated, and the rats were generally very polite. It had served nicely as a place to call home for the past couple of months, but now that winter was coming I was getting the distinct notion I'd overstayed my time in New York City. Plus it was difficult to find a bar in the neighborhood where I was sure not to run into Santa.

I didn't know where I was going. According to the papers, snow was on its way, and I wanted no part of it, so I was thinking someplace tropical. Beyond that, I had no plans.

I also forgot it was Christmas Eve. After paying for the room, I ended up in the lobby, in a beat-up old chair waiting for a taxicab to show up to take me out of town. Taxi service was turning out to be less than optimal, however. I really only needed a ride as far as, say, a bus station or something—I hadn't decided —but getting a cab to show up wasn't working out, either because of the holiday, the oncoming storm, or the fact that I was calling from a seedy hotel in a crummy part of town. For whatever reason, I ended up sitting in that chair for a couple of hours with my bags and an old steamer trunk, watching the lobby clerk/building owner finger through the race tables in the newspaper.

And of course that got me thinking about the kid again, and how frustrating it was to have been scammed by a ten-year old. An unreasonably clever and worldly ten-year old, but a child nonetheless. It was sort of humiliating. And I was giving up on a friendship because of this kid. I felt horrible about that.

If it had been anybody other than Santa I probably would have been getting drunk with him right at that moment, as we complained about the nature of *kids these days*. (This has been one of the most popular subjects in bars since there have been bars.) But he was entirely too cheerful to commiserate with over something like this. Also, if there was one thing I could think of that was worse than complaining with Santa, it was listening to the only reliably upbeat person I knew having his idea of the world dashed on the floor.

"Beautiful Pete," I muttered, shaking my head. "Can't believe I bought any of that."

"What was that?" the owner asked.

"Sorry, nothing. Just thinking about a story I heard recently."

"Good story?"

"Yeah, it was, actually. It was a really good story. Very believable."

The owner was a shrunken man with bad eyesight. It was difficult to tell, most times, if he was sitting behind the desk or standing, because there wasn't any apparent height difference. He had a sort of disapproving grandfather face that probably served him very well when it came to certain customers. He looked at me over his paper and through his thick lenses.

"Used to be a jockey by that name, I recall."

"No kidding."

"Yup. Beautiful Pete. Hell of a jock. Four-foot-eleven and hung like his horse, I'm told. Course, he's long since retired. Haven't heard that name in years."

This rattled loose an idea I had apparently been working on for a while.

"*How many* years, would you say?"

∽

It was snowing hard by the time I reached O'Shea's pub. Not quite sundown and the place was already packed with guys who'd gotten off work early enough for a few drinks before having to face their families. Santa wasn't one of those people, but I had an idea of where I could find him if I had to.

After about an hour, I called O'Shea over.

"I need a favor," I said, and slid ten dollars across the bar.

"How big of a favor, exactly, pal?" he asked, after taking my money. He was about ten times friendlier when I was there with Santa, but that was true of the entire city.

"I need to talk to a certain someone. You mind if I stand behind the bar for a minute? I'd like to stomp on your floor."

He smiled. "The kid, huh? What'd he do this time?"

"It's a really long story. Do you mind?"

"Nah, go ahead. He's a pain in my ass anyway. Just take him out back before you kick him around."

∽

Reaching into cabinets and pulling out screaming children is apparently a common practice in bars, as nobody there particularly minded. Nor did anyone get an urge to step in and help the kid, who insisted rather loudly and ardently that I was about to murder him. Given the comments I heard from the rabble, a few of these guys knew Davey already, and at least three or four owed him money.

I didn't release the kid until we made it into the alley, and then it was to drop him into a snow bank.

"What're you *doing?*" he shouted. "I ain't got no beef with you!"

"No beef. But you owe me."

"I don't owe you nothing! What the hell are you talking about?"

"Listen, kid. I don't like children and I don't trust them. I do my best to avoid them when I can. But my friend Santa is different. He loves kids, can't get enough of them, and I mean that in the best possible way. So let's get one thing clear: if you were going to piss off one of us, you pissed off the wrong one because I already expected this from you. He didn't."

"What, you want me to apologize? *You?* You didn't even tell the old man anything, don't think I don't know. He's been asking all over town for me. Some friend you are."

"Yeah, fine, I'm a lousy friend, but I'm going to make it up to him, and so are you. But first, I want what you owe me."

"And what's that?"

"An answer to one question. You can stop checking behind me for some help because I'm pretty sure you don't have any friends in that bar."

He actually looked a little nervous, because he was coming to the same realization. I could have hurt him if I wanted to, and he knew it. "That's all? A question?"

"No, that's not all, but it's a start."

"Fine, sure, go ahead. Ask your stupid question."

"The question is, how *old* are you?"

He looked speechless for a change. I'd spent just enough time with him to recognize when he was working out something in his head, but it didn't look like he was doing any of that. For once, he looked like he really was a kid. Which I was pretty sure he wasn't.

"What?"

"Just answer."

"Look at me, how old do you think I am?"

"That isn't an answer. Turns out Beautiful Pete was the nickname of a real jockey, but he retired six years ago. How many years ago did you run away from that orphanage?"

"C'mon, mister. It's embarrassing. I don't want to say."

"Embarrassing is getting outsmarted by a ten-year old. But you're not a ten-year old."

"I'm *twenty-one*, okay? But look at me! I'm like, a midget or a dwarf or something."

"You're not a dwarf. A twenty-one year old dwarf would still need to shave. You ran up to puberty and stopped. No, you're something else."

"Oh, so you know what I am, do ya? You think I ain't heard

that before? The nuns thought they knew what I was too, why do you think I ran off? They kept throwin' holy water on me, and worse. It was messed up. I mean, I guess I can't blame 'em, right? All the kids my age kept getting taller and looking older and I just stopped for no reason, and there wasn't no amount of praying to fix that. And hey, I'd *love* to ask my parents what the deal is with this, but I can't do that either, can I? What are *you* gonna do that's any different? I already know you're a nutso."

"I might be. But I know exactly what to do here. We're going to go see Santa."

"You're *crazy*. What for? So we can tell him I'm a freak too?"

"That's not why little boys go to see Santa, kid. They go to ask for something special for Christmas. You still have time."

～

My friend was sitting on his throne at the end of his final Christmas shift for the year. The day was winding down and the line of children waiting to sit on his lap was gone, because everyone understood you had to give Santa at least a little time to get in his sleigh and start delivering toys or nobody was going to have a proper holiday.

The store itself was still very busy, because last minute shopping has been a thing as long as there have been stores that stayed open through Christmas Eve. But the corner on the top floor where Santa sat was dim and empty, and he looked a little sad sitting up there alone.

He perked up when he saw me, though. It was nice how happy it made him, but I think I would have preferred it if he was angry.

"Stanley! My goodness, where have you been?" He climbed off his chair gave me a hug. "I couldn't imagine what had happened!"

"Sorry," I said. "I have a lot to explain."

"You do! I'm sure it's quite a story!"

"It is, Santa." I turned him around and pointed him back to his chair. "It's a heck of a story, but I only know part of it. You're going to have to fill me in on the rest."

"I don't understand."

"I know. But you promised *me* a good story, so before I tell you mine I want you to tell me yours."

"What do you mean?"

"You never told me about your son."

I saw that same dark cloud pass over his face as before, memorable for the fact that one doesn't see that sort of expression on someone like him.

"But that's not a *happy* story. Christmas should only be about happy stories. March! March is a good time for a sad story. I'll tell you then."

"I'd like to hear it now, if that's okay. Let me decide if it's happy or not."

He sighed. "All right. What do you know about us?"

"About imps? Not as much as I could, and I can never tell when one of you is prevaricating, so it's hard to ask."

"Excellent choice of words, yes! Prevarication is in our nature, isn't it? Well, here is something true about my kind. As it happens, we are not exceptionally good at reproduction, which is a blessing, really, given our lifespans. I daresay we'd overrun the planet otherwise. But no, there is a very *specific* time in our lives in which we—the men, I mean—are able to… I'm sorry, I am *very* uncomfortable talking about this particular thing in this particular chair."

"It's all right, I get the basics. So it was your time, and you met a girl."

"I met a girl! Precisely! She was a beautiful young thing, and she loved me, and I loved her, and it was all nearly perfect, except for one thing. She was human and I am not. In most regards, that's not an issue. We could still…"

"You could still get a visit from the stork."

"Yes! But then, tragedy struck!"

He was poised to launch into the rest of the story, but stopped himself and remained quiet for much longer than was customary for him. He looked like a man wrestling with a dilemma.

"What kind of tragedy," I asked, to jump-start the tale.

He shook his head. "I'm sorry, Stanley, there are at least a dozen different versions of this story I could tell you. All are quite stirring, and three or four are *guaranteed* to make you weep openly. But I am old and tired, and I don't have the energy any more. I've been looking for the boy since the day at the track, did you know? I can't find him anywhere. He's disappeared, much as I thought *you* had. Now here you are asking me the *strangest* question. But... here's the truth, my friend, without any gift-wrapping. Her name was Laura, and she was lovely, and she found out what I was and couldn't cope with it, and so she left me. My chance to have a son and pass on my legacy left with her."

"I'm sorry."

"Thank you for your sympathy."

"Was it the age thing?"

"You could say that, yes. She had issues both with my current age at the time and with the notion that she would grow old at an advanced rate by comparison. Of all the people in the world I imagine you are the only one with a full understanding of that sort of problem."

"You're probably right. That happened here, didn't it? In New York?"

"I never said so, but yes. Why do you ask?"

"Because I think this Laura of yours actually did have a son. She dropped him off in an orphanage not far from here, in 1934."

"How could you *possibly* know that?"

While we were talking, Davey—who had been hiding behind a display and listening—had wandered down the velvet rope path to the front of the line.

I gave the kid some credit. With only my vague promise of answers and a guarantee he wasn't in any kind of trouble, he could have easily taken this opportunity to sneak off. Instead, he stuck around and listened. He passed himself off as a street tough, but he wanted answers more badly than he let on.

Standing at the "Wait Here" sign at the end of the line, he looked a lot more like a scared ten year old than a stunted young adult. And the truth is, he was somewhere in-between. Davey was perfectly normal; he just wasn't a human.

"Is it true?" Davey asked. "Your story, about Laura. Is it true?"

Santa looked at Davey, then at me, then back at Davey.

"It can't be!" he said, to me.

"I'm pretty sure it can."

To Davey, he said, "Why, I... yes! Yes it's true. All of it! The year is right, and... oh my goodness..."

"So my dad is Santa Claus?" Davey looked at me when he said this.

"It sounds a little crazy when you put it that way."

"Yeah, a little," he said with a shrug.

Santa was crying, meanwhile.

"Are you okay?" I asked.

"Yes, yes... I'm just happy... Davey, come here. Give Santa a hug."

"Yeah? I dunno."

"Oh for goodness sake, kid," I said.

"All right, all right. Geez."

He walked over and let Santa pick him up and give him a proper hug, and while he would never admit it, the boy looked like he needed that hug just as much as his father did.

"Merry Christmas, Santa," I said. "Looks like we found your happy ending."

*S*anta had a penthouse. This was something he'd told me already, but I didn't quite believe it because as much as it made perfect sense somehow for him to live at a location that offered a downward view of the city, it was difficult to take anything he said at face value.

But a penthouse it was, and the view was really lovely, especially once snow covered the top of the city.

He also had expensive enough liquor to make one wonder why he spent so much time in dive bars. But imps need places with people to tell stories to, so it wasn't all that difficult to fathom.

I was on his balcony, looking down on the city and drinking some of his expensive brandy, and feeling unreasonably good. I couldn't stop smiling for some reason, and wondered if this was how everyone else experienced Christmas.

"I told you snow, makes all the difference," Santa said, on joining me. He had the entire bottle in his hand and wasn't bothering with a glass.

"It does indeed, especially from this angle. How's the kid?"

To say Davey was uncertain about how to cope with all of the information he'd had thrown at him was an understatement. He had always known he was different, but not *that* different. Not *something other than a human being* different.

"He's confused. I half expect he won't be here when I wake up in the morning, but I'm not concerned. If he sneaks off, I'll just have to go out and find him."

"The apartment is a good selling point."

"I know, did you see his eyes light up when he saw it? That was precious."

"He's probably just pricing your art."

He laughed. "Puberty comes late for imps. Having an extended childhood makes story collecting much easier, I've found. He'll blossom soon, and grow into an adult quite quickly.

This time next year, I expect. I can't believe I didn't recognize him for what he was. Shameful."

"Well, he needed a bath."

"Cheers, to the best Christmas present Santa's ever gotten."

I touched my glass to his bottle and we drank.

"And then there's you, my friend," he said, after a long swig.

"What about me? You haven't decided I'm an imp too, have you? I'm not."

"No, no. I mean you still owe *me* a story! I will be eternally grateful for what you've done this evening, but don't think you're getting out of an explanation."

"Why I left the track, you mean?"

"I didn't know what to think! You had me *very* worried! Why did you do it?"

"I chickened out."

"I don't understand."

"It doesn't seem like a big deal now, but someone had to break the news that the kid was stringing you along the whole time, but I didn't want to be that person. Not right before your favorite day of the year."

He remained utterly puzzled. "Stringing me along in what way?"

"You know: the story about Beautiful Pete and the jockeys laying down. He made that all up to get you to place the bet and change the odds. He had a side bet that the odds would move. You must have realized some of this by now."

"Did he *really*? How tremendous. You know, I should have seen that much sooner too, that gift for storytelling. Assuming he's here in the morning I must ask him how he came up with such a remarkable tale. Do you think he made it up on the spot?"

I was confused. "So you still believed the story? But what did you think when the horse lost? By then you had to have known something was wrong, didn't you?"

"Ah you see, this is where we're getting tripped up. I couldn't understand where you'd run off to or why little Davey failed to appear afterwards, but if the horse had *lost*, it would have made much more sense. I had no reason to think such things, though, because *Bacchus Doubtful* won that race."

"You're kidding."

"On my honor as Santa Claus, I swear it's true. You can look it up if you don't believe me."

I didn't really know what else to say then, so I just started laughing.

"Another toast," he said, also laughing. "Hold up your glass, Stanley."

"All right. What are we toasting?"

"We are toasting the first Christmas miracle an immortal man has ever seen! May there be many more happy Christmases and many more miracles in your future."

I held up my glass. "I can certainly drink to that!"

THE IMMORTAL CHRONICLES

Regency IMMORTAL

Gene Doucette

REGENCY IMMORTAL

I don't know how I ended up in Vienna.
This happens more often than it probably should. It's fair to say I simply don't recall what circumstances resulted in my being there because I'm talking about 1814, and that was a long time ago. It's equally reasonable to say that history is full of little gray periods in which nothing happened, nobody did anything, and everybody died quietly and unnoticed. Furthermore, it's entirely fair to assume that a man who has been alive for sixty-odd thousand years—hi, that's me—is going to have a gap or two in his memory.

However, in my case I probably can't remember because I had been drinking.

This is not to say there's no merit to the "gray periods" argument, because that's also sort of true. If you want to know what it's like living as long as I have, try and imagine the most bored you have ever been in your entire life. Now imagine what it's like to be *that* bored for entire centuries.

When you've reached that level of bored, there are going to be gaps in the record, where you can't remember what happened because absolutely nothing *did* happen and your brain didn't bother to record the minutia. This is why it's not all that hard to convince someone they could have been abducted by aliens and had their memories erased, because that explanation is much more interesting than the possibility their life was so incredibly boring their own brain wasn't even paying attention.

Not that I'm saying there are aliens. There probably aren't. I've never met one, though, and I've met an awful lot of weird things.

I'm digressing. The point I wanted to make is that history, as a whole, was powerfully boring. Sure, every few months something a little memorable can happen, and every couple of years there may be a genuinely exciting event. Once or twice a generation, just to break things up, there's an outbreak of abject terror, which is exciting only not in a really good way. Like volcanoes, or Huns. But mostly? Dull and boring. History is written about the exciting things, but life is mostly lived in the boring parts in-between.

Vienna in 1814 wasn't one of the dull moments, because that was when a number of important people showed up to figure out how to divide Europe before someone started another war. This happened all the time—war I mean—and would continue to happen after the congress was over, even when France ran out of Napoleons. Every civilized collection of city-states goes through the same cycle that only ends when everyone gets together to discuss why it is they keep having wars if nobody is enjoying themselves, and they all agree to work on their anger management and megalomania, and then things are quiet for a while until they aren't any more. Repeat.

But the congress was still a nice idea. And as I said, there were a lot of important people in Vienna for this congress, which has nothing to do with my being there. I know I've already said I don't know how I ended up in Vienna, but I can state for a fact that my importance had nothing to do with it, because I'm not an important person. Or, I should say, I'm not a publicly important person. This is mostly by design.

On average, important people don't enjoy long lives. Some of them don't even survive their tribe's first bad crop. Since I don't care to be blamed for things that are out of my control—blight, comets, plagues of locust, and so on—I strive to be unimportant. I would rather be the guy in the back of the room that nobody knows the name of than the one at the front of the room taking responsibility for big decisions and leading people into battle. Also, I'd rather not go into battle.

But despite being often unimportant, I do find myself in situations now and then that require me to do semi-important things. Vienna was one of those times. You can read all you want about the Congress and everything that was accomplished there. What you won't read about is the assassin who was in Vienna with the delegates. The reason you won't is that I was there to stop him.

Well, not just me.

~

Her name was Anna. I never got a last name, but she may not have had one to give. That was a pretty common thing for a long time. If you didn't have a title or some sort of highborn lineage you might have still had a family name, but nobody much cared what it was. And a lot of the time it wasn't even a name at all; it was whatever your dad did. Thus, a world full of Smiths.

I didn't bother to invent last names to go with the first names I'd also invented, unless I was traveling in the kind of crowd that expected one, and then it was tricky. I've invented entire royal bloodlines—and, on a couple of occasions, entire countries—just to get into decent parties, a trick that only works until someone does a little research.

Anna was beautiful and smart and just the right kind of dangerous to get me killed, which was often what I looked for in a woman, to be entirely honest. The interesting ones are somehow almost always the ones who come with life-threatening risk on the side. It keeps my life exciting, and might also explain why I have trust issues.

When I first saw her she didn't look like someone who had no last name. She was in a powder blue dress with bright white lacing, which in this particular part of town drew attention the way a newly blossomed flower would catch the eye in a bed of weeds. If the outfit had been more threadbare and dirtier, she might have been mistaken for a prostitute; otherwise, the obvious conclusion was that she was an out-of-place noblewoman.

I'm not saying that was what she was, I'm saying that was how she dressed. Noblewomen tended to wear clean dresses, and sport a lot of layers. About fifty years earlier, it was possible to tell how close a woman was to royalty by the number of layers one had to remove to see them naked. I never undressed a queen, but based on what was involved in unclothing a lady-in-waiting I'm guessing doing so would require a skilled lock-pick, a small axe and a tremendous amount of patience.

Anna dressed like someone from court—the English court—and wore enough finery to make it plausible for her to have breathed the same air as a king somewhere along the way. She had raven-black hair tied in a complicated set of knots that brought it down past her shoulders in a tight curl, and a dress that was off the shoulders –she had a wrap around them—and showed off an impressive bosom.

When I found her she was standing in an alley, looking deeply perplexed. That perplexity had nothing to do with the dirt or the alley, or even the rough part of town where the dirt and the alley were located. It also had nothing to do with the unwashed gentlemen milling about not far from her, looking as if they meant to either hire her for prostitutional duties or harm her in some more rapacious way for free.

I doubt I looked much better than those men in her eyes. (Her eyes were a deep coffee brown, by the way.) I had on nicer clothing than they did, but I'd been wearing them for a few days. This wasn't unusual—down at the peasantry level having more than a couple of outfits wasn't too common—but I was actually traveling with a decent sum of funds and could afford to not be seen in the same coat over and over, provided I remembered to get back to the flat I was renting before I passed out, rather than after. It had been a few days since that had happened.

She was out of breath, and her eyes were searching all of our faces and then the walls and the windows. It was a cloudy day but visibility wasn't too terrible because cities hadn't invented pollution yet, so there were no hidden mysteries. Whatever she was looking for, she couldn't find it.

More importantly for her immediate wellbeing, she'd largely ignored the men nearby, up until the closest one decided to offer a lewd suggestion, the general gist being that perhaps what she was missing was located in his pants. When she didn't reply, he worked a little harder to get her attention by putting his hand on her shoulder, which was just a huge mistake.

"Remove your hand, sir," she said. There was an iron in her voice that should really have been enough of a warning to leave her alone.

It wasn't enough, because the hand went from the shoulder down the front and on a misguided journey toward her cleavage. He wasn't going to be getting that far though, because a moment later she'd broken his wrist.

He shouted out in pain and fell over, which just drew more attention. It also didn't do anything to dissuade the men whose wrists hadn't been broken yet. That in itself showed an amazingly poor self-preservation instinct, because the effort she expended to break bone was not at all extensive, and it's not easy to do that. I can do it, but I've had a lot longer to practice.

"Now why did you do that to my friend?" said the next nearest gentleman, who was neither a gentleman nor a friend to the injured man so far as I could tell.

"That wasn't nice," agreed a third man. "You should try to be nicer."

I was nearby, emerging from a different alley only a few paces away. (I was in the alley for reasons involving my bladder. The streets were dirt and we had no toilets—I swear to you this was normal.) If there hadn't been any rape-minded men wandering by, I expect I would have concocted some excuse to engage the lovely noblewoman in the wrong end of town all on my own. The slowly assembling mob presented a much better excuse, however.

I had a sword with me, which was just a happy coincidence, as I didn't always travel around town with it on my hip. It was a good sword, the kind that convinces people not to give the owner an excuse to use it. So a few second after the third man spoke, my sword was resting on his shoulder. This caused him to freeze, which is what blades do to people whose necks they touch.

"*I* think you good fellows should return to your tavern," I said. "I'm sure they miss you there."

Anna, who had widened her stance as much as her dress and boots allowed, knees bent and in a defensive crouch, looked at me with something less than love in her eyes. "I can protect myself," she said. Her hand—which I had taken to be holding her dress out of the mud—was actually fingering the hilt of a knife sewn into one of the layers of her skirts.

"I'm sorry, would you like to kill them yourself?" I asked. "Gentlemen, do you care which of us kills you?"

"Seems to me, sir, this has been a misunderstanding," said the one with the blade on his neck. His able-limbed companion was already backpedaling while the one with the broken wrist was getting to his feet and thinking that going through life left-handed was preferable to not surviving the day.

"I'm certain you're right," I said. "Why don't you walk away from the lady and discuss it amongst yourselves."

I lowered the sword and waited to see if anybody was foolish enough to see how good I was with it. I happened to be very good with it, so it was always a little disappointing when nobody challenged me. Honestly, the first time I held this sword there was a better-than-even chance I'd get to use it on a bunch of pirates. Who knew that was going to end up being my best chance at really swinging the thing? I mean, none of these guys even *had* a sword. It was depressing. I miss the fifteen-hundreds.

Anyway, the area cleared out pretty quickly. There were still a couple of dangerous-looking malingerers at the edge of my vision, but none of them looked like they were prepared to take on a swordsman. Unfortunately.

"I told you I didn't need your help," Anna growled, showing me the blade.

"Yes, I heard you, and that's a really impressive little dagger, but my sword was a more peaceful resolution and it's hard to get blood out of a petticoat. Why don't you put it away?"

"*You* are still here," she pointed out. And indeed, she had an excellent point. My sword and I were far more dangerous to her than any of the men she'd been prepared to dispatch. I'm sorry if that sounds like I'm bragging.

"Of course. My apologies." I slid the sword back into its sheath. She didn't do the same with her knife. "Now before I leave you to your sharp little blade and whatever mob those ruffians are no doubt organizing at the pub up the street, I wonder if you want to tell me who you're looking for? Mind, I am in no way suggesting you *need* my help, but if you *want* it, I'm completely free of other engagements."

"What makes you think I'm looking for anybody?"

"If you were looking for a *thing* you have failing eyesight, as there are no things in this part of the city. There's only mud and squalor and men like the one you explained the fragility of wrists to. You're after a someone, and unless it's me—in which case I'm very flattered and it's a pleasure making your acquaintance—you've failed in locating them."

Briefly, and only briefly, something that looked like amusement colored her eyes. Then it was gone. "Why would you help me?" she asked.

"Because you're very pretty, and I'm very foolish. I'm also useful, and currently sober. You could do worse."

"In this part of town, I'm sure I could do *much* worse." She put the knife away, which was about the closest thing to a handshake I could expect to get under the circumstances.

"I'm looking for a… murderer," she said. "I chased him here, and then he was gone. I think… sir you will find this absurd."

"I might," I agreed. "Say it anyway."

She blushed, which added a dimension to her features that was unreasonably appealing. A small gang of threatening men didn't raise her heart rate in the slightest, but the idea of saying something I might think was crazy raised her color. This was an unusual woman.

"I swear to you," she said, quietly, as if it could be truer if uttered in hushed tones, "it was a vampire."

"A vampire."

"On my father's grave."

"I see."

Well, it wasn't a vampire. I knew this immediately, but not for the reasons she might have been expecting. No doubt she was anticipating some manner of condescending *vampires don't exist, silly girl* reply, and I didn't have one of those, because they certainly do exist, albeit not in as scary a form as people expect.

The problem was that she was telling me this in the daytime. I grant it wasn't a sunny day, but since vampires actually do burst into flames in sunlight—I've seen it happen and it's gross—most of them wouldn't risk being caught outdoors when the clouds parted. Also, she'd clearly been chasing it, and I don't care what kind of shape the woman is in, no human in full skirts is going to be able to pace a vampire. Vampires can outrun horses.

"And... this vampire... did someone harm?" I asked.

"It did. It killed a man, not half an hour ago. Right in front of me."

"Ah," I said again. "Then I'm afraid I don't believe you."

"As I said, sir. Now leave me to my imaginary creature hunt."

"But there are other creatures who could be mistaken for one. Perhaps you should explain how you arrived at the notion that it was a vampire?"

She stared at me for a long time, as this was not the direction she anticipated this conversation turning. "What other creatures?"

"The world is full of nightmares, milady. It would be far more efficient if you summarized what you know and let me list out the options than to provide a complete taxonomy."

"I see." It was maybe just then occurring to her that the only thing worse than finding someone who didn't believe her vampire story was finding someone who *did*. "At this time I am wondering if you are a madman, sir."

"And you the madwoman, for claiming to have seen a vampire."

"Indeed. And I question my own rightness of mind. But while I'm in close communication with my own intellect, yours is a worry."

"We can be lunatic in tandem, if you'd like. But it would be an excellent idea if we were to practice our lunacy in a different location. This alley will soon sprout ears and eyes. I can recommend a tavern not far from here if you'd like to accompany me at least that far."

As it happened, the tavern I had in mind took us along the same path my new friend had followed on her way to the alley of disrepute, and with a little convincing I got her to agree to retrace her steps first. She was reluctant. I assumed that was because the path was supposed to terminate at a dead body.

Vienna is reasonably grid-like in design, as are most cities that were built to *be* cities. A distressingly large number of roads became roads after livestock decided on a particular path, meaning most of the older ones were effectively designed by cattle. I hate learning my way around those kinds of cities, but at the same time I greatly prefer them to the rigidity of a grid. There's no charm in a grid.

An uncomplicated city plan does have uses, though. In this instance, getting to what Anna insisted was a crime scene involved little more than heading to the end of the alley, crossing a busy thoroughfare, and then going straight down another alley. From there we stepped into a corridor that led to a private garden.

It was a private garden with a notable dearth of bodies.

"He was here," she said, pointing to a lovely collection of flowers.

"The dead man?"

"Yes. His body was right here."

"And now it isn't."

"It *was*."

I squatted down next to the bed. The flowers were mostly local, and well tended-to. Whoever owned the garden knew how to take care of plants. They made the man-sized indentation of crushed stems and broken flower heads that much more obvious. It was still absent a corpse, however, and corpses don't often get up and walk away. And if they were in the habit of doing that, they still tended to leave behind blood, and this one hadn't.

It might have been feasible that her friend had turned into a vampire after being killed—and possibly picked up all of his own blood at the same time—but that seemed unlikely.

I'm not privy to the process that turns a person into a vampire, but I'm powerfully dubious as to the accuracy of the claim that vampires are some manner of living dead things. They're obviously living; otherwise, it wouldn't be possible to kill them. It's just that their life isn't one that can be measured in the same way as the lives of humans. People make these things so much more complicated than they have to be.

"And you chased this vampire down the alley and across the carriageway."

"Yes. When I crossed the main road, I lost sight of him for the briefest of seconds while ensuring I wasn't trampled by a horse. In that moment, he must have turned to fog. Or a bat."

"Indeed."

"You still don't believe it was a vampire."

I stood up from the edge of the flowerbed and brushed dirt from my knees. "Not based on that description, no. Vampires can't do either of those things."

She cocked her head and treated me to a faint but unmistakable smile. Bemusement was something she granted only sparingly, I could tell. But she was neither afraid of me nor actively disdainful, which I considered great progress.

"You know this how?"

"I have a few vampire friends."

She waited a beat, to see if I had a punch line to go along with this. "You're being serious."

"I am. They're very nice. Not always the best company, and they have no interest in drink, which is often *all* I'm interested in, but they're okay. Hang around with me for long enough and I'll introduce you to one, if you like."

"Do you think *you're* a vampire?"

I laughed. "No, of course not."

Anna couldn't have known this, but I get mistaken for one all the time, which is what happens when you're immortal, especially when there isn't anyone else like you. My uniqueness, as the only immortal man on Earth, is probably the most interesting thing about me. But aside from not getting older and never getting sick, I'm pretty much all human. Real vampires are always confused and disappointed by this. People are too, on the rare occasion I tell someone and they believe me.

She shook her head, but in a cute sort of way. "I'm trying to understand what it is about you that makes me think you might actually be speaking the truth."

"I'm not a particularly gifted liar. To compensate, I've become exceptional at telling the truth."

She sighed grandly.

"Where is this tavern again?"

It was actually a *Heuriger*, which only served local wines and no ale or beer. It was not the sort of place I would have preferred to be—I love wine, but Austrian beer is really excellent and I can get good wine in a lot more places than good beer—but it was where it made more sense to bring a woman. This particular woman could assuredly handle herself in a less savory establishment, but I saw no reason to burden our conversation with the constant threat of violence.

We found a small table in a quiet corner where it was possible for both of us to face the room. This is something I've learned to do on days when I've pulled out my sword. It's a good habit.

With a jug of wine between us we drank in silence for a time, waiting for the warmth from the alcohol to set in and for Anna to calm down a little. Her hands had a tiny shake to them, which was entirely normal. I've been in more combat situations than I can recall, and after nearly all of them I ended up in a corner somewhere, waiting for my hands to stop shaking. Sometimes I was also vomiting and discovering wounds I didn't know I'd gotten. It depended on the battle. Adrenaline, I believe, is the culprit, although of course I wouldn't have put it that way back then.

"I'm Christoph," I told her. This was one of the names I had been using at the time. The other was Eliahu, which I employed when it was to my advantage to be taken for a Jew. They were both new, and as I said I hadn't bothered to devise last names for them yet. I'd only recently stopped using the British name Reginald Bates, both because I didn't feel like being taken as an Englishman while in Europe, and because I'd had that name for a little too long.

I can only keep full names for about twenty years. Any longer than that and people figure out I'm not aging. The name I'm using now—Adam—might stick around for longer, because the only people I give that one to already know how old I am.

"My name is Anna," she said. "I should probably apologize for earlier. You were good to step in with those men, and I appreciate your help with the... other thing. You've been very patient."

"Well, as far as the men are concerned, I think I did them a much greater favor than I did you."

"Maybe so. But this clothing slows me down. If they had a mind to assault me with some coordination I could have been had."

"Those clothes would slow anyone," I said. I decided not to offer to help her out of the clothing. "Dress like this is meant to keep a woman still, and breathing shallow. It's a wonder you were able to run without succumbing to a lack of air."

She laughed. It was a tinkling sound, like sanctuary bells.

"You're dressed above your usual station, I gather," I said.

"And you are dressed below yours. That's Damascus steel, isn't it?"

"You have a good eye. There aren't many people who would recognize it."

The sword was by then a rare and valuable antique, since people had stopped making proper Damascus steel weapons a hundred years earlier.

She hesitated for a moment before deciding I was someone she could trust at least this much, then drew the dagger I'd seen her wielding earlier. She placed it on the table.

Damascus steel has curious whorls and swirls in it, a consequence of the smelting process that makes every blade unique. Her dagger was marked in this way.

"Persian," I said. "Based on the grip."

"Very good."

"Fake."

Her eyebrow expressed surprise for the rest of her face. "Very, *very* good. How do you know?"

"It's possible to recognize a blade that has been etched *after* forging, but it would be difficult to explain exactly how. It's a quality fake, though. And I'm sure nobody stabbed by it would much care."

"I've not received any complaints yet," she said. "And I've had many offers to buy from people who ought to know a counterfeit."

"*You* knew it was fake, though."

"I did. I made it."

I laughed. "Blacksmith's daughter?"

"Something like that."

I handed the blade back. As she slid the knife into whichever one of her layers it was housed, I leaned over my cup, and in a quieter voice, said, "Why don't you tell me about the vampire?"

She nodded. "All right, what do you want? A description?"

"That would be a start."

"He was pale. Large teeth, long fingers, bulging eyes. And his mouth…" She shivered. "Like a great animal."

Vampires have been around for a really long time, which I know mainly because I've been around for longer. I don't know all there is to know about them, but what I do know is that about 99% of the mythology—and there's a ton of it, dating back to before the Greeks even—is completely wrong. I never took the time to parse the *mistaken for something else* wrong from the *somebody just invented that* wrong, but there's a lot of both.

What Anna described was a version of how most people in this era thought vampires were supposed to look. Like Nosferatu, basically. I couldn't tell you where the depiction came from, and if asked a few hours earlier I would have said it was an entirely invented monster. But she saw *something*, and she didn't strike me as the type of woman who was prone to hysterics.

"What was it doing?"

"Ripping out the man's throat with his teeth."

This is also not tremendously vampire-ish behavior, but it's closer. A really hungry one will commit all sorts of brutality, but indiscriminately, and with little regard for subtlety. I knew of one who dismembered a small village after he'd been locked up in a tomb for several months.

If there had been a killing spree in the middle of Vienna, though, I imagine I would have noticed.

"The man he killed was your friend?" I asked.

"We had business together," she said. Her eyes darted around the room, as if what she'd just said aloud was something that should have attracted attention. "I scarcely knew his name."

It was my turn to arch an eyebrow. "Business off an alley in a private garden?"

"Not *that* kind of business, sir."

"Of what kind?"

"I can't share that with you."

"The more we know about the dead man, the better we'll understand why someone wanted to eat him."

She sat back and looked me over once again. "You aren't Viennese. What's your business here?"

"I have no business here."

"A free merchant of some kind, I expect. What do you peddle?"

"It looked like a nice city, that's all. I'm not here to pursue any particular interest."

Again, I don't recall why I was in Vienna. I do recall being well off financially while there, which is a state I find myself in periodically. It's cyclical.

"I have *been* a merchant, certainly," I said, "but just now I have only the funds I'm traveling with and the freedom to do as I wish."

"You're royal, then. But not English. French?"

"I'm what you would call a jumped-up peasant. If I become bored I may at some point in the future consider a new business or title, but I'm not driven by either pursuit."

"You can devise a better lie than this, sir."

"I probably could, if I were lying. Here, let me offer a solution to our current standoff. You've already told me you are dressing above your station in life. I expect you're doing this because it opens doors for you that wouldn't otherwise open."

"You could say this about most women."

"I could, but you're not looking for a husband or a benefactor. You want to be on the other side of those doors because that's where important people are having important conversations. You asked me what my trade is and I'm telling you the truth when I say I have none at present. But you do. I would wager your trade is in secrets."

She smiled. "As you can imagine, sir, if this were so, I wouldn't tell you."

"True, but let me build upon that assumption anyway. As a person who traffics in secret information, I can't imagine a better place for you than Vienna, where the value of secrets is at a premium. Now, I have seen you neither read nor write, but assuming you can do both of those things—and I do—I believe somewhere on your person is a letter divulging secret knowledge. This letter was supposed to be going to the man in the alley, up until he was killed by a creature you call a vampire. How am I doing?"

"I'm beginning to wonder if *your* trade is divination."

A letter found its way from her bosom and onto the table. She kept her hand on it.

"How do you know these things?" she asked.

"I pay attention. But here's the solution I promised: I don't care. I don't care what's written in that letter or who it concerns, how you got it or who it was meant to go to beyond the fact that all of these things may have gotten your contact murdered. I have no interest in politics."

"Only a fool doesn't concern himself with politics."

"I concern myself only insofar as it's a better way to solve problems than having a war. But in the larger picture nearly all politics is petty and inconsequential, and I've lived long enough to learn not to care overly much about it."

"You're not so old as that, sir."

"My age would surprise you. Now can we move ahead? If you had failed to meet up with this man, what were you supposed to do?"

"There was no alternative plan."

"I know something of espionage, milady. There's always an alternative plan."

"*I* had no other plan. My cohort may have had one, but I must assume whatever he had worked out didn't include his own murder. I was told to complete my business with him and only him, and I've already violated that control by discussing this with you."

"You haven't told me anything," I said.

"That hasn't stopped you from getting very far purely on

deduction. Do you truly have no stake in the outcome of the proceedings?"

"The proceedings?"

"The congress."

"Oh, that. I'm not here for that. I *think* I probably had some business in the city and decided to stay once it was concluded."

"That was unconvincing to a staggering degree."

"It's a nice city. And this was probably many months ago. I recall seeing snow."

"Oh my God, you're an idiot."

"No, just a drunk. So?"

She sighed some more and rolled her eyes, and I don't know what it is about exasperation in women, but I find it adorable. Then she removed her hand from the envelope on the table.

It was unsealed. I picked it up carefully, slid out the letter, and unfolded it.

"Interesting," I said.

"Can you read it?"

It was in Romansh, a Swiss language that came with multiple dialects. This was, I believe, the Sutsilvan dialect, but Vallader wasn't out of the question.

Regardless of the dialect, they're Romance languages, and I can read and speak pretty much all of them with only a little effort. Not because I'm especially gifted, I just have a lot of time to practice everything. Plus, languages have root tongues—Latin, in this case. Once you know your way around the root you can navigate most of the descendants, especially if you update yourself from time to time. I do, mostly because it's easier to get food and shelter and women if I'm fluent in the local language.

"I can," I said. "But I wasn't supposed to be able to, was I?"

"No. And I don't believe you. Tell me what it says."

I was about to do just that, but then a thought came to me. "*You* don't know what it says, do you?"

"It was handed over by a man I was told to never speak to again, to be delivered to a man I never met before."

"And who are you, Anna, to be entrusted with such a vague and yet specific undertaking?"

"I am… nobody important. I can get in and out of certain places because of my…"

"…your charms."

"Yes. That makes me valuable to certain people. But I've never had to deal with a letter such as this, and I've never had to worry about a vampire."

"It wasn't a vampire."

"So you've said."

"Was this letter unsealed when it was handed to you?"

"It was. I assume the language it was written in provided its own safeguards."

"Or the one who gave it didn't want to put his seal on it."

"He was not the sort of man to have a crest of his own."

"No… I imagine he wasn't." I was skimming the letter while talking, when I should have been giving it my full attention. The problem was, I didn't follow much of the text because it involved people I didn't know, doing things I didn't understand.

I have basically stayed out of politics since the invention of politics. Part of the problem is that political concerns are generally local and extremely time-specific, and I am very much about the long-term. Learning all there is to know about a regional political reality is somewhat like learning a new language, except the knowledge isn't useful for longer than a generation, which makes it just about useless to me.

I did take a special interest in the post-script on the letter, however.

"Are you certain you'd never seen the killer before?"

"Of course not. Unlike you, I don't collect vampire friends."

"I just thought I'd ask. It's possible he saved your life."

"By not killing me as well?"

"No, that isn't what I mean. It seems the last part of this message instructs the recipient to kill the messenger if this letter is delivered unsealed."

She went a little pale. "That's a precaution. In the event I read it before delivery."

"Obviously, if you could read the language you would have known to reseal it, so that doesn't make sense. This was so the man who was to murder you would feel no guilt in doing so. The fact that according to the sender the letter was supposed to have been sealed, would have absolved the recipient of guilt and put the responsibility for your death on your own shoulders. It might have been your body in that garden instead of his. Well, pretending for the moment that his body was lying in the garden still."

"It would have been his body, only by my hand," she said.

"Yes, you're probably right."

Her eyes darted around the room. "We should find a private place, Christoph, so you can read the rest of that letter to me and I can find out what information I was meant to die for."

"You're right. I might be the only one in this *Heuriger* who can read Romansh, but ironically, I might be the only one who doesn't understand what any of it means. What did you have in mind?"

"I have quarters nearby. They should be sufficiently private."

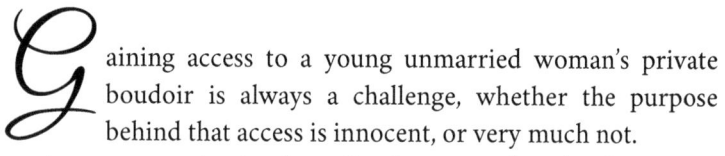

∽

Gaining access to a young unmarried woman's private boudoir is always a challenge, whether the purpose behind that access is innocent, or very much not.

Anna was staying in a boarding house run by a battle-axe of a woman called The Frau. This Frau had a moral compass that placed her somewhere above the Pope, and a tendency to eject tenants who disagreed with her minimum standards of chastity.

Or so I was told. I didn't get an opportunity to meet her, which was fortunate. Equally fortunate, for this particular devising, the women of the house had an entire system established to spirit visitors into the apartments undetected. It was a coordinated effort that required no fewer than four residents acting in concert to redirect The Frau's attentions, hold open the rear entrance, and act as lookout. Considering how efficient the entire process was, I had to think the building's tenants entertained a large retinue of men on a semi-regular basis. The Frau was probably losing a lot of money by not charging the male visitors.

The quarters were small, but very clean and plush, and much more girlish than its resident. I ended up in a chair in the sitting room on the other side of a portable screen behind which Anna was changing.

"I must apologize," she said before disappearing, " but I can only wear a corset for so long. I feel as if I'm being squeezed to death."

"As a gentleman, I feel honor-bound to offer my assistance in freeing you from this horrible experience."

"I'm sure you do," she said, with a gentle laugh that led me to think it wasn't completely out of the question. "I can hear you perfectly well from the other side of the screen, and I know how to undress myself. Read the whole letter. Let's see if we can figure this out together."

So I did. And when I was finished I read it through again. Then we started attacking it sentence-by-sentence to work out why it was important enough for someone to be killed over the contents.

The obscure dialect the drafter used was only one problem. There was also the matter of the abbreviations. As far as I could tell, the letter contained minutes from a meeting, which made it possibly the most boring piece of espionage imaginable. But this meeting involved people with names that—if written out—would have been easily recognizable to anyone looking at the page, regardless of their familiarity with the rest of the words. Their solution was to abbreviate the names. The only other way around it would have been to use a language that employed different alphabet, which is what I would have done.

"Who do you suppose RSVC is?" I asked.

Her initial response was a loud clatter. She must have had so many knives hidden in the dress she couldn't easily locate each of them, because this was the third time I'd heard one fall to the floor.

"Probably the Viscount Castlereagh. Robert Stewart."

"And he is?"

A sigh, the slap of a knife on a wood countertop, the slip of lace through an eyehole. Audio-only striptease.

"The foreign secretary of Britain," she said. She stepped out from behind the screen, wearing only a turquoise bustier and a white lace slip. She either forgot that this didn't constitute acceptable public clothing or didn't much care if I saw her in her underthings. "Please tell me you do know what Britain is?"

I couldn't really speak right away. Anna had untied her hair, which cascaded over her naked shoulders and framed her face in a way that was far more fetching than I would have expected. She had high cheekbones and striking eyes, and those two things in combination generally made for a very attractive woman when her hair was pulled back. This was true as well for Anna, but with the hair down her face was somehow more intoxicating.

And yes, I was mostly looking at her face, although there was a great deal of cleavage to gawk at as well. I could see one of her ankles, too. I have nothing bad to say about ankles.

"I do," I said, eventually. "I've even been there."

"Well thank God."

She disappeared behind the screen again, and I exhaled.

"Was Robert Stewart *at* this meeting?" she asked.

"I don't think he was, they only talked about him."

"Who are *they*, though? Where was this meeting?"

I'd read it through twice already, and that information wasn't in the letter. "If you have a pad and paper I can translate it out so I don't have to keep referring to the text for you."

"I think it would be a poor idea to keep any records we don't have to, especially one in plain tongue."

"Maybe a language only you and I know. Are you familiar with Sanskrit?"

"What is that? East Indian? No. Keep it oral."

"All right. Who do you suppose KWFM is?"

"Prince Metternich, I suspect. Was *he* there?"

I flipped through the document. "No."

She sighed. "Who *was* there?"

"Um... PGL. I think he was definitely there."

"PGL... who else?"

"PSH? Lots of P's. One T."

"T?"

"Yes, but there aren't any other letters to go with that one. Just T."

"That's unhelpful."

"I don't believe the framers of the document were interested in making this easy on someone in our position."

Anna emerged from the screen again. She had extricated herself entirely from women's clothing and had switched to a large white men's shirt and a pair of slacks that were likely meant for a boy. Her hair was in a ponytail.

Honestly, I could have spent the evening waiting for her to pop out from the screen every few minutes in different clothes.

"Who else?" she asked.

"Um... CPR. And CL."

"This is not at all helpful."

"I realize that, but I wasn't the one who wrote it."

She sat on the edge of her bed, which was a number of feet away from me. In slacks, she settled in as a man might, with her legs uncrossed and open. I wondered if she often had cause to impersonate a boy. With her hair up and tight and hidden in a hat and her bosoms tied, she could no doubt pass as one on a cloudy day. I elected not to say this, as this would not have been much of a compliment.

"What about the body of the document?" I asked. "Maybe it can give us an idea of who these others were."

The meeting these various initials had convened was inordinately concerned with Saxony, which was a detail I found more interesting than I let on. I happened to have met a Saxon duke a few years earlier, and more to the point had saved him from being stolen and ransomed. He knew me by another name, but he knew me nonetheless. Assuming he hadn't been kidnapped more successfully in the interim, he could maybe turn out to be helpful, if he was in Vienna at all.

"None of it sounds *important*," she said. "It sounds like the sort of thing bound to be discussed in the congress proper. I can appreciate certain members of the talks meeting on the side, perhaps to digest the various positions without those positions being made a part of the official record, but I see no reason to kill a man for the results of that meeting."

"Or to kill a woman," I said. "The author of this letter—assuming it was he that gave it to you—decided you were to perish after completing the task. Maybe to figure this out we should begin with him."

"Yes, only I don't know who *he* is or how to relocate him. And I'm assuming he thinks me dead."

"Maybe you should tell me how you got involved in this undertaking."

She sighed. "Would you like a drink?"

"I would always like a drink."

Anna slid open a drawer in her nightstand and extracted a bottle. After a little more digging she found a cup, which she handed over. It was a steel cup of the kind I would expect to discover aboard a ship.

"I have only one glass, I'm afraid I don't often entertain."

"That's all right."

She poured an amber liquid into the cup. "Brandy," she said. She took a swig from the neck of the bottle before I had a chance for a taste. It was subtle, but this was her way of telling me the liquid wasn't poisoned. It was a nice touch, and one I wouldn't have expected from a woman. It was also mostly unneeded, as I can't really be poisoned. I assume this is for the same reason I can't get sick, whatever *that* is.

I tried her brandy while she sat back down, ignoring for the moment the idea that if she really, really wanted to poison me, the smart play would have been to put the poison in the cup. Likewise, brandy would have been the liquor to use in such an endeavor, as most poisons are bitter and brandy's sweetness can offset that nicely.

It was fair to say I didn't think I could really trust her. I *wanted* to. We had managed to spend most of the day together by then, and I'm frankly bored of 90% of humanity after under an hour of active conversation. I just couldn't shake the feeling that one of the reasons I found her so interesting was that she wasn't telling me the whole truth, and I wanted to know what that whole truth was.

The letter was a good example. As much as we appeared to be struggling together with the contents, there was something about her responses that made me think none of it was really a surprise, not even the part where the author attempted to have her killed. I felt like I was missing an important angle.

Anyway, the brandy was unspectacular, but brandy doesn't have to be excellent to be enjoyable. It was also not bitter and probably without poison.

"A man approached me through common associates," she said.

"Some months ago. I was … not in Vienna at the time. Elsewhere."

"Britain?" I guessed.

"Elsewhere," she repeated. "He asked me to come to Vienna. He provided me with this apartment and a per diem, and established a method for contacting me when my services were required, and that was all. It was the last I saw of him. Weekly, a purse arrives, delivered to The Frau and forwarded to my door. It's a generous enough sum that I'm able to keep up the appearances of a highborn lady."

"A mercenary spy."

"I like to think of it as an effective way to earn coin without having to open my legs for someone unsavory. So far I've enjoyed a much better life than someone with my background should expect to have."

"The counterfeiting of blades strikes me as a lucrative endeavor."

"Oh, it *can* be. But I need men with titles to establish provenance, which means getting close to men with titles. So you see, my benefactor's needs coincide nicely with my own. There are more titled men and women in Vienna than ever."

This was true enough. Negotiation between sovereigns had been conducted, historically, through intermediaries—messengers, or someone with a modest title and the trust of a king. This process added a layer of complexity to any treaty, because inevitably the person negotiating was working from a slightly different agenda, and could control what information was shared with whomever he spoke for. (Telephones have largely eliminated this element.) From all I knew of the congress—which was not much at all—an effort had been made to remove the intermediaries from the talks as much as possible. That meant there were an unreasonable number of titled individual milling about Vienna.

"You've been busy while waiting for your orders, I take it."

"Very much so. I've promised to deliver authentic Damascus to a duke and two princes, representing three countries. I suspect none of them would know what to do with a proper blade, but that's not my concern. I was also asked to deflower a king's nephew, a task I politely declined."

I laughed. "Please accept my apology in advance, milady, but was it the money?"

"The money wasn't an issue, and the nephew was hardly hideous, but he didn't like girls. I could tell that instantly. I regret it will take his father much longer to figure this out. I wouldn't have minded terribly otherwise, but I really do prefer a partner with at least *some* skill to match their ardor. This little man would have had neither."

I was thinking I liked her better in men's clothing. She seemed less guarded, and I felt more at ease. So much about the way women had to dress at the time was about illusion. Waists were cinched, breasts were squeezed and shoved upward, backs were held stiff, shoulders were augmented, hair sculpted and raised, and faces redrawn. It was almost theater. But without all of that clothing and make-up it was as if we had both agreed that the illusion was over and everybody could relax.

Of course, getting me at ease and speaking freely was an entirely calculated decision on her part, but I didn't think this through until after it was too late for the realization to do me any good.

"So you received a signal?" I asked.

"One of the coins that came with the per diem was marked with an X. That was the signal. I had been given three different locations in the city, all of which I had reviewed in my travels through the city. The specific location depended on what kind of coin bore the mark."

"Should I assume there's no way to connect the coin to the location without being told ahead of time?"

"You should, yes. The associations are random, on the chance any of this was intercepted."

Spy tradecraft always sounds like it's going to be more interesting than it ever really is. It's actually the worst combination of dull and paranoid the human mind can devise.

"The location was a dead drop that contained nothing but an address."

"Now we're getting somewhere. You went to a building?"

"No. I went to a street corner. And at the appointed time a carriage stopped, and I got in. The man inside handed me this envelope and told me where to bring it, and when."

"Where did he take you?"

"A hotel. My cover was as a hired lady, and so I accompanied him inside, but not into a room. I was escorted to the back of the building, where the carriage awaited to take me back to the same corner from which I'd been retrieved, and only after riding around the city for well over an hour."

"And you don't know who this man was?"

"I only saw him clearly once when we got out of the carriage and into the hotel lobby—a fleeting look—before he handed me off to an escort. I didn't recognize him."

"But clearly someone else would have."

"I don't understand."

"He went through the effort of making it appear as if he'd hired a prostitute. He needed a logical explanation for interacting with you, and thought it was necessary to play out the charade right up to the hotel. People expecting to be watched that closely are either important enough to be recognizable or are paranoid."

"Or are spies. Always assume you're being followed, and always have a cover story."

I waved the letter. "He was important enough to get into this meeting."

"No, no, you're assuming he took the notes himself. We can't assume anything like that."

"There must be *something* useful we can get out of this man."

"I saw his face. That's useful. If I ever see him again."

I sighed. "All right, so then what happened?"

"The following afternoon I went to the garden to deliver the letter, and you know the rest."

"He didn't tell you anything about the man you were meeting?"

"No. The garden was sufficiently private that there was no need. I had a code word to use, but it's meaningless outside of that particular context."

I thought of something. "I was in that garden with you. There was only one entrance."

"So there was."

"You walked in and found this vampire standing over your contact?"

"That's correct, yes."

"You were standing between it and the only way out of the walled garden."

"He shoved me aside on his way by. I doubt he expected me to chase."

"Why didn't he just kill you? It doesn't sound like he would have been interrupted."

"I don't know, Christoph. He didn't give me an opportunity to ask."

Something really wasn't right about this story, but I couldn't get my head around what it might be. That might have been because of the brandy, or possibly the fact that the white shirt she was wearing was a little see-through at certain angles.

As much as I hate to say it, I doubt I would have questioned the last part of this story if a man had told it to me. I could accept that a creature capable of biting open one man's neck might be unwilling to combat another man, if the second man was sufficiently formidable. But as impressive as Anna was, formidable was not the first thing that sprang to mind. In truth, that was exactly what made her so dangerous, because she was not someone to be taken for granted. However, one generally needed to take someone like her for granted first in order to discover the mistake. It sounded like whatever this thing was, it fled on sight of her, and that didn't really work for me.

Yet I could think of no reason why she wouldn't tell me if she'd engaged the thing in some way. She seemed exactly the kind of woman who would brag about that.

"Fair enough," I said, keeping that last line of reasoning to myself. "So all of that is a dead end."

"I think so." She took the letter from my hands. "I'm afraid figuring out the contents of this letter is our only way ahead. Unless I can find the man who gave it to me. Or the vampire."

"There can be only so many ways those abbreviations could work."

"I agree. I have some contacts I can reach out to. But for now..."

She placed the letter on the bed, carefully, as if it might explode. I had hoped her next step would be to offer me a spot on the bed about where the letter was, but that didn't look as if it was going to be happening. Instead, she stood and extended her hand.

"I think our business is concluded for this evening, Christoph."

I stood as well, and kissed her extended hand. "If you're sure you're safe here."

Anna laughed. "You're going to stand guard at my bedside in case the vampire climbs in through the window?"

"I've already told you, this isn't a vampire. And yes, that's exactly what I mean."

"And perhaps while you stood guard we could entertain ourselves in *other* ways?"

"Yes, if the mood struck."

She reached up and brushed my cheek with her knuckles,

gently, as if I had soot on my face that required tending to. "You're a fascinating man, and I'm still not convinced you're fully sensible, but I like you. Another time."

~

The steps involved in smuggling me back out of the building were a little easier than the ones that got me in, only because it was later and The Frau was sleeping. It still involved two confederates and a shawl that I had to wear until I reached the exit, at which time I handed it over to the eye-rolling young woman who saw me out. I believe the eye rolling had to do with assumptions made regarding the reason for my visit. Specifically, she assumed I was there for sex, and given I was leaving so soon after having arrived, my prowess was not being held in high regard.

This might have been justified. There was a time when I was on my game enough to talk my way into the bed of someone like Anna. I could have been losing my edge, but there might have been something else going on that was far worse.

Being immortal can have a surprisingly negative impact on one's ability to carry on a romantic relationship. Sex, sure, I'm good at that, and I'm also pretty good at doing the things one does in order to get sex. I can be charming when I want, basically, and if I don't feel like being charming I can always find someone who's looking for money and not charm. But romance? That's more complicated.

I've *cared for* a lot of people in my life. But at the same time I keep most people at a safe remove, because emotionally I just can't get too invested when I know that even if I spend the rest of *their* life with them, it won't be the rest of *my* life. It won't even be a tiny piece of that life. And that's what love is: it's realizing you don't want to live in a world without that other person in it. Outliving someone who means *that* much to you is difficult to do once. I've done it a hundred times, and it never gets easier.

But I'm still human, and I still connect with people, and that means I still fall in love, and it's not really something I can control. It doesn't seem to matter that everyone I have ever loved is dead; it keeps on happening.

Now, I'm not saying I had fallen in love with Anna. I'm saying a part of me might have recognized that I *could*, and that was what kept me from trying a whole lot harder to get her into bed.

Although the possibility existed I just wasn't as charming as I thought I was.

It was nightfall by the time I left.

You've probably spent your entire life in a world lit by electricity and likely can't appreciate what it was like in a night illuminated only by gaslight, or before that, one brightened by nothing but stars and the moon. It was often not pleasant. Darkness to me has always meant I should expect predators, so for the longest time I was in the habit of staying where I was from sundown to sunrise. That was one reason I tended to sleep in bars, although certainly not the only one. It was also a reason a more persistent version of me might have tried harder not to leave Anna.

But leave I did, and the flat I was staying in wasn't particularly close to her building, so I had to wander the streets. It wasn't all that terrible, because in a city you're always surrounded by people and guided by secondary light sources: windows in taverns, lanterns on passing carriages, and so forth. It was also a cloudless night and the moon was near full. It wasn't pitch dark, by any stretch.

All of that was good, because my understanding of the Viennese streets was not fully comprehensive. Yes, it was a grid, but most of the streets were unmarked, and it was too dark to read what street signs did exist.

I could have ducked into the nearest tavern and spent the rest of the night the same way I'd spent most of the past month, but that meant possibly losing track of time and Anna and quite possibly the rest of the year. (It could happen. I've lost my grip on entire decades. They were boring decades, I'm pretty sure, but I lost track of them nonetheless.) Something made me think I wanted to stay sharp for as long as this congress was happening. Treaties weren't unusual things, and they usually lasted only as long as it took to dry the ink, but this one felt important. It felt like an era I didn't want to forget I lived through.

Another really good reason to stay sharp was that there was somebody following me.

I didn't notice him right away. There were enough people out in the streets—milling about in various directions and without any concern for potential large predators—that it took a while to pick up on the one person sharing the night who was also sharing a destination.

He was mostly staying back about a half a block, keeping people between us when he could, and stepping into alcoves when I stopped and/or turned to check.

It was much too dark to get a clean look—tall man, upturned collar, hat—but he had a distinctive footfall. He dragged and scuffed his right foot on the cobblestones every five or six steps. It wasn't much, but it was enough to pick him out aurally.

I opted against trying to lose him in a tavern, mainly for the above reasons, but also because I can handle myself. (In hindsight, this was a little arrogant of me. I'm very good in close combat, but only against other humans.) I could think of only one or two reasons someone might want to follow me, and they were really interesting reasons, so I didn't try and shake him. I hoped he'd catch up and I would get a good story out of it.

I kept giving him a chance to get closer—I slowed my pace

and lingered in front of empty shops, cut down vacant alleys and doubled back a few times—but he stubbornly refused to take the opportunity. It made me think he was only tailing and had no intention to engage.

And then, a few blocks from my building, he disappeared.

I didn't see this happen, but I heard it. At first I lost him in the shuffle caused by four loudly non-sober men exiting an alley between me and my shadow, but when the noise they were making faded, I couldn't hear him walking any more.

I couldn't see him either. I only had the moon by then. There were no open shops on the block, carriage lanterns required carriages and there were none, and I had no independent source of illumination. The moon was inadequate. But I didn't think he was there.

I ruminated on the facts for the next two blocks, trying to decide if I had been imagining the whole thing, when quite suddenly he reintroduced himself.

I'm ashamed to admit that someone without a gun or projectile of any kind got the drop on me, but this guy did. In my defense, he wasn't technically a "guy" at all, but I still should have seen it coming.

He launched himself from the alleyway only a few yards from the stoop of my building, and had his arm around my neck before I could do anything about it. I recognized the grip. It was the kind a strong enough man could use to break another man's neck. I'd used it myself a couple of times. There were a few defenses against it, but I needed to be still to employ them, and that was impossible so long as I was being dragged into the alley, so I let him take me there.

"Tell me," he hissed into my ear. His breath was hot, and smelled unpleasant. He'd eaten pickled eggs recently. "Who is your master?"

"Who is my what?"

He tightened his grip, which made it hard for me to use any

words at all for a few seconds. He was definitely strong enough to break my neck.

His point made, he allowed me to breathe again.

"The woman answers to you. To whom do you answer?"

"Ah, I understand. You're mistaken, she doesn't work for me."

He had an odd accent. He was speaking German, but not in the way of a native European. I couldn't pinpoint where he hailed from, though. I needed more sentences.

"Then you for her! How far does this go? Tell me and I will kill you without pain."

"That's an appetizing offer."

His grip changed subtly. The proper way to break a man's neck using this particular technique involves both arms, with one forearm pressed against the back of the neck and one around the front and jerking backwards. There are other methods, but this is the one that I've found to be the most consistently successful. I felt the arm at the back of my neck release and the one in front tighten. It happened too quickly for me to do much of anything, but since my best defense involved driving him backwards into the wall, the change in grip didn't alter my circumstances much. Or, so I thought in the half-second I had to act. After that it was too late.

"In my other hand is a dagger," he said. "The tip is pointed at your spine. I can take away your legs and saw you open at my leisure. Do not doubt this."

"I was wondering what that was."

"You joke when you should be answering."

"Right. Well thank you for telling me what your other hand was doing."

In response, he pushed the point of the knife forward exactly enough for me to feel the prick of it on my back.

I'm frankly accustomed to people attacking me without knowing exactly what they're doing, only because when it comes to hand-to-hand combat, most people legitimately *don't* know what they're doing. He did, because as I said, the best defense against being choked was a head-butt and a shove backwards until we made contact with the wall of the alley. This was especially true if his second arm wasn't pressing against the back of my neck any more. The problem was I couldn't very well propel him backwards if there was a knife between us.

More than knowing what he was doing, he appeared to assume I knew what *I* was doing too, because he had summarily removed my cleanest defensive approach. All I had left was moves that were likely to get me stabbed.

The other choice, I suppose, would have been to tell him something he wanted to hear. I just didn't have any idea what that was.

"What makes you think I'm working for anybody?" I asked.

"I am not a fool. I…"

The rest of what he was going to say got lost in a shout of surprise.

Since we were standing on top of one another I actually felt the impact of the knife, which struck him somewhere in the shoulder area. I didn't waste any time wondering who had thrown it, not when that gave me an opportunity to act on my own behalf.

I put the heel of my boot on his foot and pivoted so my elbow was inserted between us, something he wasn't going to be able to counter effectively because he needed his balance to do that, and he didn't have it as long as I was standing on his foot. It would have been tough to pull off this maneuver if he still had a solid hold of my neck, but that went away when he took the blade in his shoulder.

I shoved away from him and fell over, because I was also not in balance for having pivoted on his foot. But when I hit the ground, my neck wasn't broken and my lower spine was intact. I'm a pretty good healer, but I don't think either of those injuries are the kind I can recover from.

He shrieked, and when he did it his jaw opened wider than a human's jaw is capable of. The teeth were double-rowed and sharp. It was Anna's vampire.

"Assassin!" he yelled—not at me—pulling the knife out of his back.

I no longer had his attention. It belonged to whoever stood at the other end of the alley. This would have been an excellent time to get up and either attack him or get the hell out of the alley.

I stayed where I was.

His knife was sharp. I hadn't even felt it cut me. Not in the spine, thank goodness, but in my side. It wasn't deep, but only because it wasn't a long knife. I knew this because it was still stuck in me.

In the near-dark of the alley, there was a struggle. I heard metal against metal, and grunting, and then I saw legs running past me. He was fleeing. I didn't much care. I had just pulled the knife out, which was maybe not the best idea ever. But it was an unusual knife and I wanted to get a better look at it.

I knew what the vampire really was.

~

I woke up to sunlight on my face from an un-curtained window in my own flat. I was on the bed, propped up in a sitting position, and there were bloody cloths and a bottle of cheap whiskey next to me. The bottle was empty and the blood was mine.

There was clean dressing wrapped around my stomach. From a wood chair at the foot of the bed, a young man was looking at me.

No, not a young man. Anna.

"How do you feel?" she asked.

"A little hung over."

"You drank quite a lot. Not that I blame you. Stitches can be painful."

"Will it leave an impressive scar?"

"Probably, yes."

She moved to a spot on the bed and gave a pinched smile. The half-open lids and creases on her face betrayed how little sleep she had gotten.

"You were up all night," I guessed.

"Not all night, only the portion of it where you were still bleeding. Do you want me to check the wound?"

"No, and thank you. I don't even remember getting here."

"You almost didn't. I nearly had to carry you, and I'm not quite strong enough to do that. To an onlooker it probably looked as if you'd had too much to drink."

Loose memories were kicking around in my head. I sort of remembered getting back to the room, and I vaguely recalled getting the bottle to dull the pain I was expecting to have to deal with. I had no memory of her stitching me up, although that was probably for the best.

"Well… thank you again. You could have left me in that alley."

She smiled, and let me take her hat off so I could see her hair fall down over her shoulders. She'd arrived in the alley dressed as a boy, that I remembered. No doubt her attire drew fewer questions when she later helped me up the stairs.

"I could have," she said, "but I didn't want you to die."

I brushed her cheek with my fingers. Soft, cool skin, tired eyes but no less appealing for it. I don't know what made me think it was okay to touch her like this, but she hadn't stopped me. Perhaps we'd grown closer while staving off my imminent demise than I actively remembered. One way or another, something had changed between us, and it seemed like a good thing.

Then I immediately ruined that good thing.

"I'm glad," I said. "Considering you used me as bait."

She pulled away. "I did not!"

"Of course you did. It's all right, I lived, but I'd like to know how much of what you told me yesterday was true."

I think I must have put this together the night before. It seemed like too much of a clever deduction to make just moments after regaining consciousness. Regardless, I wasn't wrong.

She got up and walked to the window. It offered a nice view of an unsavory neighborhood. I doubted she found anything worth looking at, but it was better than facing me.

"That isn't how it was," she said.

"I think it must have been. He had to have followed us all afternoon. I never noticed him, but you did. That's why I was invited into your apartment in the first place."

"No! I never noticed him either... but I arrived at the conclusion over the wine. I need to kill this man, and yesterday I... when I invited you to in, it was to trick him into showing himself. I thought he *might* follow, because that's what I would do. He would want to know who gave my orders, and whether they came from the group in which he had insinuated himself or from elsewhere. Without that information he wouldn't know who to trust. So when you left, I followed, but I had to hold back until he showed himself."

I never noticed her following, but I was too busy focusing on him. And he on me, no doubt. "Did you catch him?"

"No. I stopped to help you instead." She still couldn't look at me. "It was stupid. *I* was stupid."

"Well that was very nice of you."

She laughed, but mirthlessly. "Nice, yes. Very nice. I lured you into the blade of a knife because I'm nice. I have a debt, do you understand? I have to kill this man to clear that debt, and I've failed twice now."

I didn't understand but she was on a roll and I wasn't about to shut her up. She'd moved from the window to pacing at the foot of the bed, still not looking at me.

"You were the solution!" she said. "But instead of letting things play out the exact way *I* set them up to play out, for some ridiculous reason that was the moment I picked to act like a girl, because I didn't want the death of a complete stranger on me. So I stopped and I helped you, and now not only have I not cleared my debt, my decision will likely throw this entire continent into war. It was a *costly* choice."

Anna's pacing, which had become a sort of frantic back-and-forth exercise that made me want to get out of the bed and hold her still, came to a sudden, arresting stop right next to me. She picked that moment to look me in the eye again, and I realized she'd been fighting back tears.

"I wouldn't say we're *complete* strangers," I said.

"We met yesterday."

"Fine, we're nearly strangers, but… Look, I don't understand any of this."

"I know."

She kissed me. It happened so suddenly I didn't do my very best to kiss back, which I felt bad about as soon as it was over. It was soft, and passionate, and she smelled a little bit like cinnamon, and it made all the pain in my side go away and my head empty of rational thought.

Then it was over and she was slapping me across the face. I enjoyed that more than I probably should have.

"Why'd you do that?" I asked.

She ignored the question, or perhaps didn't know whether I was talking about the slap or the kiss. I wasn't sure myself.

"Who *are* you? Christoph isn't your real name, I already know that."

"Why can't it be?"

"Because I asked you on five different occasions last evening and you gave me five different answers. And none of them were Christoph."

"Well all right, I have had a lot of names."

"And you know nothing about the politics of the moment, that much is very obvious."

"How many questions did you ask me last night?"

"Several. I wanted to know what kind of man I rescued at the expense of the peace."

I sort of felt sorry for her. If she asked me things while I was half out of my mind from pain and drink, she probably got a whole lot of honest responses that made no sense. I've had the sort of life that's only logical when immortality is presupposed.

"You use a series of false names, know your tradecraft, and can read the Swiss code. All the evidence says you're a spy, and I can't trust you. Yet I'm certain you are *not* a spy and equally certain I *can* trust you, and I don't understand why that is."

"It must be my charm."

She laughed. "You're not without charm, but I'm not some fainting damsel, either."

"I have noticed. And I've been a spy, once or twice. Just not recently. I'm more of a freelance merchant at the moment."

"Those words are meaningless together."

"How about wealthy drunk?"

"Better."

"The 'Swiss code'. You can read the Romansh dialect, can't you?"

"Of course I can. That letter was meant for me."

"Then who... oh, of course. No wonder you need to kill this man. You were supposed to do that in the garden. *He* was the messenger."

I should have figured this out earlier, perhaps. Like, around the time I was standing in a flowerbed and looking at a murder scene where no blood was shed. Or when I spent the rest of the day trying to figure out a letter whose contents she didn't find all that shocking. If I'd known she was the executioner-to-be and not the victim-that-wasn't, I might have realized she was stalling until the sun went down.

"Maybe you should decide to trust me enough to explain what's actually going on so I can help you in a way that doesn't involve my being sent out as bait," I said.

She laughed, but in a less charming sort of way. "I have no reason to tell you anything. You're useless to me with that wound, and in honesty I should already kill you for what you've learned. That's how it was supposed to happen, do you understand? You saw the letter, and even if you didn't understand the contents, you could *read the words*. As soon as you proved that I couldn't allow you to live. That's why this all made so much sense! Use you to draw him out, wait for him to dispatch you for me, and then kill him and the realm is saved, and *please* stop looking at me like that."

"Like what?"

"I just said I put you at risk on purpose and you look like you want me to kiss you again."

"Well, I do."

She sighed.

"You should get out of Vienna," she said. "As soon as you can. Your life is in danger."

"From you?"

"Possibly. If not at my hand, then because of me. I work for people who are considerably more ruthless. They will never allow you to keep breathing."

"These are the people you owe this debt to?"

"It's not my debt, but yes. It belongs to my family. They saved a life, but if the debt remains unpaid they'll rescind it. And now I've added your life to that equation. So. Please leave Vienna."

"I think you're wrong. I can help you."

"How do you mean to do that?"

"Did you see the knife he stabbed me with?"

Anna blinked a couple of times. "Yes. I have it here. I thought it was interesting."

"It is."

She retrieved it from a corner table and placed it on the bed.

The knife had a handle that was shaped like an H, a logical design because it was meant to be held in the fist and used in a punching motion. I hadn't seen one in years.

"It's called a Katar," I said. "From India. It's how I figured out what you're actually facing. But before I prove I'm actually useful here, why don't you tell me why the man who used it has to die?"

She nodded, slowly. This was progress.

"Have you ever heard the name Talleyrand?"

~

Hofburg Palace is the kind of man-made structure that makes me a little uncomfortable. It's vast. I have seen vastness of all sorts before—the Romans excelled at it, especially the Byzantine edition of them—but most of the time complexity is traded out. A coliseum, for instance, is a giant building, but one with a lot of empty space in it. The Hagia Sofia in Constantinople (please don't make me call it Istanbul) is giant and somewhat complex, but that complexity is mostly for visual effect, not utilitarian functionality.

But Hofburg Palace, along with a dozen other buildings across Europe and Asia, crosses that line between awe-inspiring and disturbing. I look at these places and think perhaps humanity has done something wrong if we legitimately have a need for something so artificially complicated. I also wonder—especially when I end up in a long conversation about politics, which is thankfully not often—if spaces like this are built to address a need, or if they create one. Do we manufacture spaces for secret meetings, or do secret meetings happen because we designed the space for them and don't know what else to do?

I'm also of the opinion that political problems can be solved by putting the right people in the same large room. I've shared this theory with a number of persons, throughout history, with more political savvy than I have, and all of them have told me it's preposterous because of the complexity of the issues involved. So it was a surprise to learn that this was more or less exactly the premise of the congress: get all the people together and hash everything out. They just weren't doing it in one big room. No plenary council meetings, no big central anything, just a bunch of back-room get-togethers. I couldn't decide if it was a brilliant idea or the exact opposite of that.

Anna and I weren't heading to Hofburg Palace for one of those meetings. We were going to a party.

It had been three days since she'd stitched me up, and in that time I'd recovered enough to walk around without wincing. Running was a challenge, but I could stand straight and not give the appearance that I'd recently been stabbed, and that was important, because I didn't want to draw any attention to myself at the party to which I wasn't technically invited. With any luck at all, I'd be able to move around without reopening the stitches; I was in my best suit, and blood is really hard to get out of a good suit.

I also wasn't healed enough to experience a carriage ride without some pain. This was in a time when the choices of road were dirt or cobblestone, and neither was all that great when combined with a non-rubberized carriage wheel. Every bump was a reminder that I should have stayed in bed.

"You look pale," Anna said quietly. She was sitting beside me as the coach made its way through the downtown.

"I'm in a little pain, but I'm okay," I said. "Don't worry."

"I'm worried only that you look so sickly we will be unable to enter."

"How sweet of you."

She gripped my hand gently. "I *am* sorry about the pain. But we have larger concerns."

"Nobody will notice how pale I am if I'm standing next to you. I could show up in my breeches."

She smiled, and blushed a little. "There are greater beauties than I in court. You oversell me."

I really wasn't overselling. Anna was almost dangerously stunning. We were entering an arena in which stealth was going to be important, and she had completely failed in the part where we were supposed to pass unnoticed. Every man there was going to remember the moment they first saw her.

Anna was dressed in a style that was decidedly English, but with French influence— specifically in the waistline, which was typically higher in France than in England. It was at its tightest just underneath her bosom. Practically speaking, the style allowed for a looser corset, which was no doubt a huge relief to the wearer. The rest of the dress was in a style I'd heard called Gothic, with lots of padding and ruffles, a paneled bodice, and ornate lace. She continued to favor a powdered blue/turquoise— the base was white, but with blue lacing. The dress was off the shoulder. She would have been naked from the cleavage up except for the short Spencer jacket that took care of this.

Her hair, quite long when fully untethered, was up in a bun I think she must have had someone else help with. I don't know for certain if she did, but there did tend to be an interest, historically, in dressing as if you required other people's help. It meant you could afford to hire other people to dress you. Anna couldn't afford any such person, but she lived in a building full of women who no doubt had experience with the hair of other people.

The ensemble was designed to draw attention to her breasts and her face, both entirely worthy of that attention. To that end, it might have been an effective espionage tool, because she could be carrying broadsword in her hands and nobody would notice.

It was difficult to believe she didn't know how astonishing she looked.

"We're here," she said, as the gigantic marble edifice of Hofburg threw us into shadow. The driver stopped us at the end of a long train of carriages. We had arrived, but it would be some time before we could debark.

We were staring up at the Chancellery Wing. Each wing of the Palace could house the entire city in the event of a siege, which is the sort of thing you think about when you've lived through a siege or two. I didn't fully understand the purpose of the party we were there to attend, which had no apparent connection to the negotiations. But it was known that most of the important people in town—those abbreviated names in that letter—were going to be there. All except for the T. That was Talleyrand, and he was not expected.

I now knew a great deal about the Frenchman named Talleyrand, but didn't really grasp most of what I knew. This is how I am with politics. Like in Swift's *Gulliver's Travels*, most of the time political issues sound to me like disagreements over which end of a hard-boiled egg to crack in the morning.

Talleyrand wasn't supposed to be in Vienna... for some reason or another. It was a secret, and it meant the man was holding meetings with various people of varied import *in* secret, and these meetings had relevance to the congress that I really didn't listen too carefully about when Anna explained the whole thing. (I remember "lesser powers" and "Polish-Saxony" and "Marquis of Labrador", but I couldn't tell you how they all fit together.)

In order to keep these meetings secret, Talleyrand had hired a private security force of Swiss origin, and that—provided this time I had gotten the truth from her—was who Anna actually worked for.

Roughly half of what Anna had told me our first afternoon together was true. She actually was a sleeper agent put up in the boarding house on someone else's purse, and she really did receive a signal one day, but the part about the man in the carriage steering her around town was completely invented. She also knew the people she was working for by name and by face.

"They're meeting us inside?" I asked.

"Yes. I'll make contact, you don't do anything except look for this... thing you think you can identify. We'll try to do this without Adrian knowing you exist."

"What makes you think your target is here?"

"It's the only gathering of its kind on the social calendar for the next two months. If one wanted to destroy a negotiation, one would be better off doing it near the start of that negotiation."

"And you're sure that's his intent?"

"Isn't destruction the goal of all anarchists?"

"I believe the philosophy is slightly more nuanced."

"Well don't mention this opinion to anyone inside, whatever you do."

Spies get information in ways that defy easy explanation. I never bothered to ask how her Swiss company learned that the talks—and Talleyrand specifically—were the target of an anarchist group. The likelihood was high that Anna didn't even know the answer, and if she did she wouldn't share it with me. And if she *did* share it, I probably wouldn't understand how the logical leap was made. Information like this turns on the tiniest factoids imaginable.

So taking the anarchist story as a postulate, it was further determined (somehow) that a member of the Swiss team was directly involved.

The letter delivered to Anna that afternoon in the garden served two purposes. First, it notified her, an outside agent whose association with the Swiss was not known within the team, about the progress of the secret talks. Second, it informed her that the man delivering the letter was working for the anarchists, if not the sole anarchist in a group of one.

She was supposed to kill him then, but when she drew a blade to do that very thing, he surprised her. Those shark-teeth can be a shock, no matter how well trained you are. He shoved her over —the matted flowers in the garden were from her body, not the body of an imaginary murder victim—and fled. She gave chase, and that was when we met.

~

The carriage stopped at the main door, which was our cue to get out. A footman was there to assist us, and then down a red carpet, up a set of stone stairs, down two corridors, past a set of double doors, and we were at the party.

I felt completely overwhelmed the instant we entered the main ballroom. The noise of a hundred and more people talking over one another combined with music from the band at the far end of the hall to create an unsettling discordance. Added to that was the heat all those bodies were making, the smell of sweat and powder and perfume, and the visual spectacle of Vienna's finest guests in layers of colorful and incredibly restrictive clothing.

For large parts of my life I wore little to no clothing, lived and hunted alone or among small bands, and spoke by pointing and grunting, if at all. Nearly every time I'm forced to attend a formal occasion I miss those days. I can't even imagine what that version of me would think of this version.

I could understand immediately why Anna was so valuable to a spy organization, though, because she took to the room as if she owned it. She greeted dozens of people by name, curtsied and extended her hand, exchanged girlish bits of gossip and politely declined offers to dance—as she had only *just* gotten there and surely must give the first dance to me, her charming and nearly silent escort.

I was nearly silent because I am no good at these things, and because I knew nobody's name. We had decided in advance that I was to play the part of an Englishman who spoke no German. It meant I had to communicate from time to time with people who also spoke English, but that didn't happen too terribly often.

"You need to look as if you're enjoying yourself," she said at one point. She was on my arm and speaking through a thoroughly brilliant smile. "People will notice."

"I can't believe anybody here is noticing anything about anybody. It's too busy."

"Have you spied our friend?"

"I don't think I have, but it would be difficult to tell. What would an anarchist want in a situation such as this?"

She turned us toward one side of the room. "Do you see the man near the doors at the back? Red sash, balding, tapered face."

I saw. He had several men around him, one or two self-evidently in his employ. "Who is it?"

"That's Prince Metternich of Austria. This is his party. Now look to his right about five paces. Military red coat."

"Yes."

"That's the Arthur Wellesley, Duke of Wellington. Rumor has it he's to replace Castlereagh as Britain's representative here. He's speaking to King Friedrich Wilhelm of Prussia. Behind them both, near the band, is Tsar Alexander of Russia. A moment ago, King Frederick of Denmark arrived. He's behind us near the door still, engaging Count Lowenheilm of Sweden in conversation. I can keep going, but do you understand?"

"Your anarchist isn't just a threat to *the* crown, he's a threat to all of them."

"Yes." She looked past me, over my shoulder, at someone halfway across the room. "Stay here, keep your eyes open. I see someone I need to talk to."

"One of your Swiss coworkers?"

"It's Adrian. It's his team, and he's a very dangerous man. I'd rather stand by you, but I'd also rather not introduce you to him, and I need to somehow make him understand what we're up against."

"Good luck. I'll try not to be jealous."

She kissed me on the cheek. "You are far more handsome. And I think he may be a homosexual. Now, put on a smile and find someone to make small-talk with so you don't look quite so awkward."

I watched her glide away. I couldn't see her feet due to the length of her dress, so it was easy to imagine she wasn't actually touching the ground. She moved so smoothly, it wasn't a stretch.

I realized I was sort of staring, so I forced myself to look around the room for someone to engage, but this was the kind of party where everyone knew everyone else or knew *of* everyone else, and I wasn't on either side of that spectrum. I'd already looked around to see if the Saxon duke I knew was there, but he didn't appear to be in attendance. So instead, I held my ground, alone, near an empty buffet table, and wondered what kind of food might eventually show up on it.

Anna was wrong. There were plenty of really lovely women at the party, but none of them held up compared to her. I had checked. And I wished she were next to me so I could tell her that.

That was when I decided I was probably in a huge amount of trouble, because I was thinking like a lovesick child.

I could just leave, I thought. I'd told her everything I knew about her anarchist; there was really no reason for me to be there. Considering how rarely I involved myself in affairs of state, I no doubt already *would* have left, had the person asking me to attend not had deep brown eyes and a way of saying my name that made me think I had to change names immediately because I never wanted to hear anybody else say it.

As I said, I was in bad shape.

It was while I was dealing with this *loves me/loves me not* foolishness running through my head that I took note of a low murmur trickling through the crowd. Up to that point the ambient noise had been unfocused, the product of a hundred conversations happening out of order. But something had happened near the doors that shut down some of those conversations and introduced a new topic to the rest. I caught a name in the buzz.

Talleyrand.

Evidently, the Frenchman who wasn't supposed to be in Vienna had gone from attending secret meetings to making a grand entrance in front of everyone. Points for drama, but possibly not a great negotiating tactic. But what did I know, I barely understood the issues being debated, and had no particular desire to learn more.

The crowd opened for the man, who I saw clearly for the first time only once he'd made it halfway to his apparent destination —Prince Metternich. Metternich looked not at all surprised to learn of Talleyrand's arrival, but that might have been the only way to play the moment, politically and socially.

Charles Maurice de Talleyrand was a pale man with a shock of long grey-white hair that didn't entirely compensate for a creeping hairline. Despite a reputation as one of the shrewdest men in Europe, he looked neither wise nor formidable, although there was a determination to him that I could read very clearly, and perhaps that was enough for an effective negotiator.

He walked with a limp.

This bothered me, a little at first and more when I got close enough to *hear* his footsteps, because it was a familiar cadence.

I looked around, but Anna was nowhere to be seen and I didn't know who else I could turn to, to ask: does Talleyrand have a limp? But I couldn't ask a stranger this, for one obvious reason—supposedly the man himself was walking before me, and clearly he *did*.

I could have also asked Anna if his appearance was a surprise to her. She'd said nothing about Talleyrand coming to the party, but it was possible she didn't know it was going to happen any more than I did. Surely Adrian, the man tasked with guarding the Frenchman, should have known to expect him here.

At any rate, the limp was identical to the one the anarchist had, and this seemed important. Either the Prime Minister of France was also a monster who tried to murder me in an alley, or that monster was impersonating Talleyrand, both on the streets a few nights earlier and at this very moment in front of a hundred of the most important people in Europe.

Or I was mistaken and this wasn't the man I'd met in the alley at all. It was something important to be right about, because the Talleyrand in the room was only about twenty feet from a handful of monarchs.

I didn't know what to do, but it seemed like letting the guy get close enough to stab royalty was a bad idea, so I did the either the dumbest or smartest thing I could think of: I stepped out of the crowd and directly in Talleyrand's line of sight.

"Excuse me, sir," he said quietly, seeking to step around while not bothering to look directly at my face. His head was down, addressing everyone's feet as he passed.

"You don't remember me?" I asked.

"I'm sorry, no, I meet so many..." then he really looked, and for a half-second I saw recognition. The face in front of me was unfamiliar, but I knew the eyes behind that face. And those eyes knew mine.

"*You*," he said, freezing in his tracks. "You are dead. You should be dead."

It wasn't that serious a wound, but I wasn't going to say that. I didn't say anything, actually, I just put a hand on the hilt of my sword.

We stood like that for a whole lot longer than I really liked. To anyone else, it looked as if a stranger had interrupted and threatened an important man that *everyone* knew, right in front of other important men. All the impostor had to do was play his role and eventually someone would use force to remove me. The only reason such a thing didn't happen immediately, I suspected, was that there were no guards within the party itself. A common assumption in upper class gatherings of this sort was that all the people in attendance could be trusted to not be violent on the premises. It was actually a perfect place for an assassin who looked like the French Prime Minister.

I was still holding my breath. Many of the men there had swords of their own, and more than a few were soldiers. Wellington, for instance.

Happily, the impostor lost his nerve. Triggering a gasp of surprise from the crowd, the false Talleyrand spun around and ran.

"Stop him!" I shouted. That didn't do any good, because again, nobody knew who I was and everyone *thought* they knew who he was. But I ran after him anyway, and my stitches were overjoyed about this, I promise you.

Anna met me halfway to the door. "It's him?" she asked.

"No, I just enjoy chasing Frenchmen."

"Adrian is trying to cut him off. How did you know?"

We got separated by all the people who were stubbornly refusing to get out of our way. I would have pulled my sword, but running with a sword is a good way to accidentally impale someone, all the more likely because a sword doesn't have at all the same effect that shooting a gun in the air might under similar circumstances. We didn't reunite until we were both in the hallway on the other side of the door.

"Left or right?" I asked. We heard a woman scream and commotion to the right, and took that to be an answer. We headed in that direction.

"He walked with the same limp the other night," I said, in answer. "That was what made me stop him."

"But Talleyrand has a game leg," she said.

"Well it's a good thing I didn't know that, isn't it?"

The interior of the Chancellery Wing outside of the ballroom was like an anthill if ants were somewhat larger and dug perfect right angles. Corridors upon corridors, stairs upon stairs, enough space for a thousand secret meetings, and a thousand places to hide. We couldn't let him out of our sight or he'd be lost altogether. Especially for a creature than can change his outward appearance as totally as he could.

~

*I*t's called a rakshasa. They're popular in Hindu mythology, where they turn up as shape-shifting evil creatures that eat humans and drink their blood, and can also fly, disappear, and probably do five or six other impossible things that definitely aren't true.

Mankind likes to exaggerate. It's a common affliction that has as much to do with the natural mythmaking consequences of oral tales told down generations as with a persistent belief—as a species—in magic. It's how dragons, who were large, aggressive lizards, became fire-breathing monsters with the gift of flight. And how vampires can turn into a bat, werewolves can somehow transform into actual wolves, and demons are magical creatures from the pit of hell. None of that is true, as any vampire, werewolf or demon will tell you.

Actually, don't talk to demons. They're awful, terrible things.

Anyway. A rakshasa is a real creature, but not quite as tremendous a creature as the Hindus say. They don't literally shape-shift, or rather, not *entirely*. I'd only met one before Vienna, and he wasn't friendly, but he gave me the notion that most of their talent in impersonation comes from uncanny mimicry skills and a little stage makeup. They're good enough to fool, say, a crowd of people who know a man by face and reputation, but not good enough to mislead a close friend or loved one.

This was the first time I'd met a rakshasa anarchist/assassin, but it seemed like a nice fit. Thief would also be a really good profession for them.

They weren't mimics to be thieves or assassins, though. They did it to get into private spaces, because they liked to eat people.

That part of the myth is accurate. It's what those giant teeth are for.

"I see him!" Anna shouted, grabbing my arm to pull me through yet another hallway half-occupied by people. Constantly tripping over this duchess and that lord, duke or whatever was incredibly annoying, but having them there was also a little helpful. They all had that same *was that Talleyrand that just ran past me?* expression on their faces.

The impostor was running well for a fellow who should have a game leg, really. It was nice to see; it meant I'd probably picked the right guy. I wasn't running nearly as well by comparison, because I was pretty sure my stitches had torn and I was bleeding on my suit.

Fortunately, the chase didn't last much past that realization. Adrian had somehow managed to flank us by way of a parallel corridor, which enabled him to be in the right place when the rakshasa turned a corner. The Swiss bodyguard executed a clean tackle, rolled over the impostor and to his feet. By the time the false Talleyrand regained his footing all three of us were there with blades out.

The rakshasa stood with his own knife out—another katar—spinning and hissing and lunging at us, like an animal cornered, which he sort of was.

"It's uncanny," Adrian muttered. "I stood by Talleyrand's side for two weeks and I would swear to you this was he."

"Perhaps I am him," the rakshasa hissed. "Perhaps I have always been him, and the real man was never in Vienna. Perhaps I am the *real* Talleyrand, the only Talleyrand who ever was. Perhaps."

"Perhaps not," I said. "You ran; he wouldn't have."

He hissed again.

Rakshasas can be a little snakelike, and like only a few other creatures, it's hard to imagine one of them turning out to be a nice guy with a regular job. It's the *eating people* thing, mostly. That's hard to get past.

"Who do you work with, monster?" Adrian asked. "How many are you? What was your mission?"

Adrian was a big, burly man who—no matter what Anna had to say—looked a lot more handsome than me. He had a Nordic blond shock of hair and stood taller than most, making the sword in his hand look smaller than it actually was. He was the sort of person most men would confess everything to immediately, to avoid whatever wrath he might be capable of unleashing.

The rakshasa largely ignored him. The creature was facing two men with swords and a woman with two throwing knives, and all he had to defend himself was a katar and his teeth. The teeth were pretty impressive, but not as impressive as a sword might have been. He seemed to be stuck deciding which of us represented the weakest link, and may have been ignoring Adrian because he didn't look like the weakest anything. Surrender didn't appear to be one of the options the impostor was considering, and he wasn't about to answer anything. He had his own questions.

"What *are* you?" he asked me. I was caught off-guard.

"You're asking me? Do you have no mirrors at your disposal? I'm sorry to say the wound you gave wasn't mortal. You missed."

"That is untrue, sir. *All* my wounds are mortal. I will show you."

It was only a quick wrist flick, the same sort of motion a discus-thrower might make at their release point. It was to throw the katar. Since those aren't weighted to be thrown, the attack was awkward. Effective still, but not terribly accurate. The clever part was that he targeted Anna.

I did something historically stupid, and it was the exact thing the rakshasa had anticipated: I threw myself in the way of the blade.

Under different circumstances I might have trusted her to dodge the clumsy assault. The knife throw was telegraphed. Anybody paying attention would have been able to step aside, even someone without the kind of training needed to handle people throwing sharp things. But it was Anna, and more than that, I realized just before the blade was in the air exactly what the rakshasa meant by all his wounds being mortal.

The katar found a home in my left buttocks, which is not an impressive place to get a scar, in case you ever wondered.

Anna had been in the act of responding to his attack when I made my awkward rescue attempt. She still released her own knife, and thankfully not into any part of my body. It hit the wall behind the rakshaka.

Then, of course, I was on top of her and with a knife in my butt, and neither of us was in a position to do anything other than lie there. It was the opening the impostor was looking for.

He probably would have escaped then, except his plan required Adrian to be slower than he was, and holding a shorter sword than he had. The rakshaka didn't get more than a couple of steps—heading for the space I had vacated in my foolhardiness — before the Swiss was on him. A second after that, the creature's head was bouncing on the floor. Thankfully, beheading kills most monsters.

"*What* are you doing?" Anna exclaimed.

"Saving your life?"

She pushed out from underneath. Realizing I had a knife in me, I chose to remain on the floor, on my stomach. Adrian helped her to her feet and then knelt down beside me to take a look at the knife.

"Don't move," he said gently, as if I needed to hear this. Considering Anna had been trying to keep me a secret, his reaction to my involvement seemed pretty positive.

"Such a clumsy attack, I could have avoided it," Anna insisted.

I think I embarrassed her by behaving in a manner resembling chivalry. In hindsight, it was just as likely she was embarrassed at my having done this in front of Adrian, the man who had sent her the rakshasa for execution in the first place. She was supposed to be able to handle herself.

Again, this was hindsight. In the moment, I was sort of annoyed.

"You might have avoided it, but I couldn't risk that," I said.

"Why not?" she asked. "Do you think I can't tolerate a cut? I can—"

"Not from this kind of knife," I interrupted.

"Hold still, I'm going to pull it out so we can move you," Adrian said.

"Be very careful with the blade," I said to him. "It's poisoned."

Anna gasped.

"Don't worry," I added. "The last one he stabbed me with was poisoned too. I'll be fine."

~

I ended up in a room with a bed. It wasn't the room where all my stuff was, in the seedy part of town, and it wasn't Anna's room. It might have belonged to Adrian, but after the incident at Hofburg I didn't see him again, so I couldn't ask.

Piecing together what happened right after I was wounded is a little tough, because a lot of people got deeply involved very quickly. Adrian had a team of cohorts that all seemed to be doubling as members of the service staff: footmen, drivers, aides, kitchen staff, and so on. They were on the scene and acting with the sort of efficiency that made it clear this was not the first time they'd been called upon to dispose of a body quickly and discreetly.

I wasn't the body being disposed of, thank goodness. That belonged to the rakshasa. I could understand perfectly why they didn't want him lying around any longer than necessary, both because this was not the sort of place where dead bodies should be expected and because he still looked a lot like Talleyrand. Not as much in death as when alive, but enough to raise questions. It wasn't as if nobody saw us chasing him around, either.

I couldn't walk all too well. I tried hopping toward the exit, but that tended to make me bleed more—in two places since my stitches had definitely opened up—so they decided to put one man on either side and carry me out.

We left through what may have been a large window. It wasn't the front door, certainly, and I don't know how many other entrances were options, but there didn't seem to be anyone near this exit so I'm thinking it might have been a window. I can't remember. Whatever it was, soon I was in the back of a carriage and hating the bumps in the street twice as much as I had when we rode in to the party.

Worse, Anna wasn't with me. In the bustle to get me out and the fake Talleyrand mopped up, she and I had been separated.

The carriage ultimately took me to the room and the bed, where I did some more bleeding, and got some more stitches—this time from a surgeon—and drank some more to dull the pain. Bleeding, cheap whiskey, and stab wounds is how I remember Vienna now, which could be why I haven't visited since.

Anna came by after a few days. She was dressed simply, as a common woman rather than as noblewoman or a young man. As with every version of her, the description *common* didn't come near explaining how amazing she looked.

I was really happy to see her. I nearly jumped out of the bed, but my stitches might have had a complaint or two about that.

"How do you feel?" she asked. It was evening. The window shades were drawn and the only light was from a candle. The flame danced in her eyes.

"Well enough. It'll be a while before I ride a horse again, but I'll survive it. Where have you been?"

Aside from the surgeon and the housemaid who brought me food and emptied the chamber pot, I had only been visited by serious men I didn't know and who didn't introduce themselves. These men turned up on three separate occasions to ask how I was feeling. At first I assumed the organization I had accidentally aligned myself with was actively concerned with my health due to my self-evident heroics, but now I was beginning to think otherwise. These were not happy, grateful men. Confused, displeased, and possibly constipated was how I would describe their demeanor.

Anna sat on the bed and put her hand on my forehead. "No fever," she said. "Your eyes are clear. You're sober?"

"I am." I ran out of alcohol the day before and nobody had brought me a new bottle, but I wasn't going to tell her that.

"Good, because we have a problem, and I'm afraid you may need to test yourself on a horse sooner than you would otherwise hope. The pig died."

"Are you speaking euphemistically?"

"No, Christoph. A very literal pig. On the night you were brought here, Adrian stuck it with the knife to see if there was truly poison on the blade. Though the wound wasn't mortal, the pig screamed in agony for a full day before someone decided they could no longer stand listening to the cries, and slew it out of mercy."

The poor pig. "What kind of poison was it?"

"No-one knows. This organization has knowledge of many poisons and many kinds of people, but they have never seen a being such as the one we killed, and they have never encountered this poison. It was designed to make a man suffer enough to beg for death. And you… you look fine."

"Lucky for me."

She smiled. "This isn't luck. You're different. I've known that since the moment you pulled out a three hundred year old sword from a cheap leather scabbard. Maybe that's why I couldn't see you bleed to death in that alley. But... while I have a lot of questions about who you are, at the same time I know *exactly* who you are. Not everyone feels this way."

"I kind of... *saved* everybody, didn't I?"

"You did. But the man we killed didn't look like Talleyrand on the day he was sent to me. We think it's likely that..."

"Rakshasa."

"Yes. That creature likely killed the man we *thought* he was, perhaps some time ago. It could have been how he infiltrated the organization's ranks. And now that they know such a thing is possible nobody is sure who can be trusted. It seems all they can agree on is they *can't* trust the strange man who is immune to poison and seems to know far too much about monsters."

She looked down at her hands, which were balling up the sheets on the bed.

"They're going to be questioning you in the morning," she said quietly.

"About what?"

"About your connection to the impostor. And you connection to me, whom they no longer fully trust because of all this. And about anything else they can think of accusing you of doing."

All of that sounded really bad, and illustrated why I don't involve myself in the world very often. The consequence of doing a good thing sometimes outweighs the good thing itself. The number of times I relearn this after the fact is a little alarming.

"I don't have anything to tell them, so..."

"So they won't care. We're past that point."

She leaned forward and kissed me on the lips. It was a whole lot better than the last time she did it, if only because I was more prepared and more sober. I was about to make a joke about re-opening my stitches when she pulled back and held my head in her hands.

"We have to leave tonight," she said.

"What?"

"You and I. It's the only way. You can't go alone in your condition and I can't let you escape not knowing if you've made it to safety. So, we leave together, and we leave right now."

I was a little stunned. Some of that might have been the kiss. "We would be fugitives," I said.

"Oh, definitely. Adrian's organization has tendrils in every government in the Western world. I doubt they'll rest until they've run us both down. There would be constant peril."

"For some reason you make that sound like a lot of fun."

She gave me a broad smile, and my heart fell into my stomach. "Doesn't it? Now get your pants on, we don't have much time."

~

We fled in the night, past two unconscious men—I assumed they were only unconscious—who were supposed to be guarding me. Anna had horses waiting for us, and all the things from my rented flat. And she had my sword.

It was probably a good thing, then, that I had said yes.

The horses didn't take us too far—just out of Vienna and to a safe house she promised was off of Adrian's radar. If I had been in better condition we could have traveled farther and for much longer, but a knife wound in the buttocks is what it is, and I couldn't stay a-horse all that long.

It was far enough. We holed up for a week there, and then when my condition improved, we disappeared into Prussia.

Anna was right. Adrian didn't stop looking. He kept us on the move for a while, not quite catching up until…

Well. I'd tell you more, but this is a story for another time.

ACKNOWLEDGMENTS

Special thanks to Sue London for the rakshasa, and also for Anna, who I'm not giving back

ABOUT THE AUTHOR

Gene Doucette is a hybrid author, albeit in a somewhat round-about way. From 2010 through 2014, Gene published four full-length novels (*Immortal, Hellenic Immortal, Fixer,* and *Immortal at the Edge of the World*) with a small indie publisher. Then, in 2014, Gene started self-publishing novellas that were set in the same universe as the *Immortal* series, at which point he was a hybrid.

When the novellas proved more lucrative than the novels, Gene tried self-publishing a full novel, *The Spaceship Next Door*, in 2015. This went well. So well, that in 2016, Gene reacquired the rights to the earlier four novels from the publisher, and re-released them, at which point he wasn't a hybrid any longer.

Additional self-published novels followed: *Immortal and the Island of Impossible Things* (2016); *Unfiction* (2017); and *The Frequency of Aliens* (2017).

In 2018, John Joseph Adams Books (an imprint of Houghton Mifflin Harcourt) acquired the rights to *The Spaceship Next Door*. The reprint was published in September of that year, at which point Gene was once again a hybrid author.

Since then, a number of things have happened. Gene published three more novels—*Immortal From Hell* (2018), *Fixer Redux* (2019), and *Immortal: Last Call* (2020)—and wrote a new novel called *The Apocalypse Seven* that he did not self-publish; it was acquired by JJA/HMH in September of 2019. Publication date is May 25, 2021.

Gene lives in Cambridge, MA.

For the latest on Gene Doucette, follow him online

genedoucette.me
genedoucette@me.com

ALSO BY GENE DOUCETTE

SCI-FI

The Spaceship Next Door

The world changed on a Tuesday.

When a spaceship landed in an open field in the quiet mill town of Sorrow Falls, Massachusetts, everyone realized humankind was not alone in the universe. With that realization, everyone freaked out for a little while.

Or, almost everyone. The residents of Sorrow Falls took the news pretty well. This could have been due to a certain local quality of unflappability, or it could have been that in three years, the ship did exactly nothing other than sit quietly in that field, and nobody understood the full extent of this nothing the ship was doing better than the people who lived right next door.

Sixteen-year old Annie Collins is one of the ship's closest neighbors. Once upon a time she took every last theory about the ship seriously, whether it was advanced by an adult ,or by a peer. Surely one of the theories would be proven true eventually—if not several of them—the very minute the ship decided to do something. Annie is starting to think this will never happen.

One late August morning, a little over three years since the ship landed, Edgar Somerville arrived in town. Ed's a government operative posing as a journalist, which is obvious to Annie—and pretty much everyone else he meets—almost immediately. He has a lot of questions that need answers, because he thinks everyone is wrong: the ship is doing something, and he needs Annie's help to figure out what that is.

Annie is a good choice for tour guide. She already knows everyone in town and when Ed's theory is proven correct—something is apocalyptically wrong in Sorrow Falls—she's a pretty good person to have around.

As a matter of fact, Annie Collins might be the most important person on the planet. She just doesn't know it.

∼

The Frequency of Aliens

Annie Collins is back!

Becoming an overnight celebrity at age sixteen should have been a lot more fun. Yes, there were times when it was extremely cool, but when the newness of it all wore off, Annie Collins was left with a permanent security detail and the kind of constant scrutiny that makes the college experience especially awkward.

Not helping matters: she's the only kid in school with her own pet spaceship.

She would love it if things found some kind of normal, but as long as she has control of the most lethal—and only—interstellar vehicle in existence, that isn't going to happen. Worse, things appear to be going in the other direction. Instead of everyone getting used to the idea of the ship, the complaints are getting louder. Public opinion is turning, and the demands that Annie turn over the ship are becoming more frequent. It doesn't help that everyone seems to think Annie is giving them nightmares.

Nightmares aren't the only weird things going on lately. A government telescope in California has been abandoned, and nobody seems to know why.

The man called on to investigate—Edgar Somerville—has become the go-to guy whenever there's something odd going on, which has been pretty common lately. So far, nothing has panned out: no aliens or zombies or anything else that might be deemed legitimately peculiar… but now may be different, and not just because Ed can't find an easy explanation. This isn't the only telescope where people have gone missing, and the clues left behind lead back to Annie.

It all adds up to a new threat that the world may just need saving from, requiring the help of all the Sorrow Falls survivors. The question is: are they saving the world with Annie Collins, or are they saving it from her?

The Frequency of Aliens is the exciting sequel to *The Spaceship Next Door*.

∾

Unfiction

When Oliver Naughton joins the Tenth Avenue Writers Underground, headed by literary wunderkind Wilson Knight, Oliver figures he'll finally get some of the wild imaginings out of his head and onto paper.

But when Wilson takes an intense interest in Oliver's writing and his genre stories of dragons, aliens, and spies, things get weird. Oliver's stories don't just need to be finished: they insist on it.

With the help of Minerva, Wilson's girlfriend, Oliver has to find the connection between reality, fiction, the mythical Cydonian Kingdom, and the non-mythical nightclub called M Pallas. That is, if he can survive the alien invasion, the ghosts, and the fact that he thinks he might be in love with Minerva.

Unfiction is a wild ride through the collision of science fiction, fantasy, thriller, horror and romance. It's what happens when one writer's fiction interferes with everyone's reality.

∾

Fixer

What would you do if you could see into the future?

As a child, he dreamed of being a superhero. Most people never get to realize their childhood dreams, but Corrigan Bain has come close. He is a fixer. His job is to prevent accidents—to see the future and "fix" things before people get hurt. But the ability to see into the future, however limited, isn't always so simple. Sometimes not everyone can be saved.

"Don't let them know you can see them."

Graduate students from a local university are dying, and former lover and FBI agent Maggie Trent is the only person who believes their deaths aren't as accidental as they appear. But the truth can only be found in something from Corrigan Bain's past, and he's not interested in sharing that past, not even with Maggie.

To stop the deaths, Corrigan will have to face up to some old horrors, confront the possibility that he may be going mad, and find a way to stop a killer no one can see.

Corrigan Bain is going insane ... or is he?

Because there's something in the future that doesn't want to be seen. It isn't human. It's got a taste for mayhem. And it is very, very angry.

∼

Fixer Redux

Someone's altering the future, and it isn't Corrigan Bain

Corrigan Bain was retired.

It wasn't something he ever thought he'd be able to do. The problem was that the *job* he wanted to retire from wasn't actually a job at all: nobody paid him to do it, and nobody else did it. With very few exceptions, nobody even knew he was doing it.

Corrigan called himself a fixer, because he fixed accidents that were about to happen. It was complicated and unrewarding, and even though doing it right meant saving someone, he didn't enjoy it. He couldn't stop —he thought—because there would always be accidents, and he would never find someone to take over as fixer. Anyone trying would have to be capable of seeing the future, like he did, and that kind of person was hard to find.

Still, he did it. He's never been happier.

His girlfriend, Maggie Trent of the FBI, has not retired. Her task force just shut down the most dangerous domestic terrorist cell in the country, and she's up for an award, and a big promotion.

Everything's going their way now, and the future looks even brighter.

Unfortunately, that future is about to blow up in their faces…literally. And somehow, Corrigan Bain, fixer, the man who can see the future, is taken completely by surprise.

Fixer Redux is the long-awaited sequel to ***Fixer***. Catch up with Corrigan, as he tries to understand a future that no longer makes sense.

∼

FANTASY

The Immortal Novel Series

∼

Immortal

"I don't know how old I am. My earliest memory is something along the lines of fire good, ice bad, so I think I predate written history, but I don't know by how much. I like to brag that I've been there from the beginning, and while this may very well be true, I generally just say it to pick up girls."

Surviving sixty thousand years takes cunning and more than a little luck. But in the twenty-first century, Adam confronts new dangers—someone has found out what he is, a demon is after him, and he has run out of places to hide. Worst of all, he has had entirely too much to drink.

Immortal is a first person confessional penned by a man who is immortal, but not invincible. In an artful blending of sci-fi, adventure, fantasy, and humor, IMMORTAL introduces us to a world with vampires, demons and other "magical" creatures, yet a world without actual magic.

At the center of the book is Adam.

Adam is a sixty thousand year old man. (Approximately.) He doesn't age or get sick, but is otherwise entirely capable of being killed. His survival has hinged on an innate ability to adapt, his wits, and a fairly large dollop of luck. He makes for an excellent guide through history ... when he's sober.

Immortal is a contemporary fantasy for non-fantasy readers and fantasy enthusiasts alike.

∼

Hellenic Immortal

"Very occasionally, I will pop up in the historical record. Most of the time I'm not at all easy to spot, because most of the time I'm just a guy who does a thing and then disappears again into the background behind someone-or-other who's busy doing something much more important. But there are a couple of rare occasions when I get a starring role."

An oracle has predicted the sojourner's end, which is a problem for Adam insofar as he has never encountered an oracular prediction that didn't come true ... and he is the sojourner. To survive, he's going to have to figure out what a beautiful ex-government analyst, an eco-terrorist, a rogue FBI agent, and the world's oldest religious cult all want with him, and fast.

And all he wanted when he came to Vegas was to forget about a girl. And maybe have a drink or two.

The second book in the Immortal series, Hellenic Immortal follows the continuing adventures of Adam, a sixty-thousand-year-old man with a wry sense of humor, a flair for storytelling, and a knack for staying alive. Hellenic Immortal is a clever blend of history, mythology, sci-fi, fantasy, adventure, mystery and romance. A little something, in other words, for every reader.

∽

Immortal at the Edge of the World

"What I was currently doing with my time and money ... didn't really deserve anyone else's attention. If I was feeling romantic about it, I'd call it a quest, but all I was really doing was trying to answer a question I'd been ignoring for a thousand years."

In his very long life, Adam had encountered only one person who appeared to share his longevity: the mysterious red-haired woman. She appeared throughout history, usually from a distance, nearly always vanishing before he could speak to her.

In his last encounter, she actually did vanish—into thin air, right in front of him. The question was how did she do it? To answer, Adam will have to complete a quest he gave up on a thousand years earlier, for an object that may no longer exist.

If he can find it, he might be able to do what the red-haired woman did, and if he can do that, maybe he can find her again and ask her who she is ... and why she seems to hate him.

But Adam isn't the only one who wants the red-haired woman. There are other forces at work, and after a warning from one of the few men he trusts, Adam realizes how much danger everyone is in. To save his friends and finish his quest he may be forced to bankrupt himself, call in every favor he can, and ultimately trade the one thing he'd never been able to give up before: his life.

~

Immortal and the island of Impossible Things

"I thought I'd miss the world."

Adam is on vacation in an island paradise, with nothing to do and plenty of time to do nothing.

It's exactly what he needed: beautiful weather, beautiful girlfriend, plenty of books to read, and alcohol to drink. Most importantly, either nobody on the island knows who he is, or, nobody cares.

"This probably sounds boring, and maybe it is. It's possible I have no compass to help determine boring, or maybe I have a different threshold than most people. From my perspective, though, the vast majority of human history has been boring, by which I mean nothing happened, and sure, that can be dull. On the other hand, nothing happening includes nobody trying to kill anybody, and specifically, nobody trying to kill me. That's the kind of boring a guy can get behind."

Nothing last forever, though, and that includes the opportunity to *do* nothing. One day, unwelcome visitors arrive in secret, with impossible knowledge of impossible events, and then the impossible things arrive: a new species.

It's *all* impossible, especially to the immortal man who thought he'd seen all there was to see in the world. Now, Adam is going to have to figure out what's happening and make things right before he and everyone he loves ends up dead in the hot sun of this island paradise.

∾

Immortal From Hell

Not all of Adam's stories have happy endings

"Paris is romantic and quests are cool. But the threat of a global pandemic kind of sours the whole thing. The good news was, if all life on Earth were felled by a plague, it looked like this one could take me out too. It'd be pretty lonely otherwise."

--Adam the immortal

When Adam decides to leave the safety of the island, it's for a good reason: Eve, the only other immortal on the planet, appears to be dying, and nobody seems to understand why. But when Adam—with his extremely capable girlfriend Mirella—tries to retrace Eve's steps, he discovers a world that's a whole lot deadlier than he remembered.

Adam is supposed to be dead. He went through a lot of trouble to fake that death, but now that he's back it's clear someone remains unconvinced. That wouldn't be so terrible, except that whoever it is, they have a great deal of influence, and an abiding interest in ensuring that his death sticks this time around.

Adam and Mirella will have to figure out how to travel halfway across the world in secret, with almost no resources or friends. The good news is, Adam solved the travel problem a thousand years earlier. The bad news is, one of his oldest assumptions will turn out to be untrue.

Immortal From Hell is the darkest entry in the Immortal series.

∾

Immortal: Last Call

"I'm something like sixty-thousand years old, and I've probably thought more

about my own death than any living being has thought about any subject, ever. I used to be unduly preoccupied with what might constitute a "good death", although interestingly, this has always been an after-the-fact analysis. What I mean is, following a near-death experience, I'll generally perform a quiet review of the circumstances and judge whether that death would have been objectively good, by whatever metric one uses for that kind of thing. I'm not nearly that self-reflective while in the midst of said near-death experience. Facing death, the predominant thought is always not like this."

A disease threatening the lives of everyone—human and non-human—has been loosed upon the world, by an arch-enemy Adam didn't even know he had.

That's just the first of his problems. Adam's also in jail, facing multiple counts of murder, at least a few of which are accurate. He may never see the inside of a courtroom, because there remains a bounty on his head—put there by the aforementioned arch-enemy—that someone is bound to try to collect while he's stuck behind bars.

Meanwhile, Adam's sitting on some tantalizing evidence that there might be a cure, but to find it, he's going to have to get out of jail, get out of the country, and track down the man responsible. He can't do any of that alone, but he also can't rely on any of his non-human friends for help, not when they're all getting sick.

What he needs is a particularly gifted human, who can do things no other human is capable of. He knows one such person. He calls himself a fixer, and he's Adam's—and possibly the world's—last hope. That's provided he believes any of it.

Immortal: Last Call is the sixth book in the *Immortal Novel Series*, and also the end of a long journey for one immortal man.

∾

Immortal Stories

∾

Eve

"...if your next question is, what could that possibly make me, if I'm not an angel or a god? The answer is the same as what I said before: many have considered me a god, and probably a few have thought of me as an angel. I'm neither, if those positions are defined by any kind of supernormal magical power. True magic of that kind doesn't exist, but I can do things that may appear magic to someone slightly more tethered to their mortality. I'm a woman, and that's all. What may make me different from the next woman is that it's possible I'm the very first one..."

For most of humankind, the woman calling herself Eve has been nothing more than a shock of red hair glimpsed out of the corner of the eye, in a crowd, or from a great distance. She's been worshipped, feared, and hunted, but perhaps never understood. Now, she's trying to reconnect with the world, and finding that more challenging than anticipated.

Can the oldest human on Earth rediscover her own humanity? Or will she decide the world isn't worth it?

∽

The Immortal Chronicles

∽

Immortal at Sea (volume 1)

Adam's adventures on the high seas have taken him from the Mediterranean to the Barbary Coast, and if there's one thing he learned, it's that maybe the sea is trying to tell him to stay on dry land.

∽

Hard-Boiled Immortal (volume 2)

The year was 1942, there was a war on, and Adam was having a lot of trouble avoiding the attention of some important people. The kind of people with guns, and ways to make a fella disappear. He was caught somewhere between the mob and the government, and the only way out involved a red-haired dame he was pretty sure he couldn't trust.

∾

Immortal and the Madman (volume 3)

On a nice quiet trip to the English countryside to cope with the likelihood that he has gone a little insane, Adam meets a man who definitely has. The madman's name is John Corrigan, and he is convinced he's going to die soon.

He could be right. Because there's trouble coming, and unless Adam can get his own head together in time, they may die together.

∾

Yuletide Immortal (volume 4)

When he's in a funk, Adam the immortal man mostly just wants a place to drink and the occasional drinking buddy. When that buddy turns out to be Santa Claus, Adam is forced to face one of the biggest challenges of extremely long life: Christmas cheer. Will Santa break him out of his bad mood? Or will he be responsible for depressing the most positive man on the planet?

∾

Regency Immortal (volume 5)

Adam has accidentally stumbled upon an important period in history: Vienna in 1814. Mostly, he'd just like to continue to enjoy the local pubs, but that becomes impossible when he meets Anna, an intriguing woman with an unreasonable number of secrets and sharp objects.

Anna is hunting down a man who isn't exactly a man, and if Adam doesn't help her, all of Europe will suffer. If Adam *does* help, the cost may be his own life. It's not a fantastic set of options. Also, he's probably fallen in love with her, which just complicates everything.

Milton Keynes UK
Ingram Content Group UK Ltd.
UKHW021624160923
428812UK00021B/551